TRASH CAN DAYS

A MIDDLE SCHOOL SAGA

Teddy Steinkellner

DISNEP•HYPERION BOOKS
NEW YORK

Printed in the United States of America
First Edition
10 9 8 7 6 5 4 3 2 1
G475-5664-5-13091

Library of Congress Cataloging-in-Publication Data
Steinkellner, Teddy.
Trash can days : a middle school saga : a novel / by Teddy
Steinkellner.—1st ed.
p. cm.
Summary: Four diverse seventh and eighth graders at southern
California's San Paulo Junior High tell, from their unique perspectives,
of a tumultuous year of changing friendships and romantic interests as
they are learning to be themselves.
ISBN 978-1-4231-6632-0
[1. Interpersonal relations—Fiction. 2. Maturation
(Psychology)—Fiction. 3. Middle schools—Fiction. 4. Schools—Fiction.
5. Family life—California—Fiction. 6. California, Southern—Fiction.]
I. Title.
PZ7.S826432Tr 2013
[Fic]—dc23   2012015327

Reinforced binding

Visit www.disneyhyperionbooks.com

SUSTAINABLE FORESTRY INITIATIVE   Certified Sourcing
www.sfiprogram.org
SFI-00993

THIS LABEL APPLIES TO TEXT STOCK

To Mom,
I'll love you forever

1 • Jake Schwartz

Danny grew half a foot this summer. Six full inches—maybe a little more if you count his hair now that he's started spiking it. Three months ago he wasn't allowed on most roller coasters. Now all of a sudden he's walking right into R movies without being stopped, and he's even touching the rim on basketball hoops. Maybe my sister put it best—tonight at dinner she said that Danny had gone from "shrimp to pimp."

I never fully realized what was happening as it was happening, and yet somehow it happened. If you look at the picture of us from sixth grade graduation in June, we are literally the exact same height (I've actually got the edge since my Jewfro was extra puffy that day). But if you look at the two of us now, it's absolutely no contest. It's more than just apples and oranges. It's like comparing an apple to a much taller apple that has a wispy mustache.

Now, I don't want to give the wrong impression here. This whole growth-spurt deal didn't have, like, this big cosmic impact on our lives. Danny Uribe is still my best friend, and that's not something a stupid pituitary gland can get in the way of. This height thing hasn't defined the summer at all. These past three months have been legendary for so many other reasons:

1

1. Danny and I got to see four Laker playoff games from my dad's luxury box.
2. My family kept the pool heated up all summer so Danny and I and occasionally my sister went night-swimming a bunch. Kind of spooky, actually, but so fun.
3. Danny and I went to camp for a month, where I got my first kiss courtesy of Becca Wolfson. Plus, Danny got a tongue kiss from Jordan Meyer, one of the hottest girls there.
4. My parents took us to Europe as a graduation present. Churros in Spain, gelato in Italy, real live boobs in France.

Best summer in all of human history. I actually feel a little guilty at how awesome it all was.

Here's how awesome it was: I just looked at my pictures from the summer on my laptop while listening to a bunch of cheesy memory-type songs like the Hawaiian version of "Somewhere Over the Rainbow" and "Good Riddance (Time of Your Life)" by Green Day. As I got to the end of the slide show, my eyes actually started to tear up a little. Don't get me wrong, I'm not someone who cries a whole lot, but there was just something about seeing all those memories at the same time.

Like there's this one from the last-day-of-school party at San Paulo Beach of me, Danny, and some of the other sixth grade guys catching sand crabs. We're all really into it, and some of us are pretending to eat them or make sand crab mustaches out of them, and you can see all the girls in the back and they look way grossed out. I think one of them barfed.

Then there's this picture from my family's vacation of me, Danny, my mom, and Hannah (my dad had to leave halfway through for work), and we're all in front of the Leaning Tower of Pisa, and me and Danny are both pretending to hold the tower up with our butts and we both have constipated looks on our faces and it's absolutely hilarious.

So yeah, I guess this is the kind of stuff that gets me worked up emotionally. Not sappy love stories or profound poetry, but crustacial hair and constipated faces. I know that makes me seem kind of insane, but, honestly, more than that, I take it as proof that I just had a ridiculously epic summer. It's been by far the best three months of my life and I never want it to end. And of course I'm saying that now because junior high starts precisely . . . tomorrow.

Junior high. Middle school. Seventh grade. Tomorrow. I don't know how I feel about it yet. I don't feel that normal pre–first day of school mix of nerves and excitement. I don't feel curious or nauseous or even pissed. I'm just a little . . . I don't know. Sad?

See, I already know what San Paulo Junior High is going to be like. I've seen what Hannah's friends are like. I know the drill. I know that thanks to the maaaagic of hormones, all the people in the hallways are going to look like giants, or at least like NBA players. I know that everyone's going to be all familiar with the latest hit songs and cool clothes, and I'm not really good at keeping up with all that stuff. Some of the kids will have probably already tried beer or drugs or making out or even sex or all four, and for sure that's all anyone's going to want to talk about. Kids are going to text in class and all through passing period, and they'll be updating their statuses all the time, and they'll start dancing and freak dancing and dating, and basically school's not going to be about school anymore. And sure, I guess I've still got my group of friends from elementary school, but they've kind of changed, too. Since midway through last year, all they've wanted to do is either skate or come up with new ways to hit each other in the nuts.

And I value my nuts!

Danny's nervous too, but not really in the same way. He's more excited-nervous. He said that it might be scary getting older, but that we're also getting the chance to try a lot of cool new things. He's also pretty psyched about going to a much bigger school with a bunch of different kinds of kids. And he made a good point when he reminded me that there is going to be pizza every day.

Maybe Danny's right. Why shouldn't I like junior high? After all, I've got to remember: I've got a cell phone that I can use to text, same as everybody else. I've got stories from camp that I can use for bragging purposes. Hey, I've even got nuts to bash if it comes to that. And most importantly, I've got allies. First there's Hannah, and she isn't exactly the most generous big sister on Earth (I'm not even sure that she ranks in the top three billion), but she was a "sevvy" just last year and she remembers what it's like and she can show me the ropes.

And Danny will be there. Granted, we're only in two of the same classes because I'm starting Honors and he's doing the general track. But still. I'll always have someone to hang out with at lunchtime and after school, and that's more than so many kids can say. I've got to remember that as lame as school could possibly get, what with middle school supposedly being the worst years ever and all, I'll still have Danny through everything. Even when I'm at home, his house is what, a thirty-second walk away? I mean, my parents employ his parents. What a cool deal for us. I don't even have to leave the property to hang out.

Above all, that's what I've got to remember. I have to know that even when I most feel like giving up or crying, I'm always just thirty seconds away from my best friend. Just thirty seconds away from my brother.

Well, thirty seconds and six inches.

n first day jitters . . .
go · Comment · Like

Ashley Clarke 8th GRADE, HOEZ! LETS MAKE THIS THE BEST YR OF OUR LIVES!
4 minutes ago · Comment · Like

Bryce Sherman 1. english-morales 2. french-chamorel 3. social studies-fortson 4. pe-wade 5. algebra-montez 6. science-pittsnogle 7. journalism-collins . . . who has classes wit me?
5 minutes ago · Comment · Like

Kristen Duffy got her braces off just in time for picture day!
8 minutes ago · Comment · Like

Avery Sinclair i wanna haze some sevvies tomorrow . . . whos in lol
9 minutes ago · Comment · Like

Meghan Moore do we need a graphing calculator for algebra?
11 minutes ago · Comment · Like

Hannah Rose Schwartz has it narrowed down to 3 potential outfits.
15 minutes ago · Comment · Like

Nisha Patel is going to bed early tonight. like i'll be able to sleep.
17 minutes ago · Comment · Like

Brian Fenton ATTACK OF THE KILLER ACNE!!!!!!

17 minutes ago · Comment · Like

Jamie Mackintosh does anyone have some 0.7 lead that i can borrow tomorrow?

20 minutes ago · Comment · Like

Rachel Sloan helping hannah choose her outfit. crisis mode.

22 minutes ago · Comment · Like

Chad Beck school starts tomorrow. and i am feeling awesome. because im chad beck. thats a haiku haha.

23 minutes ago · Comment · Like

September 1
Letter to yourself assignment
English, Morales

Dear Danny,

Right now you're sitting at your desk in fourth period writing this letter to yourself. It's a big waste of time, but at least it's better than learning about real things.

You're supposed to write about how the first day of seventh grade has been so far, how you thought it would go, all that kind of stuff. Basically your feelings.

You don't really know how it's gonna be yet but you feel okay, you guess. This place is pretty cool. When you walk down the halls, you can actually hear people speaking Spanish to each other, which is tight and way different from how it was at Arlington. Also the teachers are chill and they seem kind of easy. Plus there's pizza for lunch every day and it's mad cheap.

Man, you want some pizza right now. Ten minutes till lunch.

But you have to keep writing for those ten minutes. The teacher said your pencil isn't allowed to leave the paper for the entire time and that you have to write whatever you are thinking. Here's what you are thinking: blah blah blah blah blah blah blah blah blah blah blah.

Okay, that's boring. If that's all you're gonna write then you should just crumple this paper and throw it in the trash can. You don't want to read that stuff a year from now.

You wonder what it's gonna be like a year from now. For sure you'll still basically be the same person. You've always been the same person through your whole life. Moving to Jake's big fancy house in Seabrook five years ago and meeting him and his family didn't change you. Having your parents work as the maid and gardener for your best friend's parents didn't change you. Going to Arlington Academy from second grade until now and being like, the only brown kid in the whole school didn't change you. Growing a crap ton of inches over the summer didn't change you.

Those kinds of things just change the way people look at you, that's all. And for sure people look at you different here than at Arlington or ever before, really. For one, there's a lot more people who actually look like you and are like you, so you don't have all the white-bread kids staring at you funny. Also you're one of the tallest people at school, instead of being all little like before, so you actually have girls looking at you. Noticing you. So yeah, people treat you different. In a good way.

Doesn't mean you're gonna change, though. You don't want to be one of those kids who was really cool in elementary school and then started to suck in middle school and everyone stopped hanging out with them. Well, you weren't even cool in elementary school so things can only go up from here. You should tell that to Jake. That will make him feel better maybe.

Oh sick. That's the bell. Pizza time. Okay, have fun, Future Danny. Stay true to yourself and to your friends and stuff. Oh, and most important of all, get some.

Your friend,
Danny

P.S. Get some.

2 • Dorothy Wu

Friday, September 4

I awake to the sound of my little brother, Darrell, laughing like a psycho villain. He is laughing because he has just consumed two bowls of Crunch Berries and also because he has the ten-year-old crazies. I am very annoyed because I was just having a dream in which Link from the Legend of Zelda series was serenading me with his ocarina. Link was looking especially handsome in his green tunic, and I was feeling especially beautiful in a shimmery white maiden's robe. But alas, no more dreaming. I am awake. It is Friday.

I get up and I get dressed. I choose the same outfit as always: black pants and a black zip-up jacket with no hood. It is not that I am Goth, it is just that I enjoy black. Because I bathed last night, showering is unnecessary. Also I have no time for it. School starts in eleven minutes! I determine that I have just enough time for my daily ritual of brushing my hair 151 times—once for each of the original 151 Pokémon. However, before I am even able to get to Gengar (#94), I hear my father shouting at me. We must leave NOW, DOROTHY! he says. I leave.

For the duration of the seven-minute car ride, I make up a story. The story is about a young warrior who finds a crystal with magical properties. The crystal can transform him into anything he desires, and so he chooses to become a winged bear. However, the warrior stays in winged bear form for too long and so he is unable to turn back into a human. The rest of the story is about his adjustment to life as a winged bear. He frequents air markets and cloud salons. I think that maybe the story will end with him becoming lord of the sky. I have always wanted to title a story "Lord of the Sky."

I am still thinking about my story as I wander into math class four minutes late. It is already my third tardy even though the school year is just four days old, and so I have been assigned detention for today. This means I will not be able to get home in time to watch *Rurouni Kenshin*. Drat.

Math class is dull, as always. The boys that sit behind me expect me to be great at math because I am Asian, but I defy my stereotype by getting poor scores, worse than them even. Math is usually an excellent time to develop stories because I never pay attention, but today we have a quiz. It is a review of things we were supposed to learn in elementary school. I attempt to add and multiply fractions just like every good Chinese girl should, but eventually I give up. I am expecting a C minus. However, I did draw some neat things on the back of my paper. Two broadswords and a narwhal. I hope Mr. Peterson enjoys my drawings.

In health class we are beginning a unit on nutrition. If it is so important to consume fruits and veggies, I wonder why our school's vending machines are stocked with only cookies and candy and Flamin' Hot Cheetos? And cream cheese for people to smear on their Hot Cheetos. Our school would be a much different place if people actually behaved the way they tell you to in health class. I think about that a lot.

I have Mr. Morales for English. He is new to this place and he is also quite the hunk. Don't tell Link LOL. We begin our class with some very boring but fairly necessary grammar exercises. I am the smartest person at them besides that curly-haired, pen-chewing whiz boy, Jacob Schwartz. Then Mr. Morales tells us to clear the desks so we can play word games. We play a rhyming game in which we attempt to make limericks as a group. At one point it is my turn, and we are doing a limerick about money. The only word that I can think of that rhymes with "coins" is "groins," and so I shout out "GROINS!" People laugh a lot at my antics. I am not sure what kind of laughter it is.

Fourth period I have Spanish. I am already regretting the fact that I am in this class. I wanted to sign up for Latin with Mr. Gates, but my father said that I had to take Spanish because it is more useful in everyday life and because Latin is a dead language. I do not *gusta español*. Many of the students in the class can already speak Spanish anyway, which does not seem fair. Then again, what are they supposed to take instead—Latin? Latin is a dead language.

At lunch I go to the library, same as I did during my days at Truman Elementary. San Paulo has a big library with a really nice manga section and some funny comic books too. I think I will enjoy it here. Also, the librarians let me eat inside even though it is against the rules. Since there are not that many students who come to the library for lunch, the ones that do are kind of part of this special club where eating is allowed. I call us The Lunch Club. The other members of The Lunch Club are as follows: Devon Adams and Willy Kreutzkampf, who like Internet role-playing games, Micah Trotter who looks at military books and atlases, and Whitney Dealy who draws pictures of horses and girls that resemble Whitney Dealy riding horses. If we ever got together to hang out as a group, I think that I would be the spunky leader. The librarians, Ms. Glass and Ms. Dooling, are like our spiritual guardians who assign us missions. I think that I will end up writing a Lunch Club story before it is all said and done.

In Life Science we are learning about the scientific method. I am most frustrated because the kinds of problems I want to get to the bottom of do not seem like they can be solved by the scientific method. For example, I want to know why men do not carry pocket watches anymore. I want to know if dragons really existed. I want to know why rolling backpacks like mine are not more popular at school. After all, they are so efficient! I think about a lot of things.

Next I go to Social Studies, where we are learning about prehistory, which means history before writing. I do not like thinking about a world without writing. How did people record their stories, just with cave paintings? I do not think I could very effectively convey a complicated story like "Lord of the Sky" just by using cave paintings.

P.E. is my final class and it is the worst part of the day. All I have to say about it is UGH! I wish they would just let me use judo for P.E. credit. I wish my father would let me take judo.

Detention is not nearly so bad. I get some good writing and drawing done. The only downside is that some of the annoying boys from my math class are there too, but they are more focused on talking about soccer and sexual things, and so they do not notice me until the very end. As a result, they do not have time to make a single joke about my lack of mathematical abilities. That is one small step for Dorothy Wu, one giant leap for Asiankind.

On the bus ride home, I try to come up with ways of explaining my detention so I do not receive punishment. I fail in coming up with a reason that does not blame my father too much, and so I end up getting grounded for the evening. That is all right. I planned to spend the rest of my day and night in my room anyway, going on various message boards and playing computer games.

I venture out of my room at 10:37 p.m. to finish the last of my brother's Crunch Berries. What a rude awakening he will have tomorrow morning. I smile thinking about it.

Ah, is this not the life?

SAN PAULO JUNIOR HIGH SCHOOL
Morning Announcements—Thursday, September 10

ALL STUDENTS: Next Monday, September 14th, is School Picture Day. Wear nice clothes and don't forget to bring your smile!

If you still haven't purchased a locker, go see Ms. Devlin in the business office. Bring a check for 25 dollars made out to San Paulo Junior High.

Attention All Athletes! The fall sports season is here! This season's sports are boys soccer, girls soccer, boys flag football, girls flag football, and co-ed cross country. If you would like to join one of these teams, meet outside the gym after school today for an informational meeting. Tryouts are next week. GO PIRATES!

The Cesar Chavez Social Justice in Action Club (CCSJIAC) will be holding meetings starting next Tuesday at lunch in room 120. See Ms. Montez for details.

Please observe the Dress Code. School rules prohibit any wearing of tank tops, clothes with bared midriffs, hats, baggy shorts, or Oakland Raiders jerseys.

In observance of September 11, there will be a one-minute moment of silence tomorrow during 2nd period from 9:04–9:05. Please be respectful.

Remember, starting this year, San Paulo is a no gum, no iPods, no cell phones school! Those found with any of the aforementioned items will be given a detention. No exceptions.

3 • Hannah Schwartz

Tuesday, September 15

So, essentially my problem is this: Kristen likes Alex, but Alex is torn between Avery P. and Meghan. Avery P. kind of likes Avery S.—which would be really cute, right? Two Averys dating? But Avery S. is fully, completely, madly in love with Rachel Sloan, and he even hooked up with her for like seven seconds during spin the bottle at Lauren Gardner-Smith's birthday last weekend. But everyone knows that Rachel doesn't want a relationship so soon after breaking up with Creepy Tyler, and since that's like common knowledge, Avery S. told Spenser Walker that if he can't get Rachel then he wants Kristen instead, and so then Spenser passed that along to me and so now I'm not sure if I should tell Kristen, because that would definitely ruin everything.

I know. It's hard to believe that all this could have happened in the last week, but that's San Paulo for you. If you're not checking Facebook every five seconds, you're going to miss something huge. And if you're the last person to hear the big news, you're going to look like an idiot.

I'm just glad I've been able to stay out of it so far. I mean yeah, there were some rumors that that unusually cute sevvy Jeremy Farnsworth liked me, and of course it's only a matter of time before people start asking each other to the Halloween

Dance, but mostly I just want to keep away from all the drama and focus on school stuff.

That's much easier said than done, though. No matter what, boys will always be a major part of my life. I mean, well, hmm. That came out wrong. I'm not saying that *I'm* the one who gets so involved in all the relationship drama. I personally think boys are a waste of time. I mean, after all, I'm the only one out of all my friends who's never had a boyfriend, and I plan on keeping it that way until at least sophomore year of high school.

But I have to admit that the gossip is fun to follow. Keeping track of all that stuff—who's dating who, who cheated on who, who gave who a hickey the night before picture day—it's sort of like our school is Hollywood and I'm like *Us Weekly*. Someone call the Fashion Police! Oh gosh, I wish we did have a Fashion Police. I would have totally arrested Corinne Allison today on two counts of first-degree frumpy. She needs to save her overalls for when she marries an obese farmer. Which will happen.

I mean, it's all in good fun. I think we all realize at the end of the day that while we do say some heinous things, there's no deeper meaning behind them. Like, just because you call a certain girl slutty doesn't mean it's actually *true*. Well, in the case of Ashley Clarke, it is. But she knows what she did.

Or rather, *who*.

Johnny Graham. Johnny Graham. Johnny Graham. Can I just say *bom chicka wah wah*. . . .

Oh I know, I know. That's probably not true and I shouldn't spread it like it is. Okay, time for a New School

Year's Resolution: don't be a yotch. That's almost as bad as being a slut.

I was talking with my mom tonight when we went out for sushi, and she said that when she went to middle school, there was hardly any gossip or social scene at all. Like, they had maybe one dance a year, and if they even so much as said a boy's name, a nun would slap them across the face with a ruler. All I have to say about that is thank GAWD my mom moved to L.A., went to USC, and met my dad. And thank JEHOVAH they decided to let me go to public school when I begged them till I cried.

I could not imagine going to a boring junior high. I would definitely die a slow and painful death without my friends to keep things interesting. I mean it's not like I totally hate the school part of school—I get A's and everything. It's just that I find it difficult to really care about isosceles triangles and sedimentary rocks and the effing Preamble.

It's funny because my little brother is the exact opposite. Like, he could not be more into school—he takes notes for all his classes and reads for fun and stuff. But when it comes to the social side of things, I mean yeah, Jake has his friends, but they're all pretty lame and dorky in a sevvy-type of way. Well, except for Danny, I guess—but Danny doesn't even really count, because he's the son of our maid and gardener. Of course he and Jake are going to hang out.

I actually kind of want to help my brother out now that he's at middle school with me, but it's hard—he's just so clueless. Like, get this: a couple of weeks ago, Jake and I were back-to-school shopping at the mall with my mom and Danny. We were at the Gap and I had the credit card and I tried to buy Jake these cool jeans. They were standard fit, vintage wash, pretty expensive, and I showed them to him and I said, "These are yours if you want them." And do you know what he did? He actually flinched. Like these were haunted pants or something. Like these were Horcrux jeans with a piece of Lord Voldemort's soul in them. Like it was going to kill him to actually wear something acceptable for once. God. I guess if they're not sweatpants or pasta-sauce-stained shorts, then Jake's not gonna wear them.

Danny took me up on the jeans offer. He knows what's up.

Look—it's not as if I'm totally obsessed with being popular, like a skinny blond cheerleader from a Disney Channel show or something. It's just that I'll take being a little bit cool over being completely lame. Jake is so close to becoming one of those kids who becomes defined by what a loser they are, and I just don't want that. Like, that's embarrassing for me. There's this other sevvy I heard about, this Asian girl Dorothy something, and I've heard the funniest stories about her—like I heard that at her old school, she had no friends, and so she'd just walk around during recess, talking to herself and making animal noises, and when someone came near her, she'd meow and ribbit until they went away or whatever. I just don't want Jake to be considered in the same league as her.

But why waste my time talking about such irrelevant humans. Allow me to move on to a subject much nearer and dearer to my heart: Chad Beck.

I heart Chad Beck. I heart him so much. I know I said before that I would never date until sophomore year, but . . . well . . . it's Chad. I mean, his name is CHAD, for God's sake. That's pretty much like, "Hotness: the name."

(Other contenders for Hotness: the name—Sky, Brody, Heath, Aiden, Luca. But sorry, I just don't see how any of those can beat Chad.)

Chad is basically unattainable as far as guys go. Even though every girl from Arlington has been secretly in love with him since like, 4th grade, he's never had a real relationship. And honestly, why should he? I mean, he's just better than the rest of us. I have no chance. So I should just be like, indifferent, right? I should just forget about it and treat him like any other boy.

But oh GAWSH—when I saw him on the first day of school this year it just really really clicked for me. He's like this crazy science experiment—every hot guy element mixed together into one perfect package. He's got the cute surfer/skater look, the sandy hair, the gorgeous green-blue eyes, the butt to end all butts, he's super-nice, and I even heard that he writes poetry in his spare time.

And I think he might like me, too. I mean, when we talk to each other in science or P.E. or whatever, both of our flirt-o-meters are definitely set on "pursue." So yeah, I'm not making any promises—I don't want to jinx it—but as we get closer to Halloween we'll see where this thing goes. . . .

But I mean, like—I don't want a boyfriend. I definitely do not want a boyfriend.

4 • Danny Uribe

Saturday, September 19

Today was a good day. I had the Schwartz mansion all to myself. Jake and his sister and his parents were off at some bamitzvah in L.A., and my parents were cleaning the house they work at on weekends, so I got to kick it wherever I wanted on the property. The master bedroom. The dining room. Jake's room. The TV room. The other TV room. The pool. The hot tub. The wine cellar. The Sport Court. The putting green. Anywhere as long as it wasn't my family's stupid little shack.

This morning I mostly hung out in Jake's room and played Xbox. Then I got hungry, but the Schwartzes ran out of Hot Pockets so I ordered a pizza with the money that Mrs. Schwartz left for me. It's funny how much she gave me. Forty dollars. If it had been my mom, she would've given me three dollars. She would've said, *Go get two things off the dollar menu, and a drink, and don't forget to give me back that change.* But it was Jake's mom, so I got forty instead. Livin laaaaarge.

I took a shower in Jake's bathroom just because I felt like it. He had mad good-smelling shampoo. I need to borrow that stuff from him more often. If I'm gonna start getting some ladies this year, I need to have nice-smelling hair. Girls are all over that. I used Jake's deodorant too. It was super fresh. I don't think it even got opened before today.

After that I was thinking about shooting a few j's or playing some more Xbox or maybe trying out the sauna, but I realized that I still had some homework left to do. At first I was all kinds of pissed to have work over the weekend, but it wasn't that bad. I just had a couple of math problems and this work sheet for English. I'm glad I finished it early. So far the work at San Paulo is pretty cinchy.

The people at SP are sick. There's lots of different kids with different backgrounds. A lot more color in the hallways. Everyone's way chiller than at Arlington, too. They're not all obsessed with who has the nicest things or whatever. They don't treat me like a Mexican charity case, either. I just like it better than I've ever liked school. I don't think Jake's that happy with his classes so far, but he'll be okay. He'll stop whining. He's always loved school before.

Before the family left this morning, Mrs. Schwartz gave me one responsibility for the day and that was to feed the koi fish while the family was gone. But right when I was about to get the fish food, I got a text from my cousin Javy. Him and my other cousin Carlos were hanging out and they wanted to know did I want to come over to the Eastside and chill. Getting that text was kind of a surprise. I haven't seen my cousins that much in the years since me and my parents moved to the rich part of town, only at some random family birthdays and Quinceañeras. It's cool that I get to see them more now that we go to the same school. It's cool that they thought of me today. I texted them, *Yeah let's kick it,* and put on my shoes and left the house right then. So I forgot to feed the fish. That's okay. Fishes can live without food for eight days or something like that. I think that's true, at least. I'll ask Jake.

My bus ride over to the Eastside was mad funny. There was this gray-haired woman, like a bag lady woman, and she had like, five gray hairs on her chin. It was so funny. Old white people are crazy.

When I got to my cousins' house, them and some of their friends were all just kicking it in the front yard. It was their usual crew.

There was Javy and Carlos, of course, who have always been cool to me. They've never made a big deal to their other friends about how I live in Seabrook and stuff. Javy is just one of the chillest guys. He makes me feel tight with dudes I just met, just by talking and making everyone feel part of the same group. Carlos is quieter, but just as nice and one of the best taggers you've ever seen. His graffiti is seriously like art.

Edgar dominates everyone at soccer. He doesn't even have to try. He rules every sport and he knows it. When he gets famous he's going to get himself free Gatorade for life, and sometimes he'll give me sips. That's what he said.

Junior knows all these good dirty jokes. He's probably the hardest on me out of the guys, but he still treats me good. He's a little bit older, that's all.

Then there's Martín, who is really fat, so we all call him "Gordo." It's funny how every group always has a fat guy. Gordo can make me laugh so hard. Like this one time, Javy fell asleep at one of my baby cousin's baptisms, and when no one was looking, Gordo woke Javy up by rubbing his man boobs all up in Javy's face. He was all, Who's getting baptized now? It was the best. I can't help but smile more when I'm around Gordo.

All of those guys are eighth graders. I'm the only one who's in seventh. I used to be by far the shortest out of all of them too, so when I saw them they would always call me "Danielito." Now that I've grown so much over the summer, up to like five feet eight now, I'm actually taller than all of them except Javy, but they all still call me "Danielito" anyway. I'm tired of that nickname.

All of us are Mexicans, of course. Well I'm only half Mexican since my dad is from El Salvador, but basically I'm full Mexican like them. To everyone at SP, I'm full Mexican.

To everyone at Arlington, I was the only Mexican. That was a lot to deal with. Sometimes I wonder if that was the reason I didn't really have friends there besides Jake.

It's weird. At Arlington it felt like I was, I don't know, too Mexican or something. But today I was worried that my cousins and their friends would think I'm less brown than them since I'm the only one out of all of us who went to Arlington.

It's messed up. Yeah, it's tight to have my parents working for the Schwartzes, and yeah, I do like living on their huge property with the pool and the basketball court. And yeah, it was a good opportunity for me to be able to go to a nice, smart school like Arlington. But it's still been frustrating for me. Like today, all of the guys were asking annoying questions about where I've been all summer, why wasn't I at

Javy's birthday, why wasn't I at church on Sundays. What am I supposed to say to that? Do I tell them that I spent July at a swank summer camp in Maine with my best friend, Jake? Do I say that during August I went on a big expensive cruise across all of Europe with the family of a famous movie producer? Not unless I want to get laughed at and left out of the group. Not unless I want them to start calling me "Jew-lover" or "gay" or "gay Jew-lover."

I got them to stop bugging me by telling them that I'd been busy with summer school. Summer school is something they can all understand. "Sorry man," they said. "That sucks."

We didn't do much. Went over to the courts and played some basketball. I played okay. My shot wasn't falling, but I got some good rebounds and put-backs and a couple nice steals. After we were playing for like, an hour, some older and bigger guys joined our game. Real *cholos*, like from gangs. Like from gangs where they stab people. People like that kid who died. Anyway, I'm pretty sure these guys were from San Paulo High. They all had like, mustaches and hats with the sticker still on and everything, and they were mad hard to play against. It's not so much how skilled they were, but they were strong and they had all kinds of dirty tricks.

In the middle of the last game, there was this one fool. He was real tall, like taller than me, like almost six feet, I think, and I can still picture him because his head was shaved all gangster-style and because he had like this one big, thick eyebrow that went across his forehead. Jake said it's called a unibrow. He said it's like something a werewolf would have on his face when it's in people form. Anyway, this guy was a scary-looking fool. Way thugger than a wussy wolf. I was running up the court on a fast break, and the dude came up to me and pushed me to the ground really hard for no reason. It skinned my knee up pretty bad, but I didn't want to show anyone how much it hurt. And the eyebrow guy was just laughing with his friends the whole time.

Once the high school guys basically kicked us off the court, we went to Chapala Market to get Gatorades. Junior and Gordo also stole some Pica Limon when the cashier wasn't looking. I've never seen them steal anything before today. But they said that it's just candy and they've been doing it all summer and that I'd know that if I hung out with them once in a while. Then they called me a gay Jew-lover. Those guys are wack sometimes.

We got back to Javy and Carlos's and I told the crew that I had to get back home. I didn't say my reason why, which is that I still felt bad about not feeding the Schwartzes' fish. We all bumped fists, and they said that it was really cool having me over to hang out and that I should do it more often. I told them I would, and I will. It's tight hanging out with those guys now that we're all at the same school, part of the same world.

On my bus ride back I saw the bearded lady again. I don't think she ever leaves the bus. What a crazy, crazy lady. I wish I had a beard like her, though.

I got back to the Schwartz house and fed the fish first thing. Then I ordered another pizza and watched some TV on their plasma screen for a while. Finally I was tired, so I decided to head back to my room, lie down on my bed, and relax. That's when the Schwartzes got back, so Jake came over and asked if I wanted to play video games. I told him that my thumbs were tired from playing all day. He said okay and went back to his house. I'm not sure why I lied.

From: rmorales@spjhs.org
To: qgreene@spjhs.org
Subject: Extra Funds?
Sent: 9/27 7:10 p.m.

Hey Quentin,

I have a question about funding a special project for my classes. Hope the principal's office isn't too busy today.

We just started a unit on poetry in all of my classes, and I was thinking it might be fun to do a special art project to go along with it. I'm calling it "Poetry for the Eyes and Ears." The kids would write their own poems and use art to bring them to life. It would be great if we could buy some parchment, calligraphy pens, maybe some papier-mâché too.

If we could secure the funds to do this project, then I would be quite grateful. The beginning of the school year is a tough time, especially for the seventh graders. I want to make the experience as fun and easy as possible for them.

Please let me know what you think.

Thanks,
Ruben Morales

From: qgreene@spjhs.org
To: rmorales@spjhs.org
Subject: Re: Extra Funds?
Sent: 9/28 9:33 a.m.

Hi Ruben,

I appreciate your message. Unfortunately, times are tough right now, so what I'm saying to you is no. A project like the one you suggest is simply beyond our means at this point.

Perhaps you could check with Peg Quinn in the art room and see if she has anything for you. Colored paper, crayons, that kind of thing.

Poetry and creative assignments are all fun and good for the end of the year, but for now let's stick to the basics, shall we?

Best,
Quentin Greene
Principal, San Paulo Junior High School

5 • Jake Schwartz

Thursday, October 1

I remembered to say "rabbit rabbit" this morning. If it's the first thing you say on the first day of a new month, you're supposed to get good luck. I'm not saying I'm a big believer in luck or anything, but I forgot to say "rabbit rabbit" last month and September ended up sucking, so, you know, I didn't want to take any chances.

Today started off pretty good. In science we got to play quiz games, and in health we got to design our own food pyramids. In English I asked Mr. Morales if I could take a look at my letter to myself from the first day of school—I wanted to change one thing—but he said I have to wait until June. He seemed to think he hurt my feelings by making me wait, so after class he gave me a watermelon Jolly Rancher. Guilt candy: tastes good.

My run of luck seemed as if it was going to continue in fourth period, when Mr. Armstrong said that I didn't have to make up the algebra quiz I missed when I was at Yom Kippur services on Monday. Obviously, this rules. Score one for the chosen people.

Of course, one important detail I should mention is that Armstrong gave me that news in front of the entire class. So then a couple minutes later, when he started teaching again,

Brendan Wheeler, who sits right next to me, sneezed "JEW!" under his breath. And, well, okay, I guess it was actually kind of clever. When you think about it, "Jew" does sound a lot like "achoo." And it's not like it was surprising. "Jew" has basically become my nickname these days. So I guess little stuff like that is more fun than mean. I shouldn't let it bother me. But still.

It doesn't hurt my feelings exactly, but it makes me feel kind of limited. Really—that's all I am? Three letters, one syllable, and I'm this greedy little gnome-person who cares only for shiny things?

That's school nowadays. People are all, "Hey, let's find one defining thing about each person, and that's all we'll ever talk about when we see them."

It sucks. Danny was talking about it with me at lunch today. His big thing is that he really hates it when people call him "*cholo*." And I get what he means. People assume that since he's Mexican, he's going to wear a big black T-shirt or a Raiders jersey to school and that he's not going to do his homework and that he's going to join a gang and stuff. Actually, it's not even right for people to assume that he's Mexican in the first place—Danny especially hates when people do that, because he's half Salvadoran.

The thing I don't get about Danny though, is while he doesn't like being seen as a tough cholo guy, he also doesn't like when people think of him as a preppy Arlington kid. He doesn't even want people to know that he went to Arlington, or that he lives in Seabrook. I suppose I can sort of understand why he doesn't want people knowing those things. Most of the kids from Arlington are jerks, all my sister's friends included. But on the other hand, Danny should realize that it was a great place for us with awesome teachers and a sweet playground and that it felt a lot more like school than SP ever will.

Pretty much all the Arlington kids go to SP because the Honors classes are supposed to be good here and because the private middle schools are druggy and far away. There's still no comparing Arlington and SP, though. At Arlington, the teachers never handed their students a work sheet and then tuned them out for an entire hour. The kids didn't pretend to be so cool that they couldn't remember your name even though they've known you since first freaking grade. Danny never left halfway through lunch so he could go hang out with his cousins.

Okay, I know I'm overreacting to that. But come on! I'm moody! I'm angsty! I'm hormonal!

At least I will be once I actually start puberty.

Look, it wasn't even a big deal when Danny left. There were only fifteen minutes left in lunch anyway, and our conversation was kind of dying and I still needed to study for my vocab quiz in Latin. The extra fifteen minutes gave me time to go to the library and do just that. And I got an A on my quiz, so it all worked out. When Danny told me that he had to go see his cousins because he promised them he would hang out today, I should have just said, *"Flocci non facio."* In Latin that basically means, "I don't give a crap."

Instead, what I said was "Have fun, man."

Obviously yeah, of course, I want to hang out with Danny since he's my best friend and my brother, and since he's the funnest to talk to. But I still get to see him for health and P.E. And it's not as if he's my only friend. I've got Sean and Robert and Russell, and I've known all those guys since I was five, and those are good guys. Do they have a slight preoccupation with hitting each other in the nuts? I mean, yeah. Sure. But, you know, they just . . . love the thrill of it. Or something.

Not that I know what it's like to get hit down there. When I take a Wilson or a Penn to the nuts—yeah, it hurts, but not the way people say it's supposed to. I don't feel that awful pain like the world is ending or anything, and that's because, well . . . I think I'm still light-years—light-decades away from even starting puberty. My mom said Dad was a late bloomer too, and it's just—dang it. Why is my body so behind the times? Mr. Morales told me that I'm at a college reading level. Why is it that when I look in the mirror, I see a third grader?

Danny and I played one-on-one after school today, and the difference in physical-ness was so obvious. When we used to play, it was really competitive. Every single time. He's always had some nice jukes and a quick first step, but I could usually keep it close with my three-point range. But when we played this afternoon it was just unfair. He posted me up down low, grabbed every rebound without jumping, and he even blocked a couple of my threes. He blocked my threes! It was like he had stretchy arm powers. But what kind of superhero blocks his best friend's shot?

Eleven to one. That was the final score. And I'm pretty sure that even the point I got was a pity bucket. It was near the end of the game and Danny kind of slipped and fell in an unrealistic way.

But whatever. It was fun to hang out, and Danny said that I have more game than some of the guys he plays with over on the Eastside. That was nice to hear.

After we played, we went inside and I helped him with his math homework and a writing assignment. Then we grabbed some Popsicles and played Xbox for a while. It was good times.

When it comes to that side stuff—Danny going over to the Eastside, "kicking it" with his cousins, hanging out with older kids . . . I mean, that's all fine. Whatever. *Flocci non facio.*

"Nuthin' but a Grammar Thang"
By Dr. Dre, Snoop Dogg, and Mr. Morales
Special for Mr. Morales's English Classes

One, two, three and to the fo
It's your boy, MC Mo, gonna drop a little flow
Ready to teach you somethin, so listen up
'Cause we 'bout to bring your test scores up

Yes, I'm your teacher first, but see I'm more than just a nerd,
I'll pimp smack you with syntax 'cause I'm a mixmaster of
*   words*

Aint nuthin but a grammar thang, baaaaabay!
Without structure, we'd all go craaaaazay!
You'll need it for all your essaaaaays!
Time to put our English skills on display!

But, uh, back to the lecture at hand
A sentence without grammar is like a beach without the sand
From a young teach's perspective
Writing stuff that makes sense is our number one objective
You wanna write the right quotations, man
Exclamations, man, get crunk on punctuation, man
Now y'all know I ain't no joke, my students,
I'm the teacher with the beat here so to listen would be
*   prudent*
'Cause I'm bomb with the commas like my man Obama
I'm the best, bros and hos, so go tell yo momma

Just sit tight, aight, and delight in my turn of phrase
And in no time y'all be makin' A's

It's like this and like that and like this and uh
It's like that and like this and like that and uh
It's like this and like that and like this and uh
So just chill till the next episode . . .

(tomorrow's class!)

6 • Dorothy Wu

Wednesday, October 7

The Club Chronicles
Part 12: Vengeance Strikes Back
By Dorothy Wu

"This is your last chance, Lunch Club," the gray ogre growled as he licked his purple lips. "Give me the secret to your powers or else I shall destroy this entire junior high."

"You will never get away with this, Moo-dar!" cried Dorothy, her raven hair glistening in the library's fluorescent light. "Our powers must be earned, and all you have earned is a one-way ticket to Ugly Island!"

"Clever girl . . . " the elephantine ogre whispered, licking his lumpy lips again. "Do you know what happens to clever girls? They end up . . . **DEAD!***"*

He motioned toward the children's section of the library, where Dorothy's fallen comrades lay on the ground. Whitney, Willy, Devon, Ms. Dooling . . . only some of them had in fact been clever girls, but all of them were slumped on the floor, dead and bloodied and rotting. Now the fate of the whole school—nay, the whole city—nay, the whole county, depended on Dorothy, Micah, and Ms. Glass.

"This is our last chance, Lunch Club!" shouted Dorothy in spunky leader fashion. "Let us send this baddie back to

Dark Plunder where he belongs!"

"Right!" shouted Ms. Glass. "It is Transformation Time!"

There was a bright flash and the heroes took the form of their spirit beasts. Micah became Lieutenant Lemur, obedient and proud. He also had super-vision. Ms. Glass transformed into a kangaroo who could pull anything from her pouch. Dorothy became a warrior mermaid maiden with the power to fly. Her beauty was stunning and her gaze was fierce. The Lunch Club was ready to fight.

But Moo-dar was also ready . . . for them. Using his summoning staff, he conjured a fire force field that surrounded them before they could unleash any potent attacks.

Dorothy tried to break free, but the flames were burning hot. Yowch!

What were they to do? All the hope in the universe was lost.

Just then, there was a smashing through the front door. In jumped a handsome hero wearing a bronze mecha-suit. He was serious and brave, but he had a smiling look in his gold-brown eyes.

"You are finished, Moo-dar!" the dashing savior cried. Dorothy looked at him with wonderment and glee. He struck an impressive figure in his metallic battle armor, and his poof of hair was quite a sight to behold.

The hero made a swift motion with his hands and suddenly there was a huge heart-shaped blast. The Lunch Club stood in awe. Moo-dar cowered. The super savior had summoned the power of

As you may be able to tell, I have not yet finished this story. I began writing it last month and I just love it so far, but I do not think I will be showing it to any others. I have never shown anybody any of my stories, not because I think the stories are poor, but because I do not think the world is ready. One day I will unleash all of my stories at once, and I think that I will probably make quite the heart-shaped blast in the world of literature. But until then, I must hone my craft.

This particular story is a good one. I am not sure if it ranks up there with my best. It is no "Magick Rabbyt" or "Lord of the Sky," and it definitely does not compete with any of the tales in my classic trilogy, *Vortex Quest: The Tomorrow Dimensions*. However, I believe that if I work on it enough, I can develop The Club Chronicles into my next grand series. The main element that I must work on is the budding romance between Dorothy and the savior.

Behind every great work of fiction there is a classic love story. Think of Romeo and Juliet. Cinderella and Prince Charming. Sailor Moon and Tuxedo Mask. What would they be without their burning passions? Love is what makes characters feel alive—it is the force that keeps heroes moving past all their obstacles. Without his love for Princess Peach, how could Mario maintain the strength to make it past all the Koopa shells and warp pipes and Goombas in his way? He needs love. We need love.

Love is probably the most necessary thing there is. However, while it is important to fall in love, it can be difficult to tell whether you are, in fact, in love or not. Take me. I develop affections rather easily, and perhaps too easily. For example, in my younger years, when I was playing Metroid on my family's old Nintendo, I developed a mondo crush on the character Samus Aran. Samus is everything you could want in a mate: brave and adventurous, with an impressive armored suit that features a cannon, missiles, and beams. But there is a catch—when you complete the game, it is revealed that Samus is in fact a girl! And I am a girl! A heterosexual girl! That made me think about some things. *Yipe.*

Then there was that time I fell in love with this tattooed man that I saw one time at the gas station, only to never see him again. Also there was the occasion in fifth grade when we were studying the Civil War and I began to "like-like" Confederate General Robert E. Lee. Very cute, but very forbidden. Oh yes, and then later on in fifth grade, I started to have sneaky feelings toward this first grader named Zachary. Yet I think I was mostly attracted to his lunch box. It is only natural for a girl to pursue a man for his Speed Racer lunch box.

Surely, I was quite confused about love after these numerous embarrassing experiences. However, I rediscovered my sexual preferences this year in English class when I first laid eyes on Mr. Morales. Ohh, Señor Morales. As they say in the movies, "What a catch!" Or, as I sometimes say to myself, "Holy Table!"

(An explanation of the phrase "Holy Table": I wanted to start saying exclamations that begin with the word "holy," but I did not feel like glorifying "cows" or "smokes" or "molys" or the s-word. So I came up with "Holy Table." After all, who does not love tables?)

As I was saying, Ruben Morales is every girl's dream. He is very aesthetically pleasing, from his boyish smile to his nerdy glasses that he sometimes wears to his sandy skin (well, it is sand-colored, but smoother than sand, mehopes!). He is extraordinarily funny, kind, and cute in that smart-cute way that I especially like. Also, he wrote and performed that bomb-diggity rap for our class. I will never throw my copy of the lyrics away. Doing that would be like throwing away an expensive porcelain cat, and I am still enraged at my father for doing that.

But when I think about it, I realize that what exists between Mr. Morales and myself is not love. It is just my girlish mind playing tricks on me. He is an adult with his own life to worry about, and I am just a tween. We are from different worlds. It can never be. I love him not. I feel lust for him—that is all.

So whom *do* I love? That is the question.

And after much pondering, I will say that right now I do not know. I must love someone, but it has to be the right kind of someone. Someone who understands me. Someone who finds me physically enchanting. Someone who enjoys my stories. Someone who loves to have silly times. Someone who likes the same video games and mangas that I like.

Oh yes! I know the person whom I love!

. . . 'tis me!

lilbeachbabe777: hey

CHAD4lyfe: hey hannah

CHAD4lyfe: hannah bannana

lilbeachbabe777: lol

CHAD4lyfe: sup

lilbeachbabe777: nm u?

CHAD4lyfe: nm

CHAD4lyfe: my moms making me clean my room

CHAD4lyfe: im like mom noooooo

lilbeachbabe777: lol

lilbeachbabe777: that is so funny

CHAD4lyfe: haha yea

CHAD4lyfe: so wats up

lilbeachbabe777: omfg

lilbeachbabe777: i was over at kristens house

lilbeachbabe777: after club vball practice

lilbeachbabe777: and alex came over

lilbeachbabe777: and so we were like lol what r u doin here

CHAD4lyfe: yea

lilbeachbabe777: and alex just smiles

lilbeachbabe777: and he holds up this big sign that says "kristen—go to the halloween dance with me or lose at life"

lilbeachbabe777: omg it was the cutest thing ive ever seen

lilbeachbabe777: literally ever i think

lilbeachbabe777: im so happy for krist shes been crushing on alex forlikever lol

CHAD4lyfe: i heard about that

lilbeachbabe777: o yeah?

CHAD4lyfe: yea

CHAD4lyfe: actully

CHAD4lyfe: *actually

CHAD4lyfe: the way he asked her

CHAD4lyfe: was my idea

lilbeachbabe777: really

lilbeachbabe777: ???

CHAD4lyfe: yea

CHAD4lyfe: we were talkin bout it yesterday and i came up wit it

lilbeachbabe777: well arent u the little romantic ;)

CHAD4lyfe: yea

lilbeachbabe777: but wait

lilbeachbabe777: whats gonna happen now

CHAD4lyfe: ?

lilbeachbabe777: now that like

lilbeachbabe777: u used up ur best idea on how to ask someone to the dance

CHAD4lyfe: well i wouldnt go that far lol

lilbeachbabe777: haha well like

lilbeachbabe777: have u asked someone...?

lilbeachbabe777: i mean like, u know

lilbeachbabe777: ur chad beck

lilbeachbabe777: everyone wants to go wit u haha

CHAD4lyfe: even the dudes?

CHAD4lyfe: jk lol

lilbeachbabe777: lol

CHAD4lyfe: haha gay lol

lilbeachbabe777: but like u know what i mean?

CHAD4lyfe: yea i no

CHAD4lyfe: hey check out this poem i wrote

lilbeachbabe777: ok

CHAD4lyfe: its called "her"

lilbeachbabe777: im excited

CHAD4lyfe: i want to hold those hips

CHAD4lyfe: i want to kiss those lips

CHAD4lyfe: and feel her fingertips

CHAD4lyfe: yea that would be heaven

CHAD4lyfe: she puts me in a trance

CHAD4lyfe: so let me take a chance

CHAD4lyfe: and say will you go to the dance

CHAD4lyfe: with me, lilbeachbabe777

lilbeachbabe777: omg!!!!!!!1!!

lilbeachbabe777: yes of course i will

lilbeachbabe777: OMG im so excited

lilbeachbabe777: that was a beautiful poem chad

CHAD4lyfe: thx

lilbeachbabe777: :)

CHAD4lyfe: yea well

CHAD4lyfe: the dance and stuff

CHAD4lyfe: should be tyte

lilbeachbabe777: :)

lilbeachbabe777: what do u think ur gonna go as?

lilbeachbabe777: like for ur costume?

CHAD4lyfe: i dunno

CHAD4lyfe: hey i have to go

CHAD4lyfe: mom said i have to get off lol

lilbeachbabe777: lol yeahhh moms are like that

lilbeachbabe777: just minimize the chat box!

CHAD4lyfe: no like i have to go now

lilbeachbabe777: ok so well talk plans at school?

CHAD4lyfe: yea yea

lilbeachbabe777: ok sounds awesome!

CHAD4lyfe: yea

CHAD4lyfe: l8r hannah

lilbeachbabe777: good night, chad

lilbeachbabe777: <3

CHAD4lyfe has signed off at 10:32 p.m.

lilbeachbabe777 has signed off at 10:32 p.m.

7 • Danny Uribe

Thursday, October 15

My best memory of elementary school was the first day of fifth grade. That was the day Jake's mom told me and him we were allowed to walk to school all by ourselves.

All through fourth grade, Jake would complain to his mom about her rule that a parent had to take us to school and back. Her rule made no sense. The Schwartz house isn't even a mile from Arlington. It's like a ten-minute walk. Mrs. Schwartz said, It's safer if I drive you. Jake said, Mom, you should trust us. Jake's mom said, I do trust you guys, it's the strangers I don't trust. Jake got all upset whenever this happened.

My parents have always been cool with me doing stuff by myself, but I never wanted to walk to school without Jake. That's what made the first day of fifth grade so sick. Jake's mom came into the kitchen while we were eating breakfast, and she smiled and told us she had some big news. She said that it was time. We knew what that meant. We were hyyyped. We celebrated so hard.

In fifth grade that was like our little way of growing up. We went from riding with Jake's mommy to taking ourselves to school.

Now that we go to San Paulo, it's way too far to walk, so

this year I've gone back to driving with Jake's mom. I don't like it too much.

Every time Mrs. Schwartz drives me, Jake, and Hannah home after school, she asks us all to share the most interesting parts of our day. Both of the Schwartz kids get really into it. I think it's like the highlight of Hannah's day. She talks about who's getting fat, who's dating "an ugly," all that gossip stuff. That girl loves the sound of her own voice.

Jake always shares something lame like, "Oh, today in science we got to dissect a sheep heart!" or "It was awesome! My Latin teacher let us do class outside!" Seriously, no one should ever get that excited about class. It seems like Jake's trying extra hard to act all happy, like he's trying to convince himself his life is dope. I feel bad for the guy. I wish he liked seventh grade better.

Whenever Mrs. Schwartz asks me about my day, I say nothing happened, even though that's never the truth.

I think she would have a heart attack if I ever told her about all the "interesting" stuff I really do see at SP. Like last week, when they found two bags of weed in Luis de la Garza's locker and he got expelled, and they sent him to juvie because it wasn't his first time. Or yesterday, when Juan Salcido and Chuy Hernandez got in this big fight during lunch because their brothers are in different gangs. Juan reps the Destroyers because of his brother, and Chuy reps the Raiders because of his brother, so of course both of them wanted to prove that theirs was the best. I'm glad they only got suspended, though. It was just a few punches thrown, nothing serious.

This is the kind of stuff that's going through my head on the car ride home. Some big-time stuff. But it doesn't belong in Mrs. Schwartz's car. When I'm in there, I have to sit and listen to the most boring stories. Hannah freaks out because she can't think of the right costume to wear to the Halloween Dance. A witch would be too boring, but a pirate would be too slutty, but a Disney princess would be too cutesy. Unless it was Jasmine, which would be too slutty. And oh man, all this stuff. She's gonna look good anyway, so who cares? Jake goes on and on about his classes, and lots of times he complains about his teachers and all the time he's trying to compare stuff to how it was at Arlington, and it's like, dude, we left that place behind. And finally there's Mrs. Schwartz, who just won't shut up about brunch with the moms, or tennis with the moms, or which movie star's house she just decorated, and why isn't Mr. Schwartz home more often, and after a while I really do not care. It's just not my scene.

That's why today, I realized it's time for me to grow up. I need to get the hell out of Mrs. Schwartz's car, just like I did in fifth grade.

So today I started taking the bus home.

It's so tight. Now instead of heading straight back to the Schwartz mansion every day, I can go and chill over on the Eastside whenever I want. I'm mad tired of Javy and Carlos giving me a hard time for getting picked up in that big white Lexus SUV after school. Now I can roll with them instead. Then I can go back to Jake's house when I actually want to.

It's not like I don't like Jake's house anymore. It's not that.

I'd just rather have the choice of where I wanna go. Sometimes I feel like hanging with my people, that's all.

Mrs. Schwartz didn't seem happy about my decision, but she said it was up to my parents. My parents are cool with it as long as I get home in one piece. Hannah doesn't know and probably doesn't care. Jake said I'll "regret" my choice because I'm gonna "need" him after school to help me with my homework. That kinda pissed me off. So I won't be able to do five cinchy-ass math problems by myself? And that's assuming I'll even want to do my homework. Whatever, man. I don't need his help just because he's in Honors. That whole program is bull anyway. Everyone knows the only reason they even have different classes for Honors and regular is so the Seabrook parents will feel okay putting their kids at SP in the first place. I know Jake's parents almost didn't even send him and Hannah here at all—they wanted them to go to some private school, like Costa Blanca or something. My mom heard them talking one time.

Today was my first day riding on my own. It was cool. I felt all old. Like, Jake has to wait until his bamitzvah in June to be an adult, but I'm basically one already because I'm riding with my homies in a city bus to the Eastside instead of in Mommy's luxury car to Seabrook. Thug liiife.

I'm kidding, okay? But yeah. Today was pretty tight. I rode over to Javy and Carlos's with them and the normal group of homies—except for Junior who was off chilling with some older guys. Actually Junior was with the same cholos who roughed us up on the basketball courts that one time. I used to think those guys were in high school since they're so big, but it turns out they're in eighth grade at SP. Probably some of them have gotten held back a couple times. They're the guys like Luis de la Garza, the kind of fools who get in real trouble, not just small stuff like stealing candy. Some of them are in gangs. Maybe even most of them. There's this one guy, Guillermo Torres. He's the same guy who pushed me hard to the ground on the courts, the fool with one eyebrow. He's a real *veterano* in the Eastside Raiders. From what I heard, he's one of their main shot-callers even though he's still in junior high, and man, they're the biggest gang in SP. Guillermo's the one in charge of recruiting little kids for them, like elementary-school-age kids. Babies. It's scary thinking about it.

So yeah, I guess that's where Junior was today, off doing whatever with some of the Raiders. Maybe he wants to join the gang. Maybe he'll show up to school tomorrow with a bald head and black eyes and that whole deal. I don't want to think about what he might have been up to. I hope he keeps clean. But me and the other guys like Javy, Carlos, Edgar, and Gordo, we don't want none of that scene. We're just happy doing what we were doing today. Hangin', ballin', maybe chillin' with some fine ladies now and then. I guess in a way we're like our own little gang.

But like, I'm not actually gonna start using that word to describe us. For one, if I say "gang" at SP and a teacher hears me—or if I flash a sign, or wear Raider gear, or do any gang-ster stuff at all, even as a joke—they'll slap a suspension on me so fast. They've had a lot of problems with people from our school and gang violence. They're trying real hard to cut down. Plus, another reason I don't want to describe me and my friends as a gang is, like, what if they all get into it? What if Javy and Carlos decide that it's cool and then all of a sudden they want to get a name and colors and they want to start recruiting? And then what if the other gangs started thinking about us as a legit gang? And then what if they tried to war with us? It would all be so scary. My mom would kill me, if someone else hadn't already. And Jake would be disappointed.

Overall I'd say yeah, I'm happy to be riding the bus to the Eastside most days. But it's good to know that if things ever get too rough, I'll always be protected. I was thinking about it this way: I may not like riding home in Mrs. Schwartz's Lexus, but if I ever need to ditch the hood scene, I know that it's the perfect getaway car.

From: qgreene@spjhs.org
To: rmorales@spjhs.org
Subject: Parental Concerns
Sent: 10/22 3:30 p.m.

Hi Ruben,

It's just come to my attention that in your class two weeks ago you performed a rap song you wrote entitled, "Nothing but a Grammar Thing." From what I've heard, you entered your classroom wearing a large chain and a do-rag and you sang this song, which features words such as "pimp," "crunk," and "ho."

I have received several parental complaints about this performance. One woman even told me that her son was in tears as a result of the vulgar way in which you danced close to his desk.

What concerns me about this song of yours is that it glorifies a certain kind of lifestyle. At a school such as ours, gang activity is no trifling matter. For some of our students, the classroom is a last refuge from "the streets." We do not need the lewd, misogynistic, violence-glorifying culture of hip-hop music permeating the halls of San Paulo.

I need you to start teaching the material the way it is supposed to be taught. This is the last time I should be sending you a message like this.

Best,
Quentin Greene
Principal, San Paulo Junior High School

From: rmorales@spjhs.org
To: qgreene@spjhs.org
Subject: Re: Parental Concerns
Sent: 10/22 10:11 p.m.

Hi Quentin,

I appreciate your feedback. I think I have an idea of how I can teach creatively without causing any controversy. Let's see how it goes!

Thanks again,
Ruben

WHO LOVES RAP?
HOW ABOUT MOVIES?
COMIC BOOKS?

DID YOU EVER WANT THE CHANCE TO TRY WRITING 'EM?

If your answer is "uh—yeah!" then join the crew of Write On!—a new club being started by Mr. Morales.

Every Tuesday at lunch, bring your pencils and your creative juices to room 213.

P.S. FREE FOOD!

Saturday, October 31 at 2:33 p.m.

Hannah Rose Schwartz is setting up the gym for the dance!!
about a minute ago via Twitter · Comment · Like

Corinne Allison this is halloween this is halloween lol
2 minutes ago · Comment · Like

Avery Patterson what to wear . . . what to wear . . .
2 minutes ago · Comment · Like

Kristen Duffy is watching scary movies w/ her date :)
3 minutes ago · Comment · Like

Tyler Bell gonna groove with some ladies toniiiiiight
12 minutes ago · Comment · Like

Emily Colman cant wait to see what Spense looks like in his ninja costume
17 minutes ago · Comment · Like

Chad Beck sexiest viking this school has ever SEEN
21 minutes ago · Comment · Like

Whitney Dealy hehe can i take my horse to the dance, i need a date
25 minutes ago · Comment · Like

Ashley Clarke has a new phone. gimme your #s, hoez
26 minutes ago · Comment · Like

Jamie Mackintosh FINALLY came up with her costume idea. procrastinate much? haha

30 minutes ago · Comment · Like

Lauren Gardner-Smith is bingeing on candy corn

32 minutes ago · Comment · Like

Brian Fenton my face itches

32 minutes ago · Comment · Like

Jake Schwartz is waiting for the Great Pumpkin.

33 minutes ago · Comment · Like

8 • Hannah Schwartz

Saturday, October 31

Oh where do I begin . . . where do I begin . . .

Do I start the story at 7:22 p.m., when he held my hand for the first time . . . ? Or should I start it at 7:46 p.m., when we first slow danced. . . . Well, actually, maybe I should start at 10:28 p.m., which was when we . . .

Oh! But I shouldn't give away the ending.

How about this. The epic story of my and Chad's everlasting love for each other starts two weeks and three days ago with the cutest instant message conversation of all time. Like, if they had had AIM back when *The Notebook* happened, even Noah and Allie couldn't have had such an adorable chat.

I saved the whole thing and I look at it pretty much every day. Not because I'm a dork, even though I totally am, but because it was just that awesome. Even now, when I reread "Her," the poem he wrote for me, I remember how nervous I got. Luckily we were chatting and not on Skype, so he couldn't see me hyperventilating.

That poem!—omg—it's so amazing—it's seriously like e.e. cummings status. When Chad signed off, it just hit me, all at once. I went, "OMG. The hottest guy in school is taking me to the dance." I mean, is that not straight out of a musical? Spotlight on me with tears of joy in my eyes. Even though the

Halloween Dance has been over for less than an hour, I still can't believe it.

And this story gets better and better as it goes on. The two weeks leading from our fateful chat to the dance last night were pure magic. Passing notes in class, sitting together at lunch, sending texts before bed . . . sigh. Seriously, looking back on it makes me sigh like an ingenue. An ingenue! And yeah, we weren't going out or anything, but really, we both knew that it was just a matter of waiting . . .

Waiting for tonight, October 31st. The night of the dance.

So I was freaking out all day because I had to help decorate the gym in the afternoon with the rest of the leadership class, and I wouldn't have enough time to get ready because my dinner reservations were at five since the dance started so early at seven, because the school is afraid of having, like, random late-night stabbings or something.

Long story short: I panicked a little, some tears were shed, my mom is a goddess, and by the time Chad Matthew Beck arrived at my front door at 4:30, I was a beautiful fairy princess. I had a tiara and a wand and wings and everything, and it was just the right amount of slutty for my mom to be okay with, and oh, it was perfect. Chad was dressed as a Viking and, omg, he was so hot. He had the spiky helmet and the battle-ax and the chest plate with the built-in pecs (which he totally didn't need, by the way, with the water polo man-chest he's got).

First we took some extremely cute pictures. Don't worry, they're already up on Facebook. Then my mom drove the two of us to Sapori D'Italia, which was super-embarrassing. I begged her begged her begged her to let us get a limo service, but she said that that was ridiculous and that I have to wait until high school. I mean, luckily she didn't humiliate me too bad when the three of us were in the car, but when she started talking about how me and Chad have grown up together since preschool . . . back when we apparently used to take baths together or something . . . well yeah, I had some suicidal thoughts.

When we got to the restaurant, our group was already there waiting for us. Chad and I decided to go with a small group of just our absolute closest friends, so there were only thirteen people total. Besides the two of us, there was, of course, the happy couple Kristen and Alex (they went as salt and pepper. And they ended up winning Cutest Pairs Costume at the dance. Barf), Rachel and Avery S. (even though everyone knows he wants Kristen now, so some major drama there), Emily Colman and Spenser (dressed as a geisha and a ninja, omg, adorable), Avery P. and this guy Sam from her gymnastics team (biggest forearms I've ever seen), Meghan and Bryce Sherman (boring), and playing the role of thirteenth wheel this evening—the odd girl out—was Lauren Gardner-Smith. Come to think of it, I don't think she's ever been linked with a guy before. Huh. Maybe she's a lesbian.

I guess we could've invited Jamie Mackintosh to be Lauren's lezzie date, but—oh wait, that's right—I hate Jamie Mackintosh. She thinks she's the new me, and she is so not the new me. I would never have red hair. God likes me too much.

I'm losing track of the big picture here, which is that I went to a dance with Chad #@&%ing Beck. The details of dinner are irrelevant. We all ate, some of us less than others (Avery P. barely touched her plate. Hmm . . .), and then a few of the parents gave us a ride to SP, which is where the plot truly thickens. . . .

He held my hand on the walk into the gym. Chad held my hand! The reason was that there was this whole spooky walkway with ghosts and skeletons and stuff, and even though I had helped decorate the thing like, three hours before, I pretended to be scared so my big strong Viking would protect me . . . and he totally did! His hand was like, twice the size of mine and surprisingly smooth.

So I thought my night was complete. Right there. The hand-hold was exactly what I wanted it to be. I didn't really expect too much Chad time when it came to dancing, because, well . . . dancing is probably the least exciting part of an SP dance. The guys and girls tend to split right down the middle of the gym, kind of like we're Amish or something. All the girls pretty much dance in a big group together, and we have a good time, but what we really want is for the boys to come dance, and they never do.

Most of the guys stand awkwardly in the corner. Sometimes they'll form a small circle and each of the boys will take turns attempting to do the worm or some other lame break-dance move, but that usually dies out within a few minutes, so then they have nothing to do but return to their natural habitat, the wall, where they stand for the rest of the night with their hands in their pockets like the bored dorks they are. I've heard that in high school, guys will get up the courage to dance a little, but at SP all the boys follow the same, lame, no-dancing routine. All of them: cool guys, creepy guys, geeky guys, Arlington kids, Mexicans—you name it.

All the guys, that is, except for Chad Beck. About twenty minutes after we got there, when the DJ played the first slow-ish song, Chad came up behind me and tapped me on the shoulder, and I turned around and he had this look on his face that was just like, "Why not?" And so we slow danced, and it was incredible. It wasn't the lame kind of slow dancing where there's five feet between the guy and the girl and they're barely touching. It was like . . . bride-groom slow dancing. And he wasn't singing along with the lyrics of the song. He was reciting different words, the words to a song he just wrote for me. "Song for Hannah." It was a little confusing, trying to hear all of his words over a completely different song, but it was such a tender moment. My heart was beating so hard.

Plus, Chad stayed for the fast songs after, and well . . . we may or may not have done a little freaking, too. No comment. ;)

The whole night reminded me of my mom's all-time favorite movie, which is *West Side Story*. She's made me watch it with her like, dozens of times. There's this one scene in it where Tony and Maria are at the big dance and they lock eyes and everything else goes fuzzy, and they start dancing together and nothing else in the world matters at all. That's what it felt like to be with Chad. I barely even remember what happened for most of the dance, because he was my Tony and

I was his Maria and we only had eyes for each other. The Viking and the fairy.

We danced until ten and then my mom came to pick us up. When we dropped Chad off at his house, Mom let me walk him to his door, and she had the good sense to turn away for the next twenty seconds or so. Now I'm not gonna you know what and tell, but let me just say that we ended the night in the perfect way.

And I pity any girl who isn't me today.

Song for Hannah
Chad Beck

staring into the world inside your sapphire eyes
and running my hands
through your beautiful brown brown hair
smiling to myself i realize
that i need you
and you are there

'cause you make me happy, make me hot, make me sing
you make me smile, make me laugh, make me think
you're the girl who makes everything
make sense
to me

you're not like the others in this goddamned place
you're the only chick who's really worth the chase
when i look for love among this whole human race
it's you
i see
writing a song that i'll play for you when the time is right
and texting you
and looking at a picture of you
i long for the day when we can play my song and sing all night
but until then
i'll just sit and write

'cause you make me wonder, make me hope, make me dream

you make me much more sensitive than I seem
you make me jump up
make me scream
"i love this girl"

i need you so bad 'cause you make me so good
you make me listen like a real man should
and so girl i'm wondering i'm wondering could
you be mine
for good?

so i give you these lyrics
'cause i need you to hear this
girl, the only thing that's clear is
when i'm with you, i'm . . .
fearless

9 • Dorothy Wu

Sunday, November 1

<u>Five things I like</u>
- Funnies
- Silly dreams
- Secret wishes
- Cats (especially when they make mistakes. hehe.)
- Mr. Morales's writing club!

<u>Five things I wish I was better at</u>
- Math
- Singing
- Talking in front of people
- Talking to people for a long time
- Writing stories (I am already very good, but I can always improve, even if just a bit.)

<u>Five things I do not like</u>
- Math
- The boys in math
- P.E.
- Clothes (It is not that I want to be naked, it is just that I don't care who wears what! Why does everyone make such a big deal?)

-Darrell Wu, Pest Extraordinaire

Five mysteries I would like to know the answer to
   -Aliens: fact or fiction?
   -How do geniuses like Mozart and Shigeru Miyamoto
   get their ideas?
   -How many licks DOES it take to get to the center
   of a Tootsie Pop? That darn owl always bites the lolly
   prematurely!
   -Where in the world IS Carmen Sandiego? (My guess:
   Dubai?)
   -Fate or free will? (See? I'm serious sometimes!)

Five objects that are special to me
   -My parasol that I got when I was a baby that has
   various cats on it
   -My stuffed characters (Some of them are animals.
   Some are people. So I say "characters.")
   -My yearbook from sixth grade that has all the things
   people wrote to me
   -The picture of my parents from their wedding back
   when they lived in China
   -My Pokémon/Magic/Yu-gi-oh!/baby animal cards,
   obviously (and my manga collection, double obviously [or
   "doubviously"])

Five places I would like to visit (any time period)
   -Middle Earth

- Westeros
- "The Planet" (Final Fantasy VII)
- Agrabah
- Texas (I am just curious to see what it is like!)

<u>Five things I want</u>
- The next Nintendo system years before it even comes out
- The ability to talk to animals (particularly cats)
- A theme song
- For the Lunch Club to be real
- A special someone . . .

This is the assignment we were given at the first meeting of the new club, "Write On!" Mr. Morales said that it is supposed to help people get ideas for stories. Of course, I already have numerous story ideas. In fact, I have a whole notebook's worth. Still, others may not be so experienced, so they might need something like this. Also, for what it is worth, I did consider this exercise to be a good "get to know me." Some of these facts about me I did not even realize myself until I wrote them down. Who knew I was so obsessed with cats—or special someones—or Texas?! Ah, how I surprise myself.

Write On! has had one meeting so far. It was last Tuesday and it was a smashing success. There were six people in attendance: Mr. Morales, Dorothy Wu (that would be meee!), Whitney Dealy, Jake Schwartz, Daniel Uribe, and Tyler Bell, known to some as "Creepy Tyler." I hope no one ever refers to me as "Creepy Dorothy." I would much rather be called "Strange Dorothy" or "Wild Alice." Why Alice? I just like the name, that is all.

Mr. Morales seemed disheartened at the amount of people, but I liked it. Six is the perfect number for a group. There are six Power Rangers. There are six friends on that show about the friends. Plus, the Latin word for six is *sex*. Hehe!

I would know more funny Latin words if my father let me take that class. Hehe.

Altogether though, a very nice bunch. We have a wise leader, a plucky girl heroine, a ravishing beauty/world-class equestrian, a shy-but-able boy hero, a cunning rebel, and a creepy outsider. Basically all the elements you need for a group. I should definitely start writing Write On! stories instead of Lunch Club stories—ohhh—and what if I shared them with the group? I think that that would be quite metal. Or meta. Which one is it? I should learn the proper word for that situation.

I think the reason that I am so focused on writing club these days is because it is by far the aspect of my life that I am most satisfied with. I just received my first progress report, and unlike Write On!, my grades give me bittersweet feelings. I may be rocking the house in some of my classes like English and social studies, but I am C-plussing the house in others such as P.E. and math. I shudder to think about what will happen if my father ever sees my math grade. My mother said that if I can raise it to an A by the end of the semester, then he never has to know. But we will see if that happens. I doubt I have it in me to raise my grade in the class. Part of me does not even want to try.

The other aspect of school that is occasionally a struggle is the friends part. I am not saying that I am lacking in friends, because I am not. I am not a loser. I have all my pals in my clubs, and in all my classes, and even the fellows who give me a hard time in math, I consider them friends. I have several friends.

It is just that . . . well, I suppose I was mostly feeling rotten about all this at the 'Ween Dance last night. I had spent weeks constructing the perfect dragon-maiden outfit, and I could not wait to show it off to all my club buddies. So at seven last night I arrived at the dance . . . and none of my pals were there. I had no chums to boogie with! The gym was mostly filled with eighth graders who had gone to Arlington Academy (the Populars is what I imagine they call themselves). Also I saw some of the tough guys and their gals from the eastern part of town, close to the Wu residence (I believe they are known as the Radars. Cool name). I stayed for a brief while, got some refreshments, and attempted to popularize my "dragon-maiden shuffle," but it was just not the right atmosphere for me.

So I left the dance. My father had already arranged to pick me up at ten, and I could not call him to retrieve me earlier because he has not permitted me to own a cell phone. *Zounds!*

I spent two and a half hours walking around the campus. I actually quite liked it. Seeing all the hallways dark and deserted is very interesting. A little boring, but very interesting. In addition, I found a couple of making-outers behind the portable buildings, and I got to scare them away. I pretended to be a mangy, rabid dog. How? I used my sounds. That was cool coolness as well. I had a good time.

It would have been nice to have had a companion during the slow songs, I suppose. But, ah well. That is what dreaming is for, is it not?

10 • Danny Uribe

Saturday, November 7

Sometimes it's pretty cool living with the Schwartzes.

Today was my birthday, but I wasn't planning on doing anything special for it. I thought I'd play video games with Jake. Probably I'd go and hang out across town, play some soccer with the guys maybe. But I had no idea what today was gonna end up being like. Didn't know how badass it would be.

It started at like, six in the morning. I was having a nice dream, probably about hot girls at a car wash or something, and all of a sudden I hear Jake screaming in my ear.

"DANNY! DANNY! WAKE UP! YOU HAVE TO WAKE UP! NOW! NOW! NOWWWWW!"

At first I was all kinds of pissed because I was like, "It's my birthday, not Christmas. Don't wake me up so early." I wanted to hit Jake in the face or something. I know it sounds bad now, but you can't get between me and my sleep. So I was about to tell him to get out of my room but then he said—

"WE'RE VISITING THE SET OF MY DAD'S PROJECT!"

Like that, I woke up and I gave Jake the biggest hug. Normally, I don't hug people like that, but I wanted to show Jake how happy I was.

It's been a long time, like a couple years since we all went down and visited the set of one of Mr. Schwartz's movies. It's always the funnest thing. Where else would I get to kick it with famous actors? Or see a bunch of fine supermodels up close? Jake's favorite part is when they have trained cats.

Mr. Schwartz usually isn't home much, and when he is, he's never really with the family. But when we see him on the set, he's the nicest guy in the world. Just showing us around to everyone, letting us play with the props and stuff. It's the only place I see him take his sunglasses off even though it's usually pretty sunny and bright. And he's got this big, deep laugh that you never hear at home. Once it starts it never ends. It always makes him seem so happy.

And he's got every reason to be. He's with his family, showing them around, makin' that big money, hangin' with the stars. One day I think it would be cool to be a big producer like him. I don't know if there's any Mexican movie producers, but I guess I could be the first.

So yeah, when Jake said that's what we were doing, I jumped out of bed and I was just like, screw the shower, screw breakfast, let's go to Hollywoooooood.

The ride down was pretty good. At first it was annoying because Jake kept talking and talking and talking:

"This present was all my idea!"

"Weren't you so surprised?"

"Dude, where would you rank this on your all-time presents list?"

"Number one? Maybe number two behind the scrapbook I made you last year?"

"Oh man, the look on your face when I woke you up . . . so hilarious!"

I don't know what Jake wanted from me. Did he want me to like, thank him a million times? Did he want me to cry and say, I love you man, best friends for life? What did he want?

By the time we hit Ventura, I started to zone him out. The conversation in the front of the car was way more interesting anyway. Or, well, I guess it wasn't a conversation but more like Mrs. Schwartz nodding and listening while Hannah said all this crazy stuff about her friends. Basically over the last week, it seems like Hannah's turned on her whole Seabrook-Arlington crew. Some of the smack she was talking about people was unbelievable. So interesting to hear. But I'll get to more of it later.

Because once we got to the set . . . I mean like, who cares about stupid school stuff. Middle school is a joke. Hollywood, man, that's what's real.

This movie, like all of Mr. Schwartz's "projects," is pretty much like this big action blockbuster. It's all about the world ending like how it does in the Bible, and at the end there's going to be this giant special effects fight between Jesus and Satan. It's gonna be so bomb. Also there's this love story on the side with Will Smith and some blond lady with big boobs. They were really good in the scene we saw today. I think they're both probably gonna get Oscars.

And seeing the stars isn't even the best part of being on the set. Free food represent! I ate like, ten brownies and all kinds of cheese and a buttload of sandwiches and tons of donuts, too. There was so much food everywhere. I was looking for Jake at this one part because they brought out a huge thing of pizza bagels, and that's his favorite food. But I couldn't find him anywhere.

I didn't know where Jake was for most of today. It felt like he was keeping away from me. I wonder if he thought I was mad at him. I guess I could have been nicer in the car. I wasn't really pissed at him, even. I just didn't want him to keep acting so hyper around me, like some little kid who just ate a bunch of sugar. It's embarrassing for me when he acts that way, especially when there's others around. He doesn't have to be like that.

Actually, for a big part of the day I hung out with Hannah. The two of us go way back, of course. I've lived on her property since I was seven. But this was the first time I ever really chilled with her instead of Jake. And it was mad weird because up until maybe a week ago, she would have annoyed the crap out of me no matter what she said—all that gossip about best-dressed couples and crap. But today I found all the stuff she had to say real interesting. The way she talked about her friends was different from how she used to in the drives to school. She was straight-up trashing people, and not the losers or the *cholos* or Creepy Tyler, but she was saying bad stuff about all her closest friends. It made her seem a lot more honest. A lot funner to be around. It was tight. I felt bad for her, though. She was pretty upset. What did this Chad guy even do to her?

Since Hannah was kind of sharing her secrets with me, I felt good. And it made me feel okay talking about some things that I haven't talked about with anybody, not even Jake. Especially not Jake.

I told Hannah about gangster stuff.

It's crazy. As much rumor-spreading as that girl has done over her life, you'd think that she would know the stories of everyone at SP, brown kids included. But really, Hannah doesn't know anything about people outside her special group of Seabrook friends. Like, she kind of knows that gangs exist, and she knows a couple of signs because I always see the pictures of her and her friends doing them on Facebook. But like, it was crazy. She didn't even know who the main two gangs in San Paulo were. And I mean everybody knows the Raiders and the Destroyers. Sometimes it seems like all anybody wants is to be a Raider or a Destroyer. I know fools who would give anything for one of those gangs, even their lives probably. That sounds dumb when I say it, but maybe you have to be more like me to understand it. I'm not saying I would ever want to join a gang. But I get why people would want to be part of a brotherhood, part of a family.

Maybe that's the real problem, though. All that people like Hannah and Jake and their parents and their friends know about us Latinos is the fact that we have gangs. That's a bad thing. They think we just beat up on each other for no reason and they think that's messed up. They see we don't have money like them. Then they see that some of us work for them, like my parents with the Schwartzes. So they don't respect us. They all think of us as nothing more than Mexican gangsters.

So for me to spend a day telling Hannah the stuff my

cousins told me, stuff about how the Raiders formed, when's the last time they warred with the Destroyers, which of my friends are thinking about jumping in—that's just making her think that all I care about is the Eastside, the thug life. And that's not me. That's not the whole me.

I mean, for one, I'm still mad tight with Jake. I go to his writing club with him and I even like it sometimes. And Jake's about as far away from gangster as you can get, since he's white and nerdy and emotional and stuff. Also, I'm basically a part of the Schwartz family. That's not very thug. And I don't want to be all ghetto or whatever. I want to be a big producer, right?

I can't believe that I spent the whole day talking to Hannah, all the way from the set in the afternoon to the Schwartzes' Malibu house where we stayed tonight, and I didn't even get the real me across. I mean she did a good job of smiling and pretending to be interested in my stories, but I probably seemed like such a fool to her, all obsessed with gang stuff. That's like the opposite of who I am. I don't want her to think of me that way.

Jake got sick this afternoon. He came up to me and Hannah when we were talking, and he looked all pale and sad. He said he wasn't feeling well. Then, instead of staying in Malibu with us that night, he made Mrs. Schwartz drive him all the way back north to home. I don't know how sick he really was. Maybe he was bummed out that today wasn't the perfect best friends birthday memory like he planned. Whatever. He's the one who bailed. If he doesn't want to hang out with me, then that's his deal, right?

heyyy chicaaa

wut ^ girl?

enjoying the movie?

been sleeping lol. this class is sooo retarded

if we have to watch another movie about a white girl getting her period, i'll cry

LMAO at least i was havin a good dream . . .

o ya? about certain high school boys?

i only hooked ^ wit Fabian ONE time!!!

ya but i bet u liked it . . .

¡UNA VEZ!

ya but how far did u go?

not tellin ;)

ay!!! u better watch out chica

¿por que?

u don't wanna end ^ like hannah

¿chiquita blanca?

ya, u dont want all that chisme about you

dont worry got it under control

k i believe u then

really?

NO!!!!!!!!!!!!!!!!!!!!!!!!

luv u chicle

te amo luz

11 • Hannah Schwartz

Wednesday, November 11

HANNAH SCHWARTZ IS A SLUT

That's been written on the wall of the girls' bathroom for the last week and a day. In layers and layers of Sharpie too, so it's impossible to rub off. The janitors didn't do anything about it and neither did the administration until my mom barged into Mr. Greene's office today and practically blew out his eardrums from yelling so loud. So now they say they'll paint it over first thing tomorrow. That's what they say.

Obviously it's not true that I'm a slut. Obviously! So I'm not feeling all worked up about this or anything, like it's true. I'm not filled with sadness. Just hatred.

It helps that I know who's responsible for this. Helps me direct my rage.

And it just so happens that the person who made this lie happen is the same person who wrote me a freaking love song a little over a week ago.

I'm not going to pretend like I know how boys' brains work (little demons in hamster wheels are probably somehow involved), but I can pinpoint the exact moment when all this drama started. It was Monday of last week, when I went to Chad's house to "study for our algebra quiz."

Okay, first of all, it was funny that my mom ever bought that excuse. Chad and I don't even have the same math teacher, and who studies for a quiz anyway? Adults are idiots. As long as you make up some kind of lie, you're fine. Doesn't even have to be good. I could have said, "Chad and I are going to go volunteer at the Sponge-Bathing Old People Clinic," and my mom wouldn't have batted an eyelash.

Obviously I was over at Chad's for a different reason. Only thing is, he had a different definition of the word "reason" than I did. So we're sitting on his bed, pretending to study until his mom has to take his little sister to ballet or whatever. And we were actually doing a couple of math problems, and that's when it first dawned on me that Chad is fully stupid. Like, he kept saying, "how can x be a number? X is a letter. I think the book's wrong." It would be funnier if it weren't so sad for humanity.

So Chad being painfully dumb was the first chink in the armor. But then came the massive, comet-sized dent. As soon as we hear his mom leave, I clear the books off of the bed. Because I'm like, ready to make out, right? And I put my head on the pillow and I kind of close my eyes because I want the moment to be super-cute, right? Because we've never made out lying down before, and that's kind of like a milestone. But then all of a sudden, right when I'm ready for the magic, I feel this sharp pain in my chest, and I open my eyes and that jackass is not only groping but *squeezing* both of my boobs, as if they're freaking stress balls! What was he trying to do, stunt my chest growth? Counter-intuitive much?

I took his hands off of me and kind of laughed it off at first because this was back when I used to think Chad's pathetic attempts at humor were worthwhile. And so after he let go, it got okay for a little bit. He lay down and he started kissing me and it was nice. Well, as nice as making out with a secret creep could have been. But then, Chad's hands, which had been right where I wanted them to be, palms on the bed, started moving. They made their way onto my shoulders, down my arms, around my waist, then he started playing with my belt, and then he—

And then I slapped him so hard, so effing hard, that I think there might still be an imprint, or at least pain. Serves him right. I mean, who did he think I was—an eleventh grader? The easiest girl at Camp Whorebag? Or—God forbid—Ashley Clarke? I said, *Get away from there* in my sternest voice possible, and I got up and called my mom, and she picked me up and took me home. The whole experience wasn't that scary or anything, just frustrating. I mean, I broke my no-boyfriend rule for Chad because I thought he was the best SP had to offer, and he turned out to be nothing more than a perv disguised in a cute, sensitive water polo player's body. I wouldn't say he broke my heart or anything, but he definitely shattered my confidence in boys. Probably forever.

I went straight to my room and I updated my Facebook status to "single," and I was expecting that to be the end of it. Yeah, I thought Chad might spread the story, and yeah maybe word would get around that I'm a prude, but there are worse things in life. Better than the alternative, right?

So imagine what it felt like to walk into the girls' room during nutrition break on Tuesday morning and to see *that*. That lie. Instantly I knew Chad was responsible because it was even written in his remedial-preschooler handwriting. And you know what? Maybe I was a little bit ready for a cheap trick like this. But what I couldn't have seen coming was . . . well, how much of an opportunity it provided for everyone else.

I mean, people didn't even seem *surprised*. Like, now that it was "official" that I was a big fat ho, they could just look at me and talk to me like I was . . . like I was *lesser*. And of course no one believed my side of the story. Because a dirty bathroom wall is totally more convincing than a real live human being. I could see everyone staring at me in the halls like I was that girl from that one famous book, the girl who wasn't supposed to have sex but did and everyone knew it. The girl with the big A on her boobs. I mean, Kristen and Rachel, for God's sake—who I thought were my two best friends—when I tried to tell them what really happened, they looked at me with these pointed little smirks, as if to say, "Sure, hon . . . but we know what *really* happened. . . . We know what you *really* are. . . ." And honestly, I am not going to take that crap from Kristen, because she's done way worse stuff with Alex, only no one ever gives her a hard time about it because they're "in love." People just wanted a reason to hate me, and now they've got one and no one cares if it's BS.

I guess this whole ordeal has provided me with the chance to see who my real friends are. Namely, nobody.

But my family has stepped up in a surprisingly big way. Mom of course has stayed up with me like, every night. Daddy let us visit the set this past weekend on one of his busiest days. Jake's cut down on the stupid little-brother comments. And even Danny—remember him? Little Mister I'm-gonna-take-the-bus-every-day-and-try-to-find-myself-and-rediscover-what-it-means-to-be-a-*cholo*? Yeah, he turned out to be the most stand-up guy of them all. I spent like, the whole weekend talking with him.

Honestly, I really haven't been that upset about this whole thing in a few days. Still über-pissed, yeah, but I know the truth, and over time I think I can help everyone else see it for themselves, too. Talking to Danny really helped me. It put things in perspective. I mean, when I think about it, I have it so easy. My life has essentially been struggle-free. Yeah, I'll have the occasional hair emergency, or Daddy will buy me an ugly outfit and expect me to wear it, and I wish my chest was bigger, and I wish my butt was smaller, and I really do have such awful friends, but those aren't the worst problems ever. Danny knows guys that have like, shanked each other. Now that's some real drama. Like, scary drama. So who cares if the whole school thinks I'm a slut? Right? It doesn't even matter. The important people know the truth. I don't care what a bunch of dumbasses think.

 **SAN PAULO JUNIOR HIGH SCHOOL**
MORNING ANNOUNCEMENTS—TUESDAY, NOVEMBER 24

Thanksgiving Break starts tomorrow! Before you go home today, please try and thank at least one teacher, administrator, or member of the custodial staff!

TODAY is the LAST DAY of the Thanksgiving Canned Food Drive! Put your cans into the bins in the front office. All food will be donated to the Pacific Relief Homeless Shelter.

A campus divided against itself cannot stand! Seventh and eighth graders have been fighting for far too long. Come to a special **town hall meeting today at lunch,** at which students from both grades will share their experiences and air their grievances. This event is being hosted by the leadership class.

Christian Athletes meets today at lunch in room 133. Christian Athletes: a fun place where sports and the Lord can coexist.

AFTER SCHOOL SPORTS RESULTS

Boys Soccer: La Mesa 2, San Paulo 0
Girls Soccer: San Paulo 3, La Mesa 1
          (Lydia Hernandez–2 goals)

Boys Flag Football: Mission Viejo 21, San Paulo 0
Girls Flag Football: San Paulo 14, Mission Viejo 6
          (Maricruz Perez–1 TD, 1 INT)

CONGRATS to San Paulo's November Student of the Month ... Nisha Patel! In nominating Nisha, her teachers described her as being "engaged," "industrious," and "cheerful." Congratulate Nisha if you see her, and remember that **you could be the next SPSOTM!**

After Thanksgiving Break, *all* Oakland Raiders paraphernalia (jerseys, T-shirts, hats) will be banned from campus. Any merchandise discovered will be confiscated permanently.

And as always, San Paulo is a no gum, no iPods, no cell phones, no skateboards school! Those found with any of the aforementioned items will be given a detention. **No exceptions.**

HAVE A WONDERFUL BREAK! See you on Monday!

Identity Poem

everybody wants to be
a G like you see
when you watch TV
a baller, shot-caller
a have-it-aller
with skills like Kobe
only taller
a veterano, the number-one pimp
as long as you're not
a Seabrook wimp
like me.

Not white, not brown
just in between
I'm one of their own
but haven't seen
the stuff they've seen

my home is so far
away from their scene
and to them I'm not mean
you know what I mean?
and I feel like I'm grown
but I'm only thirteen

I'm not a true beaner
I'm just a bean
with brown on the outside
and white in between

12 • Jake Schwartz

Thursday, November 26

Don't get me wrong. I love my family, I really do. I enjoy spending time with them. I *choose* to spend time with them. They are my favorite people in the world.

But Thanksgiving always sucks.

My family has a tradition as pointless as it is boring as it is cliché. At Thanksgiving dinner, everyone has to go around the table and say one thing that they're thankful for. And although we all like each other just fine, more than the average Hollywood family I'd say, that doesn't stop us from stinking when it comes to Thanksgiving. No one ever says the right things.

This year we invited the Uribes to join us for Pointless-boring-cliché-palooza. Sounds like that would make Thanksgiving better than normal, right? But, unfortunately, it still sucked. And we still all had to say what we were thankful for. It was in the back of my head the entire day. What would I say when it came to be my turn at dinner tonight?

The day went by quickly. The girls watched TV. My dad looked at scripts and made phone calls. Danny went across town to hang out and probably play tackle football or something cool like that. I stayed in my room, reading and working on my "Identity Poem" for writing club. It was one of those non-days that you can't remember anything about a week later.

Until dinner, of course. That's when plenty of memorable stuff happened, because that's when we all had to go around the table.

My dad is thankful that we're all healthy and happy. I'm not sure if he's really home enough to properly gauge our happiness. On Danny's birthday, which was one of the last times I saw Dad before this, I ended up leaving the set in tears. I'm not even sure why. I mean I know why, but I didn't think I felt bad enough to cry about it or anything. It's not like I wanted to cry, but I did. So that's probably not a sign of happiness. Not saying I'm depressed or anything, but you know. Sometimes things just don't go the way you planned them, and Danny's birthday was an example of that. My dad doesn't seem to remember. I wonder if Danny does.

Dad also made sure to include that we should all be thankful that we're so secure financially. He's feeling extra-secure right now because he recently closed a deal with a studio to green-light a third *Planet Skull* movie. I'm not really sure how it's going to work out since Harrison Ford is getting so old. But that's the thing about Hollywood. It doesn't matter if it works or not—you get paid anyway. That last sentence was an actual quote from my dad tonight, by the way. He can't go two minutes without talking about "the Industry." Not even at Thanksgiving.

My mom is thankful that all the kids are growing up so well. She talked about how beautiful Hannah looked on

Halloween night, and then she mentioned Danny's summer growth spurt and how much of a man he's turning into. Then for me, I think she realized that she didn't have anything to say. I mean, not relating to the theme of "growing up." When you're sub–five foot three, sub–one hundred pounds, you don't get to qualify as a man. Not by any measure. So yeah, Mom looked at me, she paused for a couple seconds, she smiled, and she said:

"Jake, you've got Dad's strong chin."

?!?!?!?!??!?!?!?!??!?!

DOUBLE-U.

TEE.

EFF.

?!?!?!?!??!?!?!?!??!?!

Was that supposed to be like a joke, or what? Out of all of the things in the world about me that she could have been thankful for—my intelligence, my warmth, my sense of humor, my loyalty, my, I don't know, special Jake-ness—my mom—my *mom,* who I can usually depend on for a choice compliment—*my mom who gave birth to me*—picked my chin. My freaking chin. And my chin sucks. It's nowhere near as manly as Dad's chin. Or Danny's, for that matter. This wasn't even the most disappointing part of the night.

Danny's parents, Oscar and Manuela, went next. They kind of did theirs together. It's weird with the two of them. Sometimes when I'm around them, I'll hear them joking or arguing or whatever, and I can't understand what they're say- ing because it's in Spanish, but I know that they're showing tons of personality, describing how they really feel. But when they're around my parents, they're always super-bottled up—they're all "Yes, Mr. Jeffrey" and "Okay, Mrs. Judy."

I don't think they wanted to be at dinner, actually. My parents thought they were doing this great thing by inviting them, but something tells me that the Uribes would have been happier with extended family. Tonight they said they were thankful to my parents for employing them, obviously, and for the good meal "Mrs. Judy" had put in front of us—even though Manuela had made probably ninety-five percent of the dinner with no help from my mom, who had been watching the Macy's parade and the dog show with Hannah.

Speaking of Hannah, her thanks was perhaps the most ridiculous of all. So, she's really been blowing this whole bathroom wall thing out of proportion. I mean, yeah, it's quite lame what happened to her, but really, it was one of those things that happens—like a bad grade on a test, or a pimple on the nose—that sucks for a day and then everyone forgets about it. Everyone except Hannah. She's been acting all funeral-style for the last couple weeks—wearing black a bunch, posting lines of poetry as her Facebook status, the works—and when it was her turn to talk tonight, she put on this really somber tone of voice and she said:

"I give thanks to all who have stood by me. This . . . situation hasn't been the easiest period for me, but you all made life just a little bit more worth living."

I swear, that's exactly what she said. Like she was a celebrity whose naked pics had been leaked to the Internet or something. I texted it to myself under the table so I'd be able to read it to Danny later so we could laugh about it.

Little did I know that Danny has been taking Hannah's "situation" more seriously than anybody.

It was Danny's thanks that really, really, really sucked.

Right after Hannah went—and I should have realized this earlier, but she was looking straight at Danny the entire time she talked—Danny looked at *her*, and he said, without missing a beat, "I'm thankful for you, Hannah." And then he went on to talk about how strong she's been throughout all this, and how much he's enjoyed getting to know her better, and how meaningful their conversations have been over the last couple weeks—and all this in front of all of our parents, no less. A lesser man than I might have said, "Get a room, you guys."

Of course I was horrified, but I figured, Okay, he's just leading off with Hannah since it makes for a nice transition. But then he'll get to my parents and his parents and, well, you know, his best friend in the entire world.

But nope. That was it. He stopped talking, he flashed a smile at Hannah, and then he looked over at me. Not because he had anything to say to his closest friend that he's ever made in his entire life who does lots of really considerate stuff for him, but because now it was my turn to be thankful for something.

At that moment, right after all I'd had to sit through, I felt thankful for nothing. Absolutely nothing. And I'm a terrible liar. So why even bother?

With everyone looking at me, I sat there for a few seconds, without speaking or changing my expression. Then I reached out and grabbed my root beer and I took a big sip.

"Jake?" my mom said.

And I stared at her—and then I made eye contact with each person at the table—from Mom to Dad to Hannah to Manuela to Oscar to Danny—and I said, "No thanks."

"Jake—" my dad started to say, but I interrupted him by suddenly unleashing one of the loudest, nastiest, most reverberating belches in the history of Thanksgiving. Seriously, Pocahontas smelled this belch.

And it felt so good. Here's what I'm thankful for: I'm thankful that my throat decided to do that at that exact moment in time, because the looks on everyone's faces after my epic burp were beyond priceless.

And I have no idea what happened next. I stood up, calmly went to my room, quietly closed and locked my door. No one's come to check on me or bring me food or make me apologize or anything.

Thanksgiving always sucks.

The Club Chronicles
Part 26: Poseidon's Orb
By Dorothy Wu

"Hahaha! Try and catch me!" Princess Dorothy cried as she leapt into the ocean, her turquoise mermaid's tail glistening in the faint glow of the maize sun.

"I must catch you!" her suitor called gallantly after. "For I love you!"

The young man was none other than Prince Jacobim, the same dashing young warrior who always arrived to rescue Dorothy whenever she was in peril. He stood up tall on the rock where he had just been sunning himself. He ran his hand through his poofy, coffee-colored hair, flexed his lean, muscular frame, and gave a triumphant roar.

"I must have you!" he shouted. "I must have you forever!"

He snapped his fingers and in an instant his two legs combined into one, and scales and fins sprouted from his every pore. Dorothy gasped the gasp of elated surprise. He had taken merman form so that he could become closer to her.

Jacobim dove into the waters with the grace of a swan nymph. He proceeded to swim up to Dorothy and kiss her passionately all over her face.

"Oh, my Jacobim," Dorothy whispered. "I have waited

so long for this . . . for you to kiss me all over my face."

Then, suddenly, she pulled her face away.

"But wait," she said with concern. "Are you not still betrothed to Chastity Bubblemist, the youngest daughter of Poseidon?"

". . . Yes," Jacobim admitted, his cheeks flushed. "But I have never loved her. It is you I want, Princess Dorothy, and I do not care who knows it! Not even Poseidon himself!"

Suddenly, a rumbling in the waters!

"WHAAAAAAAAAT?!?!" came a giant bellow from below.

"Oh no! Poseidon!" Dorothy shrieked.

"He has heard every word!" cried an alarmed Jacobim, less fearful than Dorothy, but still worried.

A hundred-foot-tall wall of water formed in front of them, but instead of crashing down on them as a wave, it turned into a gargantuan water face—a terrifying water face—the water face of Poseidon.

"JACOBIM, YOUUU FOOOOL! HOW DARE YOU BREAK THE TERMS OF YOUR ENGAGEMENT WITH MY DAUGHTER! NOOOOW YOUUU MUST PAY THE PRIIICE!"

Poseidon pursed his humongous lips together and began to blow a bubble. But this was no ordinary bubble—Dorothy knew that right away. This was Poseidon's Orb, the legendary prison that the Lord of the Sea created only for those that he most loathed. Once surrounded by the impenetrable walls of Poseidon's Orb, one could never hope to escape.

Dorothy was expecting the Orb to form around both her and Jacobim, as an eternal reminder of their sin. But instead it only surrounded Jacobim.

She looked up at Poseidon in surprise. He looked down at her in evil.

"LITTLE WENCH," Poseidon called to her. "YOUUU HAVE ERRED GREATLY, BUT I WILL FORGIVE YOUR MISTAAAKE. JUST STAAAY AWAAAY FROM THIS DISHONEST FOOL."

Dorothy narrowed her eyebrows and looked up at the Lord of the Sea with steely resolve.

"Never," she said, softly but strongly. "I love him."

13 • Jake Schwartz

Friday, December 4

So I have a secret admirer. Or, I should say, a Secret Santa.

It makes me so excited, thinking about it, and admitting to that makes me feel like Hannah, which makes me feel less excited. But still. How can I not be psyched? There's someone who admires me—secretly!

It all started the first day back from Thanksgiving break. I went to my locker in between second and third and there was this big green-and-red heart taped to the front of it, and taped to the heart there was a bag of Peach Rings. Now, that happens to be my favorite candy in the world, and very few people know that. So at first I was thinking, you know, that Danny or Hannah was trying to make Thanksgiving up to me. But A) those two still don't seem to realize what they did, and B) neither one of them would ever publicly give me a paper heart—Danny because he'd be seen as gay, and Hannah because she'd be seen as nice. So that's when it occurred to me that, yeah, I've got a serious secret admiring Santa on my hands.

The next day, when I went to my locker at the same time, I found another treat. This gift was a little stranger and oddly practical: a bag of brand-new Bic Ultra Round Stic Grip pens. My favorite pens. And the thing is, I actually needed some new ones because all my old ones are out of ink, and I've bitten the caps on them so much that they're all gross and disease-ridden. Attached to the bag there was a typed note that said, "So you do not have to keep asking people for theirs. XOXO Secret Santa." And Secret Santa was right. I had been asking people in class to borrow their pens for days. So I guess that's a hint. My secret admirer is someone who has classes with me. That's good. I wouldn't want it to be like, some random person.

I've been getting gifts every single day, like Advent calendar–style, and they always appear on my locker right between second and third. The crazy thing is that no one's seen anyone put anything there. I've been getting some bizarre stuff, too: superhero rub-on tattoos, origami cranes, cute little drawings, a yo-yo . . . and the present I got this past Monday was the wildest one yet.

It was a little soap sculpture of me. Just like the ones Boo Radley leaves for the kids in *To Kill a Mockingbird*, which my Secret Santa must have known is my favorite book. And yeah, I hope this doesn't mean that my Secret Santa is a creepy pale man who lives down the road. But this little carving is seriously cool. It's wearing a hoodie, just like I usually do, and the fro is just right. Carving a fro out of soap must take a long time. So this person is clearly pretty into me, and clearly that's pretty awesome.

I think I know who it is. It has to be someone who's in a bunch of my classes but who also knows me outside of that. For a while, that's the thing that was giving me trouble. Where have I said all this personal stuff? My favorite book, my favorite candy, my story about how I was the only kid in third grade who couldn't make a paper crane . . . and that's when I realized. The only place I've talked about myself that much is in writing club, in our warm-up exercises. My Secret Santa has to be someone from writing club.

My Secret Santa must be Whitney Dealy.

It feels good to say. And it feels good to be liked. I mean, I don't know if I liked her before, but I don't think I've ever really liked someone before, so I don't know how it feels, really. And now that I've put it together that it's her, I really do feel happy about it. Whitney is cute and nice, I like her long brown braid, she seems to have good fashion sense, and although I don't really understand why she's so obsessed with horses, I would be willing to learn more about them if we started dating or something. Maybe we could even go riding together.

To be honest, it's a huge surprise that someone as cool as Whitney would be interested in me. But from the note I got on my locker today, it seems pretty apparent that it is her. It says:

Jake,
You must be dying to know who I am. Be patient!
I will reveal myself at some point during the last week before break.
But until then, here is a hint: D.
XOXO,
Your Secret Santa

P.S. Omnia vincit amor

D. The first letter of her last name. That's a good hint. I mean if her name was like "Denise" or something, then it would be too obvious, because I could just guess right away. And yeah, I guess the hint is still easy this way too. But maybe Whitney wants me to know it's her.

After all, the P.S. is a super-cinchy hint too. It's Latin. There aren't even that many girls in my Latin class, so Whitney kind of tipped her hand there. *Omnia vincit amor.* It means, "Love conquers all." I guess that's a little over the top, but I understand. It's not as if Mr. Gates has taught us how to say, "Strong like conquers all." Plus, I like it. It's the kind of thing I would write to someone I secretly admired.

It will be exciting to see how she chooses to tell me. I have to admit that I'm really looking forward to it.

And I'm really really looking forward to being with a girl, holding hands with a girl . . . and, you know, kissing a girl. Okay, see, well, I've never gotten kissed before, exactly. I've told people that I've been kissed—like I told Danny that I kissed Becca Wolfson at camp—but that was less about telling the truth, and more about not seeming like a loser. This is back in the days when Danny didn't think I was an overly emotional, schoolwork-obsessed, sucky-at-basketball, birthday-ruining loser.

But D doesn't think I'm a loser. Or, I should say, Whitney doesn't. Whitney wants to be friends with me, and more than friends with me, because she really, genuinely likes me. This is someone who understands and appreciates me for what I'm actually like. I can't wait to understand and appreciate her.

14 • Danny Uribe

Saturday, December 5

I was planning on hanging out on the other side of town today. I wasn't planning on taking Hannah with me. But I did, and I'm happy I did.

This whole thing started weeks ago, back when me and Hannah first started talking more. Every time I brought up my cousins, the Eastside, whatever, she would ask all kinds of questions. And I'd be happy to tell her the truth because like, I don't really have anybody to talk about that kind of stuff with. But when she started asking if she could come and check the scene out for herself, I just told her hell no. It's not like I thought I was gonna be embarrassed by her over there. I wasn't even that worried about what Mrs. Schwartz would do to me if she ever found out, even though she would probably run me over with her SUV. It's just that I didn't want Hannah to have a bad time. On the Eastside, you never know.

But Hannah. Man. When that girl wants her way, you can't tell her no. So this afternoon when I said I'm heading out and she said I'm coming with . . . well, that's what we were doing. I told Jake, Sorry dude, I can't hang out, it's my cousin's birthday, and Hannah told her mom, Sorry, I can't go shopping, I'm studying at Kristen's. We timed our exits so

Jake wouldn't see us leave together. And we were on our way.

Well, first I made her change what she was wearing. Before we left, Hannah had this nice pink sweater on and these fancy-ass jeans with little shiny things on them and all kinds of necklaces and jewelry and stuff, and I was just like, No, you have to wear the cheap version of this. And she said, I don't own the cheap version of this. So then I said, Fine, you have to wear your P.E. clothes, and I think that made her really sad for a second, because girls are weird, but then I told her I was kidding. But yeah, she did have to put on something that would help her not stick out so much.

Not that it was gonna help. As soon was we got on the bus, she got all kinds of stares from people, stares that were like, This girl doesn't belong on the bus. Hannah didn't help herself much, either. She kept on asking me questions. Why do people keep pulling on that cord above our heads? Why aren't there any seat belts? Why does that lady have a beard?

By the time we got to the bus stop on Castillo, I decided that this was officially a bad idea. I was all ready to go back to Seabrook. But right as I was gonna tell Hannah that, she grabbed my hand with both of hers and she gave it this little squeeze. I couldn't believe how warm her hand was. Then I looked at her and she was giving me this smile, this smile with mad dimples and stuff. I don't know if brainwashing is real, like in the army and stuff, but if it is, then I bet they use hot girls. Because right then I would've done whatever she wanted.

It was just a small crew over at Javy and Carlos's. Besides

my cousins, only Edgar was there. They said that Gordo was off rolling with Junior, which means Gordo was off rolling with the Raiders. Finally, I guess. He'd been talking about jumping in for weeks, saying Guillermo this and Guillermo that, saying I'm gonna be made this position, saying I'm gonna recruit that kid. It's crazy that Fat Boy joined for real, though. I hope he's happy. And I hope he doesn't do anything stupid. But knowing Gordo, he's only gonna be happy if he's doing something stupid, like rubbing his man boobs all up in Guillermo's face or something. Oh, man.

It was a little awkward when me and Hannah first got there, but the guys were all nice to her. Only Javy and Carlos know about me living with the Schwartzes, but the rest of the guys have heard me talking a lot about Hannah before. Everyone knows I think she's cute. Everyone wants me to get some. The guys know to be cool around her.

We didn't really do too much. Just sat around and talked. Javy, Carlos, Edgar, and Hannah are all in eighth grade together, so they know some of the same people and teachers, and they talked about that. And of course I was the common friend that everyone had, so they all had a good time making fun of me. My cousins told Hannah about how they used to call me Danielito, and Hannah really liked that. She basically hasn't called me anything else since. And yeah like, it was a little embarrassing for me, but we were all having a good time.

That's when two more people showed up: girl people. And not just any girls but Luz Vasquez and Chicle Rodriguez.

Chicle's real name is Angelica, but everyone calls her Chicle since she chews gum 24/7.

I was pretty nervous when they came. They're like the Hannah Schwartz of the Mexicans at our school. All about the gossip, all about the chisme. Well, I guess Hannah isn't like that anymore, but basically Luz and Chicle are the girls who know everything about everybody. So like, if they say something, it gets around and everyone believes it. Doesn't matter if it's true. I wasn't too worried when I was hanging around with just Hannah and the guys, but when Luz and Chicle showed up . . . I was thinking that if they realized that Hannah was close to me . . . and if they told their friends, and if more and more people found out, and then even the whole school . . . well, I just knew it couldn't be good.

But that's when Hannah did something really, really smart. She said, "Hey, I have an idea. Let's pretend like this is a school dance. Let's split up. You boys can go watch sports or whatever while we girls stay here and chat."

So that's what we did. Edgar remembered that there was a Mexican Soccer League match on, Guadalajara vs. Toluca. We watched the second half of that, and that was tight. It was actually a little hard for me to understand the Telemundo announcers because it's been a while since I've heard Spanish being spoken that fast, but we had a good time watching the game, eating chips and salsa and hot sauce.

I was still worried about Hannah the whole time. I knew that if she said or did one wrong thing, Luz and Chicle could make her seem all rich and selfish and mean to the brown kids at school. And Hannah isn't like that. She's not. I want people to know that.

It turns out that I had no reason to worry. When we went back to the porch after the game, the girls were laughing like they had been best friends for life. It was such a nice surprise. I have no idea how Hannah did it. My best guess is that she shared some of her secrets and got the girls to share some of theirs, so everyone felt like they could trust each other. That's kind of what happened with Hannah and me. That girl works in mysterious ways.

Around 5:30, me and Hannah decided to head back to Seabrook. Right before we left, Chicle was like, "Hannah, please don't go!" and Luz was all, "See you at school, chica!" It was funny.

On the bus ride home, Hannah had this little smile on her face. It was like, mission accomplished. We didn't talk too much on the bus, but we both felt good. Then, a stop before the one closest to her house, Hannah pulled the cord above our heads.

"Let's walk the rest of it," she said.

I said okay. Of course I said okay. After all, I was being brainwashed. And it felt good.

We still didn't talk much on the half-mile walk up the road, past the main gate, and back to her property, but we held hands. Well, we didn't hold hands really, like we didn't walk with our hands holding, but she did the thing where she reached over and squeezed mine. She did it twice.

We stopped at the gate. We decided that we should time our

entrances so it didn't seem like we had been together all day. We decided that Hannah would go in ten minutes before me.

I wish I had been more ready for what happened next. Right before she turned to walk in, Hannah grabbed both my hands with hers and she tilted her head up at me and leaned in closer to me a little bit. I didn't do anything for a second. I wasn't even looking at her full on. I was confused and stuff, but then I got it and started to bring my head in. But then right when I got it, she smiled at me. It was one of those little smiles where the girl pokes her tongue between her teeth really quick then brings it back. A little teasing smile. Then Hannah put her head down, squeezed my hands, turned around and walked up her driveway, doing that slow butt-bouncing walk that drives every guy crazy.

I don't know why I was such a fool. Of course she wanted to kiss me. And of course I wanted to kiss her. I was just nervous, I guess. I mean like, I haven't ever actually really kissed a girl before. This summer I told Jake that I made out with this girl Jordan at camp, but I only said that because he was bragging about how he kissed this other chick. And like, it's embarrassing that he would kiss someone before me.

But you know what would be mad embarrassing for him? If I kissed his sister. And you know what? I am going to kiss his sister. Not that he has to know.

To my dearest sisterfriend in the world, Miss Emily-Bear,

So I'm sitting here in science and it's soooo boring and I want to die but OMG the funniest thing ever—literally ever—just happened. I'm sure you'll have heard about what happened with Hannah's brother by the time you get this note, but I think you deserve the whole story in all its amaaazing details. Srsly. I saw everything go down right in front of me. I swear that what I'm about to write is absolutely true.

So this was like 15 mins ago, right at the beginning of nutrition break. Meghan and I went to our lockers to re-gloss and hopefully maybe catch a glimpse of Marco, that hot new Italian exchange student. ;)

Anyway, so we're at our lockers and suddenly I see something dark moving behind the trash can in the hall. And I'm like wtf, so I walk over and I look behind the can and it's that weird sevvy Asian girl, Dorothy Yoo or whatever, the one who decorates her binder with pictures of her getting married to video game characters and stuff. And she's crouching behind the garbage, trying super-hard to keep still and quiet, wearing all black, and even though I'm right above her, she doesn't notice me, because she has her eyes dead set on the lockers across from us.

Then, without warning, Dorothy looks to her left and she makes a little gasping sound and her body kind of spasms. Like she's just seen a ghost, or a hot guy. Only what she actually saw was even better. Coming down the hallway, right where Crazy Asian had looked, was Hannah's little brother. You know, the one with the Velcro hair. And he had on this little blue polo shirt and these beige khakis just like Mommy bought for him, and he looked maybe 3% cute, 97% loserdork.

He headed straight for the locker where Dorothy had been staring a few seconds earlier. So this is when I realized—omg—love connection—he's the one who's been getting all those weird presents, like that creepy soap child. And she's his mystery gift giver. And I just know I'm about to see something classic.

So Hannah's brother walks up to his locker, and there's this sign taped to it—this red-and-green piece of construction paper—and it says TURN AROUND on it. And I'd completely forgotten about Dorothy at this point, but while Hannah's brother was looking at the sign, she had jumped out from behind the trash can and flung herself across the hall, and by the time he turned around, there she was, inches away from him, standing there in all her loser glory.

And I'll never forget what happened next. Little Bro turned around and he had this kind of confused look on his face, and he said, "Hey, Dorothy. Did . . . Whitney send you?" I think he was talking about Whitney Sheehan, the one who hooked up with Chad in the bathroom during the motivational speaker assembly last week. But he could've meant Whitney Ostertag—you know, that slut who only sweats under one armpit. Or maybe he meant that sevvy Whitney, the weird horse girl.

Anyway, Dorothy, as if he hasn't even just asked her a question, she throws her hands up in the air and she shouts at the top of her lungs, "I'M DEEEEEEEEEEEEEEEEEEEEEE!!!!!"

No idea what "Dee" is, but it must've meant something to

Hannah's brother, because he stares at Dorothy and he just starts—no joke—crying. Bawling. Full-on, streaming, mucus-mixing-in, call-the-waaambulance tears. I swear he morphed into a five-year-old right before my eyes. And before she can say anything to him, he just turns around and bolts down the hallway and ducks into the nearest boys' bathroom.

And so then Dorothy—God, she's so lame, she should've expected this, but poor girl—then she starts crying, probably even harder than Hannah's brother. And so then she turns around and runs in the opposite direction before bursting into the girls' room. Also, as she was running, some of those Peach Ring candies flew out of her jacket pockets and fell on the ground. Which . . . ew. That's really gross when you think about it. Candy in your pockets. Shudder.

So, yeah, there were maybe like, fifteen of us in the hallway who watched this whole thing happen, and once both of them ran away, we were all just in shock. We didn't know whether to like, laugh or applaud or cry or what. I mean SP is definitely a crazy place, but I've never seen anything like this before.

Wow—the bell's about to ring. I can't believe I spent the entire period writing you this story. You better enjoy it, bee-yotch! See you in sixth.

Can't wait till this weeeeekend for the party at Hannah's house and then our sleeeeepovaaaaa at ur place! So stoked. Maybe we should invite Marco lol.

Your BFF 4eva,
Jamie Boo

The Club Chronicles
Part 27: The Maelstrom of Lost Souls
By Dorothy Wu

Poseidon gave a hearty guffaw, the kind of deep laugh that makes the islands shake. Once he had laughed for several seconds, he stared down at Princess Dorothy with intense water eyes.

"YOUUUU LOOOVE THIS CAD, EH?" he roared, motioning to Prince Jacobim.

Dorothy glanced over at her beloved. Jacobim looked so pitiful and sad trapped in his eternal prison. Then Dorothy looked up at the Aqua God and nodded the bravest of nods.

"HOWWW MUCH DO YOU LOVE HIM?" bellowed Poseidon.

"Enough . . . enough to do whatever it takes to set him free!" Dorothy cried.

"ENOUGH TO . . . SELL YOUR SOOOOOUUUL?"

Dorothy knew that Poseidon was playing a dangerous game with her. Whatever she agreed to would probably hurt her very badly. But she had the chance to set Jacobim free! So what did her soul matter? After all, what are souls when compared with love?

"Yes," Dorothy said. "I would give my soul for Jacobim's freedom."

Poseidon began to smirk a devious water smirk.

"VERY WELL . . ." he howled. "YOU DAFT HUMAN!"

Poseidon blinked thrice, powerful blinks, and all of a sudden the water prison around Jacobim collapsed into a colossal splash and just as quickly reformed itself into a gigantic swirling whirlpool. Dorothy felt the current start to pull at her. She knew what this was—it was the Maelstrom of Lost Souls, Poseidon's preferred method of sending his enemies straight to the Underworld, where his cruel brother Hades awaited. The Underworld—where Dorothy would be forced to struggle forever with mundane tasks such as rolling boulders up hills and cleaning large messes. But she did not care what happened to her— Jacobim was free!

"WELL, WELL, WELL!" Poseidon shouted. "NOW THAT THE GIRL'S SOUL IS MINE FOREVER . . . JACOBIM, PERHAPS WE SHOULD LET HER IN ON OUR LITTLE SECRET!"

Dorothy, struggling to keep her face above the waves as she got sucked into submission, looked up at her liberated lover. He was . . . smiling? Maliciously?

"Dorothy, my dim-witted friend!" Jacobim screamed. "You were an idiot in the name of love! I never cared for you . . . not at all. But I knew that if I feigned love for you, if I seduced you, that together Poseidon and I would be able to capture you—just like we captured the rest of your pathetic Lunch Club comrades! Ha! Ha!"

"It cannot be true!" Dorothy cried desperately. "The

things you said to me . . . things you said no one else knew . . . please, Jacobim!"

"Oh, that is the other thing . . ." Jacobim whispered, an evil look in his eyes. "My name is not Jacobim—IT IS JAKE!"

"NOOOOOOOOOO!!!!!!!!" Dorothy wailed, her tears mingling with ocean water as the waves dragged her farther into the abyss.

"YES," Jake snarled. "You were stupid to love me."

15 • Hannah Schwartz

Friday, December 18

My family's annual Hanukkah party has always been one of the highlights of my year. And not just because it's an excuse to get dressed up. And not just because I get to watch former child stars drunkenly hit on my mom. I think I love it so much because every year it's this great night where my friends and I can get together, look classy, sneak sips of champagne, and all in all just have an amazing time living it up.

Of course, this year there was one small problem getting in the way of that: I hate all my friends. Ever since Chadgate, all my supposed bffs have turned into these awful, rumor-spreading yotch people. They want everyone to believe that I'm a slut because they don't have anything better on me and they're jealous and they're the real sluts and I hate them forever. Seriously, I would rather hang out in the barrio with Chicle and Luz than with them. I'm not even joking—those chicas are pretty fun. Ughhh, but no matter how hateful my "friends" have been, they were all still invited to the party tonight because all of their parents are still brunch companions and golf buddies with my parents. So I went into tonight expecting the worst.

And what I got was the best night of my year. Why? Well, why else? A boy.

There was a lot of buzz about the party at school today. Everyone was extra nice to me in the halls and on the black-top at lunch. They all probably thought that if they so much as brought up the bathroom wall that I would disinvite them. I definitely don't have that kind of power. But hey, if it seems like I do, then more power to me.

When that seventh period bell rang, it was a huge relief—no school for two and a half weeks. But I also started to stress really hard—I only had a few short hours to get ready for the party. And I wanted to look good. Beautiful good. Hot good.

I'm not gonna sell myself short, either. By the time 7:30 rolled around, I looked fully fabulous. I had on the emerald-green halter dress with the sweetheart neckline that I was planning on wearing to homecoming next year until I just had to break it out tonight instead, my silver *H* necklace that my mom gave me that I've only ever worn four times, and a pair of black Sergio Rossi heels that literally made me almost as tall as Danny. Every guy from school was checking me out all night—and no one more than Chad.

Who, annoyingly, was one of the first people to arrive. Like, seriously, him and his parents showed up before the caterers even sent out the first plate of hors d'ouevres. And once Chad showed up, he proceeded to not leave me alone, not for a second. When I went to go hang out in the desig-nated not-for-grown-ups room, there he was reciting his BS poems to all the idiot girls from our grade—and staring at me out of the corner of his eye. When I went to go get some food, there he was lurking by the fondue fountain. When I went to get a breath of fresh air out on the courtyard, there he was, bringing my dad a drink.

I realize that I'm conveniently choosing to direct all of my hatred toward Chad, simply because he makes for the easiest target. But don't worry. I hate my other friends too.

I hate Kristen and Alex for basically deciding to get married in eighth grade while totally ignoring the existence of everyone else. It's made both of them so much less fun. And no one likes your ugly promise ring, Krist. No one believes it, either.

I hate Emily for acting super sweet to my face tonight even though I know it was definitely her who sent me that "anonymous" e-mail about the dangers of being a teenage whore.

I hate Jamie Mackintosh for acting like she's Hannah Schwartz: Ginger Edition even though we only started inviting her to cool things like a month ago. I mean she didn't even go to Arlington—her dad's like, a Gap manager or something—and now she's acting all queen bee, and it totally disrupts the order of the universe.

I hate Rachel Sloan for wearing a dress that looked suspiciously *exactly* like mine even though I had told her specifically *not* to wear anything remotely resembling emerald.

And I hate Lauren Gardner-Smith because . . . well, I've always hated her. Even when I tolerated her, I thought she was a waste of space. And hyphenated names are so two years ago.

So, wait. Hold on. Tonight I hosted a party attended by my creepy ex and by my completely fake ex-friends. How exactly was it the best night ever?

Oh, that's right. Mr. Uribe.

It's a very sexy name to say: Daniel Uribe. I love rolling my r's when I say it. Almost as much as I love saying *"¡Daniellllito!"* But not nearly as much as I love it when he speaks in Spanish to me.

So going into tonight, my game plan with Danny was this: no communication whatsoever. No eye contact, no chatting, and definitely no long conversations. It's not that I'm afraid of being seen near him, it's not that at all. It's just that my family's Hanukkah party—attended by every gossip in Seabrook, the gossip capital of the world—would be a terrible time to make a first appearance as a boy-girl pairing. And Danny and I aren't ready to be seen together anyway, because we don't even know what we are yet. Although we might have come closer to figuring it out tonight.

So this no-communication rule was good, it was effective, but it was just killing me. For the first three hours of the party, I was trapped in endless conversations with catty phonies, and Danny had to sit there with Jake and his gang of prepubescent dorks while they made up tall tales about how much action they'd gotten last weekend with imaginary girls. And I didn't even know it was possible for my little brother to say the word "girl" in a sentence without bursting into tears and running to the nearest bathroom.

As it got later on in the evening, and as the adults got drunker, and as Chad started getting stalker-ier, I realized— screw appearances, I just want to hang out with Danny. So I went to go look for him, but when I got to Jake's geek circle,

Danny wasn't there. Oh, he just left, the boys said, didn't say where he was going. Then they resumed talking about their scrotums.

So I went looking for Danny everywhere. The main deck, the poolside grotto, the snack tables in the backyard, the open bar, the mini-golf course . . . But I couldn't find him. Anywhere. And it was really stressing me out. And I was just about to give up all hope—

But then I felt a poke in my back. So I turned around, and there he was, wearing this cute black button-up shirt that I don't know how he got. And he looked so sexy with that manly jawline of his, and he had a smiling look in his eye, and he said:

"Jake's room. Five minutes."

Jake's room. Brilliant! It would be too obvious if we went to Danny's room in his family's cottage, because then we'd have to walk across the lawn where the adults could see us. And my room wasn't really an option, because, well, I had stupidly allowed Kristen and Alex to make use of it for their . . . purposes (ew). But Jake's room. Jake's room!

At 10:49 p.m., that's where I was. Danny showed up a minute later and closed the door behind him. For a few seconds, we stood there rather awkwardly. Just the two of us, all by ourselves in Jake's room, being stared at by hundreds of lame action figures and bobblehead dolls.

Danny had been so confident and so suave in coming up with the idea to sneak in there. Now, suddenly, he looked kind of, well, thirteen years old. And yeah, he looked adorable in his little black shirt, nervous and twitchy, but he didn't quite seem ready for the moment. He coughed a couple times. He began to breathe so loud I could hear him. Come on, I remember thinking, you're at the finish line—don't choke now!

Danny coughed again and looked up at the room's ceiling.

"It's too bad," he said, but his voice cracked on "bad" so he started over. "It's too bad that there's not any, um, mistletoe or anything."

He wasn't even making eye contact with me. He wasn't going to make the first move. He just wasn't. I knew what I had to do.

"Danny," I said in my lowest, smoothest, sexiest voice. "It's Hanukkah. Who needs mistletoe?"

At that exact second I threw myself at him, and he threw himself at me and our mouths connected and it was pure perfection. So much better than a movie moment. So much real-er.

Yeah, Danny was a little tentative at first, not really going for it—I could tell I was his first kiss—but after a while he got the hang of it. Of the four boys I've kissed, Danny definitely has the most potential. He's more patient than Will, not as sloppy as Dylan, gentler than Chad.

And once we started really exploring with our lips, a little bit with our tongues, a medium bit with our hands . . . oh, it was so fun. You know how normally you can really enjoy doing something, but after a while you get kind of bored of it? Making out with Danny wasn't like that at all. It kept getting hotter and hotter as I pulled him down on to the bed, as

I jumped on top of him, as we tried making out upside down like Spider-Man for a few minutes, just to see what it's like. My heart was beating faster and harder with every kiss, with every touch of the tongues. I'd give anything to be back in Jake's room. I know I'd still be kissing Danny now if it wasn't for us almost getting walked in on.

No, we didn't get walked in on. That would have been a pretty scary ending to what I like to think of as an epic romance. But there was this moment after we had been making out for a while. It was long after I'd put my hair in a ponytail, and right when I was thinking about taking it all out again for hotness factor, when there was this loud bump against the door. Danny and I clenched each other when we heard it—Jake!—but it was just one of Daddy's friends staggering his way to the bathroom. My money's on Jerry Bruckheimer.

That false alarm was enough for us. Danny and I knew we had to get out of there. We fixed our hair, staggered our exits, and within moments we were back in our respective circles as if nothing had ever happened. The two of us didn't talk for the rest of the party, and I went back to my room without so much as a good night kiss. I haven't spoken to Danny since, and I have no idea what the future holds for us.

But we'll always have Jake's room.

jschwartzinfinity has signed on at 12:23 p.m.

jschwartzinfinity: hey dude

getsome_danny24: yo

jschwartzinfinity: didnt see you for bfast or lunch

getsome_danny24: probly cuz i was sleepin

jschwartzinfinity: oh

jschwartzinfinity: hey man its like

jschwartzinfinity: 5th day of break

jschwartzinfinity: we havent even hung out yet man

getsome_danny24: i kno dude im sry

getsome_danny24: after xmas i promise

jschwartzinfinity: so im guessin you cant hang out today?

getsome_danny24: naw man sry

getsome_danny24: cant today

getsome_danny24: after xmas is better

jschwartzinfinity: when after xmas?

getsome_danny24: idk dude

getsome_danny24: im busy all week

getsome_danny24: family n stuff

getsome_danny24: like in the new yr maybe

jschwartzinfinity: oh

jschwartzinfinity: okay

jschwartzinfinity: sounds cool

getsome_danny24: ya

getsome_danny24: g2g

getsome_danny24 has signed off at 12:28 p.m.

jschwartzinfinity: hey dude

russell0WMYBALLS: o hey jake

russell0WMYBALLS: been a while

jschwartzinfinity: u were at my familys party

russell0WMYBALLS: o right

russell0WMYBALLS: totes forgot about that lol

jschwartzinfinity: hey you doin anything today?

russell0WMYBALLS: sry man cant

russell0WMYBALLS: xmas shopping all day

russell0WMYBALLS: prob 2morrow 2

jschwartzinfinity: oh no thats cool

russell0WMYBALLS: yea

russell0WMYBALLS has signed off at 12:34 p.m.

jschwartzinfinity: hi

jschwartzinfinity: dorothy?

jschwartzinfinity: i found your sn on facebook

jschwartzinfinity: i hope thats ok

mrsgandalf88: hello

jschwartzinfinity: hey

jschwartzinfinity: ok

jschwartzinfinity: so i want to say sorry

jschwartzinfinity: for the way i acted last week

jschwartzinfinity: i was completely lame

jschwartzinfinity: and i just wanted to let you know

jschwartzinfinity: i feel really bad about it

120

mrsgandalf88: Jake Schwartz

mrsgandalf88: your apology

mrsgandalf88: is accepted

mrsgandalf88: by me.

jschwartzinfinity: thank you

jschwartzinfinity: that actually means a lot

mrsgandalf88: I appreciate your apology.

mrsgandalf88: It means we can be friends again

mrsgandalf88: for which I am grateful.

jschwartzinfinity: yeah yeah

mrsgandalf88: so how are you doing this break, Jake?

mrsgandalf88: (break Jake rhyme haha)

mrsgandalf88: are you working on any new stories?

jschwartzinfinity: hey dorothy i g2g

mrsganfalf88: very well

mrsgandalf88: as they say, "later."

jschwartzinfinity: haha yeah

jschwartzinfinity has signed off at 12:48 p.m.

jschwartzinfinity has signed on at 12:53 p.m.

jschwartzinfinity: hey dorothy?

mrsgandalf88: yes, Jake?

mrsgandalf88: did you intend to sign back on so soon?

jschwartzinfinity: what are you doing today?

mrsgandalf88: hrmmm

mrsgandalf88: interesting question.

mrsgandalf88: most likely I will remain in my room

mrsgandalf88: reading mangas

mrsgandalf88: and having a wicked break.

jschwartzinfinity: ok well

jschwartzinfinity: Dorothy

jschwartzinfinity: how would you like to come hang out at my house?

mrsgandalf88: oh

mrsgandalf88: really?

mrsgandalf88: Holy Table!

mrsgandalf88: I would like that

mrsgandalf88: I would like that a lot.

mrsgandalf88: on which day?

jschwartzinfinity: how bout today

mrsgandalf88: when?

jschwartzinfinity: how bout 2

mrsgandalf88: 2 o'clock today?

mrsgandalf88: o frabjous day!

jschwartzinfinity: callooh callay

mrsgandalf88: :D

jschwartzinfinity: let me tell you how to get here

mrsgandalf88: oh, I already know how.

jschwartzinfinity: wait

jschwartzinfinity: you do?

mrsgandalf88: I own a school directory

mrsgandalf88: and a global positioning system

mrsgandalf88: silly.

jschwartzinfinity: right, right

mrsgandalf88: so

mrsgandalf88: Jake Schwartz

mrsgandalf88: I will be seeing you at 2.

jschwartzinfinity: yeah, definitely

mrsgandalf88: definitely!

jschwartzinfinity has signed off at 12:58 p.m.

mrsgandalf88 has signed off at 12:59 p.m.

Friday, December 25 at 11:40 a.m.

Lauren Gardner-Smith happy bday jesus
2 minutes ago · Comment · Like

Chad Beck don we now our GAY apparel bahahahahahahahaha
4 minutes ago · Comment · Like

Johnny Graham got 2 ds games that he already owns. thanks a lot mom i mean santa
6 minutes ago · Comment · Like

Avery Patterson i was a good girl this yr. lil bit naughty tho ;)
7 minutes ago · Comment · Like

Meghan Moore who is parson brown?
7 minutes ago · Comment · Like

Kristen Duffy all i want for christmas is youuu ooooo babyyyyy (luv u al baby)
10 minutes ago · Comment · Like

Hannah Rose Schwartz chinese food and a movie!!
13 minutes ago · Comment · Like

Chase Sanford gimme some nog
15 minutes ago · Comment · Like

Alex Masterson i luv u krist ur my xmas miracle
16 minutes ago · Comment · Like

Meghan Moore what is myrrh?

18 minutes ago · Comment · Like

McKenzie Hall wishes every day was christmas

21 minutes ago · Comment · Like

McKenzie Hall wishes every day was chrismas

22 minutes ago · Comment · Like

Danny Uribe cant believe sum1 made him get a facebook . . . o and feliz navidad.

24 minutes ago · Comment · Like

16 • Dorothy Wu

Thursday, December 31

I think about the year that has been and I smile. This year I accomplished many marvelous things. I graduated from Truman Elementary, of course, and at the end-of-elementary-school-honors ceremony, I won several awards for my prowess in computer art. I made it through an entire family road trip without calling my little brother a pest. I became a woman in the biological sense, and yet I remain a girl in the spiritual sense. (Actually, spiritually I would say that I am half girl, half cat. But that is for the spirits to decide, is it not?) Yes, yes, yes, overall, the past 365 days have been very good to me.

And especially the last nine.

For these have been the days in which I have gotten to frolic with my dear Prince Jacobim. Now, let me be most clear about this: we are just friends. Let us not forget, he ran away from me crying in the hallway for a reason. Jake does not desire a relationship. That is what he said. He would like for us to be friends.

And what friends we now are! Ever since that fateful instant message conversation in which Jake begged for my forgiveness, we have seen each other every single day except for three. We have played video games together. We have read our stories and poems to each other. Jake even said that soon I might get the chance to visit the set of one of his father's movies. Even though I do not care much for American cinema, I still consider this very exciting!

Today was the most wonderful day of all—we went to the beach. Now, I know what one might think here: beach equals date and date equals love and love equals sex. Dirty mind! Jake does not love me. He likes me very strongly as friends do. That is all.

Of course, I would like to think that in its own special way, our day at the beach was just a small bit romantic. Jake arrived at my house in the early afternoon. It was his first visit to my home, a fact that made me exceedingly nervous. For you see, my house is roughly one-sixteenth the size of his, and so I thought he might laugh in my face upon arriving and demand to see "the real thing."

Much to my happiness, that scenario did not occur. Jake did not find my house tiny. Rather, he found it charming. He enjoyed my family as well, even my father. (Who was extremely friendly today. Why? Methinks because I gave him the impression that Jake was a math tutor. Little white lies do not hurt anybody!)

Upon seeing my room, Jake paid me the ultimate compliment. He said, "It reminds me of my room."

!!!

That is just the sort of thing I was hoping he would say! It is an accurate statement, too. Both of our rooms are, as they say, "busy." Posters and action figures and stuffed characters and piles of books and strange board games fill every nook and cranny. Furthermore, both Jake and I have the same exact poster of a large cat wearing a tuxedo and a top hat. The poster says "High Class Cat." We both possess it, but neither of us knows how we got it. I believe that this makes us kindred souls.

Ah, but what am I babbling on about my room for? I frequent my room every day. It is far less often that I get to walk along the beach with a certain Jacob Emanuel Schwartz.

Because my family lives near the Eastside, and not in Seabrook like the richies, the beach is a fair jaunt from our house. So to get to the waves, Jake and I had to travel by bike. It was quite comical. Jake had to ride Darrell's bike, which is already too small even for little ten-year-old Darrell. Jake resembled a clown on that tiny thing! But, like a clown, he was good-natured about it.

(Even though, as Jake told me, he has never much liked riding bicycles. Ever since he was little, he has always preferred trikes as a mode of transportation, that is what he said. The way he said it was mucho cute, too. That is why he is my boy.)

(Just a friend, though! My friendboy.)

When we arrived at the beach, it was surprisingly and wonderfully not crowded. I suppose that most people do not like to venture into the waves on cloudy, cold New Year's Eves. That just meant more ocean fun for Jake and me. Well, Jake was the one who really had ocean fun. The first thing he did when we got there was throw off his shirt and jump into the water screaming, "CANNONBALL!" with all the volume he could muster. All I could say was, "Bah. Boys."

It is not that I do not like playing in the waves, it is just . . .

bathing suits. I had one on underneath my black jacket and black pants, but I did not feel like wearing only it and nothing else. Jake should have known that. Perhaps he did realize it eventually, because after I watched him romp around and body surf for several minutes, he swam back to where I was on the shore and got out of the water (which made me happy) and put his shirt back on (drat!).

Sometimes when I look at dating Web sites for my own personal amusement and for tips on how to be irresistible, I notice that people, in their lists of things that they like, often say "long walks on the beach." I have always wondered why, and now I know. For after Jake's brief spell in the ocean, the two of us had the most joyous time just walking on the beach and getting to know each other better as chums.

At first, our conversation was as light and breezy as the light breeze. We talked of cartoons, of mythology, of fantastical scenarios, and all the while I helped Jake find flat rocks that he could skip on the ocean waters. He is a very good skipper; on one skip he got nine skips! He said that his father taught him how when he was little. Jake tried to show me how, but I was poor even for a novice. I can make the rock plunk into the sea, and that is about it. Sorry, fishies.

After some time, Jake skipped all the skippable stones that there were and so we sat down on a large flat rock. This was where the conversation became rather different.

At first, we talked about writing club. We talked about how brilliant Mr. Mo is, how quiet and mysterious Whitney is, how weird-smelling Tyler is. But then when we got to Danny, who

I believe to be Jake's favorite friend in the entire world, except for possibly me these past nine days, Jake did not want to talk much. I did not understand why. I still do not understand why. Did Jake and Danny have a fight? I do not think they had a fight. Yet why else would Jake turn silent and grumpy at the mere mention of his pal's name? I was vexed to the max.

So rather than continue on with that "awkward turtle" moment, I deftly changed the subject. I asked Jake when we would be able to visit the set of his father's film. Again, much to my surprise, Jake became quiet, so different from the boy I watched in the waves. He muttered something about "Knowing my dad, not for a while," and then he trailed off and it got quiet again, and so we were back to the first square.

Once more, I thought it would be prudent to save the conversation. So I started talking about *my* father, but then I realized that I never want to talk about my father. I faded back into silence after a few words, and so there we were on the big flat rock, close and far apart at the same time.

There were many things I wanted to tell Jake. I wanted to tell him about his role in my stories and about his role in my life the past few months. I knew that that would probably be a terrible thing to do, considering what happened the last time I tried to tell him things of a personal nature, but the silence was just so unbearable that I was about to tell him anyway, because I just had to, because I was feeling it so much right then, and there was nothing that was going to stop me from making what would have been a Jupiter-sized mistake, and so I was about to cry, "JAKE SCHWARTZ,

YOU DARLING CHAP, THIS IS HOW I FEEL ABOUT YOU," but then—but then—but then—

But then we saw the dolphins. A whole pod of dolphins, no more than two stone skips from where we were sitting. Holy Mother of Table, I remember thinking. There were so many of them, at least a dozen I would say, jumping and playing and smiling. (I know that the facial structure of a dolphin makes it look as if they are always smiling, but these ones really were. I know it.) I do not think that dolphins usually come out to play that late in the afternoon, or ever, but there these ones were, prancing about and celebrating New Year's Eve with us. A whole pod of chipper, cheerful dolphins. And all of them stayed out in the waves for nearly twenty minutes, putting on their private show for Jake and me. It was, as they say, a miracle.

A couple times during the dolphins' grand dance, I peeked over at Jake and I saw that his eyes were wet and that a couple of tears were sliding down his cheeks. He was making no effort to wipe them off. He did not have to. It was wonderful. Those magnificent marine mammals were just what we needed. Truly, they were a gift from Poseidon himself.

Hey, Poseidon, I am sorry about all those mean things I said about you in my stories. Thanks for the happy beach day and for sending the dolphins and really just for everything. You are all right after all. And Prince Jacobim, I am also sorry for what I said about you. You are all right, too.

17 • Jake Schwartz

Friday, January 1

My best friends are pretty great—both of them.

I think I know why Dorothy sucks at math. She sucks at math because she's weird. Allow me to explain.

She was at my house this morning, like she is most mornings these days, and I was helping her study for her math final. I know it's early to be studying—break isn't even over yet, the end of the semester is weeks away—but she's got to raise her grade. And Dorothy agreed with me on that, actually. She told me her dad said the same thing. She then added that she likes studying when it's with me. That's cool.

But she's so bad at studying! I was in the middle of explaining fraction-decimal conversion to her when Dorothy went on this ten-minute tangent about how she thinks of each number as having a different personality. In her opinion, the numbers 1 to 9 are not just numbers—they're characters. 1 is a cocky athlete, 2 is a shy librarian, 3 is a funny magician/entertainer, 4 is an older, spiritual woman, 5 is a young, streetwise pickpocket, 6 is a rebellious skater, 7 is a very popular girl who is actually very boring, 8 is a fat and loveable baker, and 9 is a sex-crazed spy. Dorothy seriously thinks of the numbers this way, as if they're her friends.

This explains her math suckitude. When I was helping her,

I would say things like, "All right, here you're gonna multiply two and five," and she would be like, "Oh, two would not do that. Two hates five. She finds him incredibly unsexy." On the one hand, it was so frustrating. But D. Wu is D. Wu, and that's what makes her great.

With all that nuttiness, we didn't get very far. I'd say Dorothy's only about one-eighth—or 12.5 percent—of where she needs to be for the final. Actually, she wanted to keep studying this afternoon, that's what she told me while we were having lunch, but I told her, Sorry, not today. I had to cut things short today. I had plans with another friend.

"Thank you for your assistance, Tutor Jake," Dorothy said to me as we hugged good-bye at my front door. "I am glad you are now what my father always thought you were, which is a tutor, Jake."

I said, "No problem, happy to help, and don't worry, we can go back to our usual schedule of board games and beach walks next time."

"What say you to this?" she said. "Perhaps next hang, I can be *your* tutor? Your *Jewish* tutor! Your rabbit, I believe they are called."

"Rabbi," I said.

"Yes, that. You need a mentor, young Padawan! Your bar mitzvah day is just five months and four days away, you know! Hehe!" She then gave me what she described as a dolphin smile.

Oh, D. Wu. I patted her on the head. She left for the bus station.

Then I went to go see my other best friend.

Danny's been busy with stuff all winter break, but in our chat he promised we could do something New Year's Day, and I intended to collect on that promise. I walked down to Danny's family's house and knocked on his window.

After a few moments, I heard his voice. "What?" he said. The blinds were drawn. Danny likes to sleep in.

"It's me!"

"Oh yeah. Gimme a minute, dude."

Danny was out a minute later. "What do you want to do?" he said.

I didn't care. Anything could be fun.

"Swimming?" I suggested.

"What? It's so cold."

"Well, we could heat up the pool, hot tub–style like last summer?"

"Gay, dude."

"Right. Well I could always . . . you know . . . help you study for your math final?"

"Shut up. That's like, a month away."

"Okay," I said. "Okay . . . um . . . "

I had one more idea, one last idea before we had to resort to just playing Xbox. It was sort of a strange idea, and I was worried Danny would think it was lame, but I'd had it in mind as a fun thing for us to do for a while. Probably since the start of the school year.

"We could go to Arlington."

Danny nodded. "Awesome," he said.

Awesome!

We walked down my driveway, past the gate, and down the road about a mile to the Arlington playground. It reminded me of a day from a couple of years ago, the first day of fifth grade. I remember Danny and I were eating Corn Pops before school, and my mom came into the kitchen and told us that, as a special surprise, starting that morning, we were allowed to walk to school every day without parental supervision. We high-fived so hard at that. I think we might have even jumped up and down, hugging. Those walks to school became the absolute highlights of our day, each and every day for the rest of elementary school. Obviously, now we go to SP, and it's too far to go by foot, and Danny takes the bus now anyway, so we haven't gotten to take one of our walks in a while. That's what made today neat. We didn't even have to talk much as we walked—we just enjoyed the old routine. I grabbed a lemon from this one tree right near the school. Danny and I used to take the lemons and put them in our mouths and have sour-face contests. We didn't do one of those today, but I put the lemon in my pocket for later, as sort of a souvenir, I guess. Now that I think about it, fifth grade really wasn't that long ago.

After we hopped the Arlington fence, Danny noticed that there was a single basketball sitting in the middle of the court, and fully inflated too, a clear sign from the gods that we should play one-on-one.

Man, he's good. Danny blocked three of my threes, jumped over me for every rebound, and even grabbed the rim at one point as he went in for a lay-up. I remember a year ago, he'd talk all the time about what it would be like to touch the rim. I thought the day would never come, at least not until college. Now it's his signature move. I wonder if he could dunk a tennis ball now. Probably. He was balling like a madman today.

Yet I didn't play too bad myself. Despite my tendency to dribble the ball off my shoe, and my characteristically Jewish lack of vertical leap, I kept things close. I shot the lights out. I moved my feet. I hustled. In an intense game to thirty by ones and twos, one of those wars that lasts forever and takes a ton out of each guy, I only lost by three points. After the game, Danny suggested that I sign up for after-school basketball with him. It starts next week, apparently.

"Are you serious?" I said.

"Yeah," Danny said. "It'll be fun."

I know he didn't compliment me exactly, but all the same, I felt like saying thanks.

I got another idea. "Hey," I said to Danny as he took his last jumper. "You wanna go on the swings?"

"No," Danny said, making a face. "What do I look like, a baby?"

"Oh," I said. I felt dumb. I put my head down. "Well, um, what about the Big Toy?"

Danny nodded at that. He smiled, too. "Yeah. The Big Toy is tight."

If walking to Arlington made me feel like a fifth grader, running onto the playground made me feel like a second grader. In that moment, Danny was arguably even a kindergartener.

"Beat you there!" he shouted, the second after agreeing to play. He ran off the court, across the lawn, and up to the play structure, flailing his arms, running like a loon. I followed him. When I got there, a good five seconds after him and out of breath, he surprise-tackled me into the wood chips.

"Sucks for you, dude!" he said as he splashed a handful of chips into my face.

Being a little kid is so fun. We ran up the slides, then slid down them, then ran up again. One of the slides gave me a static shock. I told this to Danny, who rubbed his hand on it, then ran up to me and touched my head with his electrified hand. It hurt really bad.

We played an impromptu game of hot-lava tag on top of the half-dome jungle gym, crawling around like little spiders. It's so tiring with only two people.

We climbed on top of the monkey bars, standing all dangerously on top of the upper bar that connects them, the way the yard duties always tell you not to. "But there are no yard duties during winter break, are there?" Danny said. It was the best—we just stood on top of the playground, surveying the stuff below. Danny tried to give me a purple nurple while we were up there and I almost fell off. So funny.

I don't know what it is about Danny. He's just always loved that Big Toy.

"Thanks," I said to Danny. I was still a bit out of breath from the basketball game plus the race to the play structure plus the slides plus the tag game plus the monkey bars plus the avoidance of the purple nurple.

"No, man, thank you," Danny said. "I forgot about this stuff. This was fun."

"Yeah," I said. "This stuff is fun."

Danny looked down at the playground below, then up at me. "I'm sorry for not hanging out with you," he said. "On my birthday, at the movie set. That was messed up. My bad, man."

"Oh," I said. "No, don't worry about it. It's fine. I'm sorry for freaking out that day. And . . . yeah."

Danny sort of nodded to himself. He didn't say anything.

"I guess I just don't like being left alone, you know?" I said.

Some more silence went by. Danny didn't look at me. I probably hit too much of a nerve with what I told him. He knows that he hasn't necessarily been the best of friends this year. I shouldn't have said that last thing. I decided to change the subject.

"How's Hannah holding up?" I said. "You've been a good friend to her, huh."

"Hannah's good," Danny said. "Thanks for asking."

We let some more silence go by. It was an okay amount of silence for two best friends. It would have been awkward if we were strangers. I wondered what Danny was thinking, what exactly prompted his apology about the birthday, whether he felt sorry about anything else he's done this year.

"You wanna head back?" I said. "If we leave now, we might have time for some video games before dinner. Or, you know, we could always take a nighttime dip in the pool."

Danny flashed another smile at that.

"So we boyfriends now or what?" he said.

We jumped off of the monkey bars and started home.

It was a pretty great time, now that I think about it. An epic day. Dorothy, Danny, Dorothy, Danny. My new buddy, my best friend. One is silver and the other's gold and, you know, all that stuff.

18 • Danny Uribe

Friday, January 1

I almost said I love you. The moment felt right. Lying on my bed, making out, her next to me, my hand running through her hair, my other hand on her lower back. There was this moment where she lifted her face from mine and just looked at me with those big sexy blue eyes of hers. We didn't say anything, but I know we were both thinking, I love you.

That's when the window started banging all hard behind us. Crap. I'd totally forgotten. I promised Jake we could hang out today. In our chat I told him New Year's Day and then later I told him 1 p.m. I checked my phone and there it was, 1 p.m. Damn. Hannah snuck into my room like, so early this morning, and we never even noticed the hours go by. Time flies when you're getting some.

I told Jake one minute and I got up and grabbed my shoes.

"I'll wait until you guys leave, then I'll sneak back into the house," Hannah whispered to me. "How's my hair?" she said.

It was all messed up from the bed. I helped her straighten it with my hand.

"Where are you guys going?" she said.

"No idea," I said.

"When will you be back?"

"I don't know. Soon, probably."

"Awesome. I'll be waiting for you."

She smiled with her tongue between her teeth. She always gets me with that.

"I'll miss you," I whispered.

"You're cute," she said.

I kissed her one more time, then a second later I was outside. Jake didn't notice a thing. I don't know when me and Hannah are planning on telling people about us, or who we're gonna tell. I'll have to check with her about that.

Jake had all these gay ideas of what we should do. Like seriously, man, you think I wanna take a bath with you? Really, you wanna help me learn math during Christmas break? I know my grades aren't the best, but come on. You have to come up with some better stuff than that.

But then he suggested rolling down to Arlington, and, I don't know, for some reason that sounded real fun to me. Gotta give Jake credit on that one.

The walk down was kinda awkward. We haven't really kicked it in a while, so there wasn't much to talk about. I can't exactly tell him about the main things in my life these days. He wouldn't want to know about Eastside stuff and he definitely shouldn't know about me and his older sister. So we just walked to Arlington, same as when we were little kids.

There was this weird part when Jake got a lemon from one of the trees and put it in his pocket. What's he trying to do, make lemonade?

Playing ball with Jake is fun since I can dominate him so hard. I was doing all kinds of crazy moves like the fools on the And1 Mixtape Tour, like I even bounced the ball off his forehead and stuff. I let Jake keep the game close because it's funner that way, but at the end when I decided to win, I finished him off with the sickest move. I crossed him over so bad he fell on his ass, and when I went in for the lay-up, I jumped all high and put almost my whole hand over the rim. I did it like it wasn't no thing, too. Like, after I did it, I just acted all normal. Jake was impressed and stuff. It was tight.

Jake kept talking about basketball tryouts the whole time we were playing, but he kept saying he wouldn't do them because he probably wasn't good enough to make the team. I told him it's just after-school sports, man, they probably take everyone who signs up. I said he should do it with me. It'll be fun.

Then Jake had this wack idea to go have playtime on the swings, and I was like, "The swings? What are you smoking?" But then he said let's go on the Big Toy, and I was all, "Now you're talking."

The Big Toy is so nice. I remember it was the first thing I really loved when I moved to Seabrook in second grade. Jake's house is big and cool and all, but for a little kid it's not really that fun. You can't touch anything in it. The grown-ups are all worried you'll poke your eye out with one of the Emmys. Plus I still missed my cousins and all my friends over on the Eastside. But then Jake and I went to Arlington on the first day of second grade and I saw that Big Toy, and I just knew, damn, this life is legit.

At my school that I went to for kindergarten and first grade, over on the Eastside, the jungle gym was all rusty and broken and jank. The slides were metal and they had too much friction or whatever. The monkey bars were oily and nasty. Everything made a creaking sound when you ran across it.

The Big Toy is like a million times and like a hundred thousand dollars better. I mean, no wonder. It's the playground for the stars' kids. It's got all the best slides and jungle gyms and zip lines and random steering wheels and everything.

I forgot how much I liked the thing. Jake and I messed around on it for a few minutes today. We ran across all the bridges and climbed across all the bars like we were my little cousins at a McDonald's PlayPlace or some crap. The best part was when I gave Jake a titty twister. He made such girl sounds, trying to get away. It was hilarious. After a while, we got pretty tired, so we were just standing up there, on the top of the Big Toy, on top of the Arlington playground.

I told Jake sorry for not hanging out with him more when he took me to the movie set for my birthday. That was the day he got all sad. I hadn't thought about it too much since then, but being with Jake today made me think about it. I wasn't a good friend to Jake that day. He deserves better. He's a good kid.

Jake acted kinda weird after that. He made some complaint about being a loner, and then he got all quiet like he was expecting me to say more. Like I was the one in charge of making him feel better. He was kinda acting the way girls do sometimes when they're mad. I just let the moment pass.

Then he brought up Hannah. That was weird, too. Kid needs to not get involved in things he's not a part of.

The walk back home was silent and awkward, like the

walk there. Jake didn't pick any more lemons.

Before I went into my room, I bumped fists with Jake and I told him, "Awesome day, man." And it really was. It can be fun connecting with the stuff you used to do.

I was so excited to get back in my room. I knew exactly what would be in there waiting for me. My girl. Her perfectly shaped legs, her cute little hands, her dark brown hair that curls just at the ends, her juicy lips, her beautiful eyes, her body, which is really nice but you can also tell that she eats, which I like, and of course how can I forget the best part: her donk. I couldn't wait for all of it. I couldn't wait to see my girlfriend. Happy ending to a fun-ass day.

She was in my room, all right, sitting on my bed. But she didn't look happy to see me like I was expecting. I said, "Baby, what's up?"

"You left your phone here," she said.

So what? I guess I'd left it in my room in my hurry to meet Jake. "What's wrong?" I said. "Something about us?"

"No, no one knows about us," she said. "But something happened. On the Eastside. Carlos and Javy have been texting and calling you nonstop. Luz and Chicle, too. I didn't want to respond for you."

"Give me the phone," I said. She gave it to me. I looked at all the missed calls, all the texts. They all said basically the same thing. All the texts repeated the same three words. I read them over and over. I couldn't believe them.

They got Gordo.

Twelve Arrested in Local Gang Sweep

By Aaron Marcuse, *San Paulo Spectator*

Sunday, January 3rd

In a surprise New Year's Day operation, local law enforcement officials carried out search warrants and made arrests of twelve individuals, all minors, on Friday morning for participation in an Eastside gang brawl.

The early-morning raid, which was known as "Operation Viper," came about partly as a result of widespread community outrage. Although juvenile gang violence has soared in the past twelve months, there has not been a corresponding increase in the number of youth arrests made, leading many to think of the San Paulo Police Department as lenient.

"After Viper, we're not so soft now," said Lt. Pat Ayers, a spokesman for the San Paulo PD.

No connections were made between any of the 12 arrested and the still-unresolved murder of 13-year-old Angel Calderon, which occurred last March.

In addition, no names have been released as of yet.

SAN PAULO JUNIOR HIGH SCHOOL
MORNING ANNOUNCEMENTS—THURSDAY, JANUARY 14

Finals week is coming! Exam schedules are posted in all classrooms. For an individual copy of the exam schedule, see Ms. Dooling or Ms. Glass in the library. **Now start studying!**

Tell your parents to come to tonight's San Paulo Town Hall Meeting. The evening's topic will be "Safety in Our School: How to Keep San Paulo as Well Protected as Possible." Principal Greene will be speaking along with Officer Craig Shaw of the S.P. Police Department. The meeting is at 7 p.m. in the auditorium.

Attention All Athletes! The winter sports season is here! This season's sports are boys basketball, girls basketball, boys volleyball, girls volleyball, and wrestling. If you would like to join one of these teams, meet outside the gym after school next Monday for an informational meeting. Tryouts are the week after next. Go Pirates!

Tickets for the Sweethearts Dance go on sale next week! Tickets are $7 per person, $12 per couple. The dance is Saturday, February 13. Get to it, cupids!

Seventh graders: feeling threatened by those eighth-grade bullies?
Eighth graders: feeling annoyed by those upstart sevvies?
Starting next semester, the leadership class is beginning a new school tradition: "Unity Lunches." Every Wednesday at lunch, try eating with someone from a different grade! Let's end the inter-grade squabbles! Let's get this right.

Future Scientists and Engineers of America (FSEA) meets today at lunch in Mr. Peterson's room (Room 124).

All health classes are beginning a unit on **Sex Education** next semester. Be sure to bring back your signed parent/guardian release form by the first day of classes.

On a somewhat related note, congratulations to Coach Wade and his wife, Marie, for their new daughter, **Bella Claire Wade!** We'll see you here in about twelve years, Bella!

Don't forget, next Friday, January 22, is a minimum day. Since it is the last day of the semester, students will be released from campus at 12:30 p.m. Make good choices!

And as always, San Paulo is a no gum, no iPods, no cell phones, no skateboards, no video games, no laser pointers school! Those found with any of the aforementioned items will be given a detention. **No exceptions.**

19 • Hannah Schwartz

Monday, January 18

I love having this little secret. Every single day feels like that night in Jake's room. It's amazing. We catch each other's eyes in the hallway before school and during passing periods. At home after school, I walk past him playing basketball with Jake, and when Jake's not looking, I shoot him a secret smile. Then, at night, when no one is paying attention, I slip into his room and we just go to town on each other's lips. Me and my forbidden boy.

Today was my and Danny's one-month anniversary, not that anybody besides us knows that. We celebrated by making out in Danny's room from seven to seven-thirty while Jake watched *Jeopardy!* Then we had an awesome conversation for a couple hours while Jake did homework. Then, after we were supposed to go to bed, Danny and I AIM chatted till way past midnight. And here's the best part: at the end of our chat, right before we said good night, Danny and I both typed and sent less-than-three hearts (<3) to each other at the same exact time. Obviously I had to delete the chat file right after, just in case anybody ever snoops around on my computer, but that <3 moment <3 is one I'll never forget.

I've known Danny since I was eight. They always say that the best relationships come out of being friends with someone first. I sort of feel like deep down, Danny and I have been best friends ever since we first knew each other. We just didn't realize it until this year.

I told him that when we were talking tonight. I said, "Danny, you're my best friend." He got that little confused look he gets sometimes and he said, "Wait, I thought we were something more?" So cute how he's always trying to DTR. I was like, "Well obviously we're girlfriend-boyfriend too, but, you know, saying we're best friends too makes it more special. It just does." Then Danny said, "Okay, but if you're my girlfriend, how come I'm not allowed to tell anyone?"

Danny, Danny, Danny.

That's really been the only mini-hiccup in our relationship so far. I'm very happy with the way things are, but Danny wants to, I don't know, be the talk of the school.

Who wants to be in a high-profile relationship? Imagine being one of those superstars who's always dating someone famous: Jessica, Angelina, Jennifer, Jessica, Britney, Jessica. It would be the most miserable life. Your every date, every handhold, every kiss would be watched and analyzed and criticized. Me, I'll take Julia Roberts's life. You still get all the money and glory, but instead of a big famous ego for a bf, you've got your low-profile-but-still-cute cameraman hubby who no one knows about and no one cares about and no one bothers.

I don't want the San Paulo paparazzi all over Danny and me. I don't even want to think about the commotion we would cause if we went public.

My "friends" would freak out because they can't possibly imagine someone of my eighth grade stature dating, let alone sniffing, a lowly sevvy. On the bathroom wall, Hannah Schwartz would go from SLUT to PREDATOR.

My parents would go ballistic because there happens to be an itsy-bitsy no boyfriend rule that they happen to believe I'm upholding. Oh, and in their mind, Uribes are just supposed to garden and clean their mansion, not mouth-freak their daughter.

Jake would cry so hard, and it would probably actually be sort of hilarious, but still, it's not like I *want* him to cry. I mean, it's funny when he *does* cry, but I can't *hope* for it.

And, well, there is that one other aspect to it. It's the kind of thing you're not supposed to talk about or even think about. But it matters.

It was so scary when I saw all those texts from Chicle and Luz on Danny's phone. And over the next few days, the more Danny tried to comfort me, the scarier it got.

"It's okay, Gordo's only a first-time offender. He'll be out soon."

"No one got hurt. The brawl wasn't legit. The shot callers just set it up to distract the cops while the big drug deal went down on the other side of town."

"Gordo will be fine."

"Everything is fine."

I mean, okay, it's not like I think Danny is going to turn into a gangbanger or anything—he wouldn't do that. But everything is not effing fine.

I've seen the cop cars outside our school like, every day ever since the raid happened. I know about the massively increased security they're getting for the Sweethearts Dance in two weeks. I've overheard my parents talking about sending me and Jake to "a safer school."

Translation: a whiter school.

Tonight Danny said not to worry, the gangsters never go after anyone who's "outside the system," so I "shouldn't think about them." Nothing bad will happen to me, he said. He wouldn't let anything bad happen to me.

But that's not the point. The point is I don't want anything bad to happen to Danny. He needs to stay the hell away from that whole mess.

And, obviously, so do I. I understand that Danny is going to be drawn to his friends and family, I know he loves that world, and I get that it's "home" to him or whatever, but me? Honestly, the Eastside scares me. I have to keep as far away from there as possible. That means that random people can't associate me with Danny.

And that's why we can't go public.

Danny and I really have been doing an amazing job of keeping up appearances, though. Ever since whoever-that-was-almost-maybe-walking-in-on-us-in-Jake's-room on the night of the Hanukkah party, we haven't come close to being detected. Danny chills with his crew. I hang out with my fake friends, all of whom still think I want Chad. Everyone's happy.

Danny and I can keep this up for a long, looong time if we

151

want to. I mean, the only time we've even planned to publicly be within a hundred feet of each other is at the Sweethearts Dance. But even there we can easily keep up appearances. We're going in different groups and we're not going to dance together or anything.

I don't know if I'm excited for the dance. Having a secret date sucks since I won't get to have, you know, a real date. I mean, yeah, it'll be a fun time I guess, getting dressed up and taking pictures and everything. I really do love my dress. I got it at Femstyle, this super-cute, super-pricey L.A. boutique. The dress is strapless and taffeta, with a ruffled but totally tasteful hemline, the most stunning shade of violet. . . . I sort of can't wait to see how it dances.

All right, I'm excited for Sweethearts. Impossibly excited. I'm excited to decorate the gym, I'm excited to see everyone in my group dressed up, I'm excited to see who gets voted on to the royal court—

And okay, I haven't told anyone this, because it sounds dumb when I say it and because I don't want to jinx it, but I want to be the Queen of Hearts. I want it bad. I don't just want to be nominated. I don't want to barely lose like I did in the Princess election last year. I want to win, dammit. After all that's happened to me this year, what with the bathroom wall and everything, and considering the way I've been able to come back from that . . . well, I kind of feel like I deserve this. And I mean, I *will* be wearing purple the night of the dance, and that *is* the color of royalty, so I'm just hoping the student body takes the hint.

Whenever a celebrity needs to rehab her image, she's got to do something big, bold, and badass. That's the only way to get the public back on your side. Some celebs write tell-all autobiographies. Some go on comeback tours. Some adopt Cambodian orphans. There's only one way I can make everyone at school forget that I'm a "slut," and that's if I become San Paulo Junior High's Queen of Hearts.

And on Saturday, February 13th, when I'm out there—when I'm out in the middle of the dance floor after the presentation of the royal court, when I've got a crown on my head and all eyes on me, it won't matter which random guy I'm dancing with. I know which one I'll be thinking of.

Long live my king. *Viva mi Danielito.* <3

From: qgreene@spjhs.org
To: rmorales@spjhs.org
Subject: Second Semester Changes
Sent: 1/21 9:17 p.m.

Hi Ruben,

I'd like for you to coach the boys' basketball team next semester. Mike Wade's wife just had that baby, so he can't do it this year. I think you're just the right guy for the job.

Let me know how that sounds. I'm looking forward to seeing some games this year.

Best,
Quentin Greene
Principal, San Paulo Junior High School

From: rmorales@spjhs.org
To: qgreene@spjhs.org
Subject: Re: Second Semester Changes
Sent: 1/21 10:06 p.m.

Hey Quentin,

Thank you so much for the offer. It is very tempting, but I'm not sure if I'll have the time to devote to both the basketball team and my writing club. Is there anyone else who you think might

be suited to the team? I'm no sports expert, after all.
Thanks so much again for thinking of me. Unfortunately, I think
I'll have to pass this time.

Thanks,
Ruben

From: qgreene@spjhs.org
To: rmorales@spjhs.org
Subject: Re: Second Semester Changes
Sent: 1/22 11:40 a.m.

I apologize, I should have been clearer. My offer was less a
question of preference and more of a request.

I know that the team represents an extra commitment, which
is why I'm asking you to lighten your load a little bit. Starting
next week, there will be no more writing club. I need you to
focus on being the best educator you can be for all of your
classes. You've got one hundred and fifty kids to worry about,
not just three.

Thanks in advance for understanding. I appreciate all of the
energy you bring to your job. Let's just direct it in the right
places, yeah? Those kids on the team need you.

Best,
Quentin Greene
Principal, San Paulo Junior High School

San Paulo Boys Basketball Sign-ups

**Please list your name as well as the position
you want to play. Thanks, everybody!
—Mr. Morales**

1. JAVY FLORES, SHOOTING GUARD

2. CARLOS FLORES, shooting guard

3. RUDY MARTINEZ, SHOOTING GUARD

4. CHUY HERNANDEZ, SHOOTING GUARD

5. Antonio Lopez, center

6. Guillermo Torres, MVP

7. Edgar Ruiz, point guard

8. Danny Uribe, shooting guard

9. Jake Schwartz, benchwarmer

10.

11.

12.

20 • Dorothy Wu

Friday, January 29

Twelve twenty-nine and fifty-seven seconds . . . twelve twenty-nine and fifty-eight seconds . . . twelve twenty-nine and fifty-nine seconds . . . twelve thirty.

WA-WA-WAAAAAHOOOOOOOOOO!!!!!!!!!!

Celebrate good times, come on! The semester is done, time for fun! I am so relieved to be finished with all those cursed final exams. I race out of P.E. as fast as my delightful legs can carry me and I meet up with Jake at our prearranged spot, the flagpole. To celebrate the completion of our first semester of grade seven, we have the most frabjous minimum day planned.

First, however, a somber matter. Jake and I go to room 213 to dearly thank Mr. Morales one more time for all he has done for us this semester. Mr. Morales says how sorry he is to see writing club end. He says nothing will ever replace us. He hugs both of us—first Jake, then Dorothy.

After that touching moment between teacher and students, Jake and I are ready for some good old-fashioned kids' fun. How much fun? A picnic's worth. Jake has supplied the paper plates, napkins, PB&Js, and Capri Suns. I have brought with me two bags of Peach Rings and one canister of Koala Yummies. Xtreme deliciousness awaits us.

It is a seven-minute walk to our destination, Bella Vista Park. *Bella vista* means "beautiful sight" in Spanish. The real beautiful sight is Jake's eyes, which are the exact same shade of brown as a fine mahogany desk, with a vibrant amber crust encircling the sable pupil. But I do not want to tell him what I think of his eyes. After all, we are just friends.

But we are very good friends. At the start of the walk, Jake asks if I would like to go to the Sweethearts Dance with him, not as sweethearts of course, but as friends. I say yes! Oh, I am already so anticipatory. Methinks Valentine's Day weekend cannot come soon enough.

On our five-minute walk, we see many delightful things. A hummingbird flapping and fluttering through the air. Two small dogs scampering after the same tennis ball. A tall, once-proud tree on which many young lovers have carved their initials. A beautiful biracial baby.

Once Jake and I arrive at the park, we are excited to sit down and get grubbin'. However, as soon as we set foot on the fresh grass, we discover that we are not alone.

Who else is there? A group of about ten tall gents, most of them wearing big black shirts and tall socks, like soccer player socks. I recognize them as the Radars, those infamous trouble-mongers from the eastern part of town.

"The Raiders," Jake says softly. "Do you see Danny with them?"

I look. I recognize a few hooligans from my math class, and I see a large, fearsome-looking fellow who has one thick black eyebrow like *Sesame Street*'s Bert.

And, to my surprise, I do indeed see the San Paulo Junior High Writing Club's own Daniel Uribe. He is not dressed in shiny black garb like the others, but he is talking and laughing with them all the same. I see him touch fists with Bert.

Jake has a stressed-eyebrows face. "We should eat somewhere else," he says.

I shake my head at him. Bella Vista Park is my favorite place in the entire world, and it is a rather large place, too. Hundreds of kids could spend lunchtime here if they wanted. Why must we vacate the premises?

"Come on," Jake says, and he starts to briskly walk away. I still want to stay, of course, but I decide to do what he wants and I run after him. Part of being in a relationship is compromise. Part of being in a friendship is compromise.

We spend the next several minutes trying to decide on a place to eat. I suggest the front lawn of the school, but Jake does not want the punk kids whose parents do not pick them up to stare at us. Then I suggest the beach, but Jake does not want to walk that far, or ride Darrell's two-wheeler, plus he does not want to get sand in his food. "Then why are we eating *sand*wiches?" I ask Jake with a quizzical and humorous look in my eye. Jake does not laugh. Not even a twitter.

We end up eating our food at the bus stop. Therefore, I would not call it a picnic. It is more of an on-the-go meal. Drat—I think—I should have brought Go-Gurt! Yet despite my obvious stupidity in not bringing transportable yogurt, I am still in high spirits. I am taking a merry afternoon jaunt with the person whose company I enjoy the most.

The bus is filled with such curiosities. Toward the back, I see an elderly woman who appears to have whiskers on her chin. I point at her to show Jake. "You should not point," Jake says. I do not understand why not. When people point at me, I do not mind at all.

Eventually we reach the stop on Valdez Street, also known as Wu Country. When I stand up to get off and go to my house, Jake does not budge. I ask him why is he not coming over for an afternoon of Nintendo and board games like we originally planned? He says he should probably go home. I ask why? It is only 1:21; the afternoon is so nascent. He says he just feels like it. I say all right. As I get off the bus, Jake does not even wave or smile at me. What an ornery owl that boy can be sometimes.

I am confused about Jake as I walk to my house, but I am still feeling grand. After all, I have an entire Friday afternoon to myself. There is no reason why I cannot play Nintendo and board games by myself. Well, hmm. Board games might be difficult. I cannot settle Catan solo. Well, there is no reason why I cannot play Nintendo by myself.

I notice more small pleasures on my walk. A remote-controlled airplane zipping and whipping through the branches of tall trees. Two young tykes selling lemonade for a quarter a cup. A pigeon with a deformed leg. Come to think of it, that last one is not so pleasing.

When I reach my house, I am ready to go straight to my room and hang out with myself, but I am stopped from doing so by a loud voice, a displeased voice, the voice of my father.

"Dorothy! Come in here now!"

I walk into the kitchen, wondering why my father is home. Also, I wonder what he wants from me. Perhaps Darrell left his action figures out and my father thought they were mine. Pesky Darrell is always such a brat.

"Dorothy," my father says in a very serious manner. "You got a C-plus in your math class."

This cannot be true. My father is making this up to frighten me. I could not have gotten a C-plus because Jake helped me study for the final. Also, how would my father know my grade?

"I called your teacher. Mr. Peterson says you got a 79.4 in his class. Dorothy, this is unacceptable. I have spoken with your mother, and we agree that the proper punishment is to ground you for one month."

My grade . . . my punishment . . . it is too many things to hear all at once. I feel a rush of hotness going to my head. Getting grounded used to not hurt me at all since I love my room so much. But now that I have become closer with Jake, and . . . oh no. Oh no. Please, please, no. The Sweethearts Dance. My father will never let me go now. I will never get to have that night. Jake will be so disappointed. I feel as though someone has ripped my chest open and sprinkled Pop Rocks all over my heart.

I am a stupid girl. A stupid, stupid girl.

Ms. Windler's Question & Answer Wall
7th Grade Health—Unit 12—Sexual Education

Remember that I have promised to answer all questions posted on the wall.

PLEASE don't make me take this privilege away.
ASK APPROPRIATE QUESTIONS!

Q: Ms. Windler, I get a funny feeling when I think about certain girls. Also when I wear this one pair of pants that I have. What is this?

A: *You're experiencing something we talked about in class. Remember erections? Erections occur when the penis becomes engorged with blood, usually as a result of sexual arousal or excessive friction. Don't worry—erections are a perfectly normal part of growing up!*

Q: How come the guys and girls get separated for some parts of class? I want to watch the video where the girl gets her period and the mom makes pancakes at the end.

A: *Sorry, California standards require that students be separated by gender for occasional special lessons. Believe me, I wish I could teach everything to everyone, but it's the law.*

Q: If a man has sex with a pregnant woman, is it possible for his penis to rub up against the baby inside her?

A: No. That would be very uncomfortable! During intercourse, the male's penis enters the vaginal opening. Human embryos are located in the female's uterus, safe and sound.

Q: Is it possible to have an inverted penis?

A: I'm not sure what you mean.

Q: CAN A PENIS HAVE SEX WITH AN INVERTED PENIS?

A: Please, everyone, let's take the Question & Answer Wall seriously.

Q: How many inverted penises does it take to screw in a lightbulb?

A: Please only post genuine questions that you have.

Q: I HAVE TWO BONERS FOR LEGS! IT HURTS TO WALK! BUT IT FEELS SO GOOOOOOOOD.

A: That's it. You've all lost your Question & Answer Wall privileges.

SAN PAULO JUNIOR HIGH SCHOOL
Sweethearts Dance Royal Court
Official Ballot

Please make a clear check mark or X next to your choice.

The results will be announced at the dance tonight!

8th GRADE KING

___ Chad Beck

___ Jonathan Graham

___ Antonio Lopez

___ Alex Masterson

___ Juan Salcido

___ Spenser Walker

8th GRADE QUEEN

___ Kristen Duffy

___ Jamie Mackintosh

___ Nisha Patel

___ Avery Patterson

___ Hannah Schwartz

___ Luz Vasquez

7th GRADE PRINCE

___ Sam Alker

___ Asher Bennett

___ Andrew Chen

___ Jeremy Farnsworth

___ Jaime Ochoa

___ Danny Uribe

7th GRADE PRINCESS

___ Taylor Doran

___ Gabriella Gomez

___ Brianna Hart

___ Chloe Khademi

___ Andrea Molina

___ Shannon Murray

21 • Hannah Schwartz

Saturday, February 13

I'm going to tell it straight through, just like it happened.

I had to get up early this morning. Painfully early. The only people who should be up before ten on a Saturday are farmers and the elderly.

I had to get to school to help set up for the dance with the rest of Leadership. I thought I'd sneak into Danny's room and give him a good-morning kiss before I left, but he was outside on the Sport Court helping Jake with his dribbling moves or something. What a good person.

The atmosphere at school was crazycakes. Gossip was flying everywhere. Apparently Kristen and Alex are on the rocks because she wants to do something super-special for Valentine's Day tomorrow—like, hundred-dollar-fondue special—but he wants to take it low-key. And I guess last night, Chase Sanford cheated on Corinne with this sevvy girl Taylor something, which . . . I mean, no offense, Corinne, but that's what two straight months of wearing pajama pants and Ugg boots will get you.

Of course, the main thing on everyone's minds was the election for the royal court. While we were all setting up in the gym, some of the Leadership kids who didn't get nominated were counting ballots in the other room. I wanted to be a fly on that wall so bad. But I couldn't know the results ahead of time. No spoilers. It'd be like prematurely flipping to the last page and learning the secret twist ending of a crappy Dan Brown mystery. When the counters finished and came out, I avoided eye contact with them. It had to be a surprise when I won.

If I won.

When I won.

The next few hours blurred by. I started to feel sick, got better, tried on my dress, hated the way I looked, showered, haired, makeupped, loved the way I looked, and Facebooked every second in between. By the time my group showed up at my house to take pics at five thirty, I was a vision in violet. The only downside happened when I tried to sneak a visit to Danny again. I went to his room, but he had already left for the Eastside where he was meeting up with his *cholo* group. I was bummed, but not devastated. I knew I'd get a kiss out of him eventually, even if I had to wait till hours after the dance.

Picture-taking and dinner were both quite awkward. Get this—out of my entire group of sixteen, literally every person was part of a couple except for me and . . . yes, the notorious Chad Beck. I almost feel like he planned it that way. So yeah, it was horrendous. When we all took the group picture, I had to grin and bear it as Chad held me with his big, gross gorilla hands. I guess the two of us could have stood on different sides of the group, but that would have looked bad.

I kept hope alive, though. All throughout having to stand

there with my Cro-Magnon ex-boyfriend, all throughout having to listen to Kristen and Alex's endless boring lovers' quarrels at dinner, and all throughout me not getting to be with Danny, I just kept my eyes on the prize: the crown.

Finally we got to the dance and I was ready to cut loose, footloose. Speaking of that, I actually wish the DJ had played a little more '80s and a little less bad hip-hop, but the girls and I had a fabulous time regardless. I was out there on the dance floor for I don't remember how long—dropping it like it was hot, leaning back, getting low, to the window, to the wall, till the sweat dropped down my . . . well, hmm. Changing the subject now.

It being a Valentine's Day dance, there were also quite a few slow songs. I made sure I was off the dance floor for all of them, so I was able to avoid Chad, and that was fine. But it felt wrong, just wrong, just *so* wrong, to look out there and see Danny swaying back and forth with Luz or Chicle or any of the Eastside *hermanas*. At one point I even saw Chicle brush her hand against Danny's butt. She better have just been looking for a place to stick her gum.

During the last slow song before they announced the election results, I was looking at Danny and some other rando chica, and she was looking at him all adoringly through her way-too-eyelinered eyes, and I just could not take it anymore. I ran back to my group's table to sit down, avoid eye contact, reapply makeup (tastefully), and mentally prepare myself for the prospect of maybe, just maybe being named queen. But when I got to the table, who did I find waiting for me but . . .

my little brother? I didn't even know he was planning on coming to the dance. Jake looked tragically dorky in a gray blazer and a red bow tie, of all things.

"Hannah," he said. He was out of breath. He looked upset. "Can we talk?"

"Not now," I said.

"Hannah, really quick, come on, please," he insisted in that whiny voice he has. "I have a question about you and Danny."

What was he playing at? I was not going to take this, not right before they announced the results.

"*Go away,*" I told him.

"Are you guys together?"

I didn't say anything. It's hard to come up with a good lie when all you can see are strobe lights and all you can hear is hip-hop with the curse words cut out.

"Are you with Danny?"

I felt cornered. So it *was* Jake who had walked in on us at the party. So he *had* known about us this whole time, and not only that, but he had chosen to reveal it to me at the exact wrong moment. What a little jerk.

"Okay, smart one," I said. "If you've known about us this whole time, then why didn't you just bust us when we were on the bed in your room?"

Jake drew his head back. His little wiener eyes widened.

"Wait, you guys are *together*? *Together* together?"

Dammit, me! So he had been naive enough to not know about us, but I had to ruin it with my big mouth anyway.

Whatever, whatever. Jake was bound to learn eventually—he's stupid, but not that stupid. So he was in on the secret now. The three of us would have to work it out. But I could deal with all this later. Not at Sweethearts. Not at my coronation.

"*GO. AWAY.*" I said it in my most pissed-off, momlike voice possible. He went away.

Before I had any time to dwell on that unexpected unpleasantness, the DJ suddenly turned the sound down and handed the mic to the principal, Mr. Greene.

"*San Paulo . . . the moment you've all been waiting for. The announcement of the royal court.*"

Applause, applause, blah, blah. I ran to find my friends. They were standing in the middle of the floor, already linking arms like the last few girls on Miss America. The announcement for queen was so so close.

"*Let's start with grade seven. Your Princess of Hearts is . . . MS. TAYLOR DORAN!*"

That girl who hooked up with Chase . . . interesting. She looked pretty skanky and incredibly cliché in a hot pink strapless bubble dress. But I didn't care that much about her. After all, the seventh grade winners don't matter.

"*Your Prince of Hearts . . . MR. DANNY URIBE!*"

Uh . . . whoa. Well, that made me care. God, I mean, I remember that Danny had been nominated. In fact, I had something to do with it . . . but for him to actually win? I thought there was no way. I guess it makes sense, since he knows all the Mexicans and he knows all the Seabrook kids and he's extremely likable and really cute to boot, but . . . wow.

Well, so what, though? This didn't matter either. This didn't like, out us or whatever.

"Your Queen of Hearts . . . MS. HANNAH SCHWARTZ!"

Oh, it was a perfect movie moment. The DJ played "Isn't She Lovely," by Stevie Wonder, or maybe it was just blaring full blast in my head. Either way, I cranked up the lovely. I put my hands over my mouth as my girlfriends mobbed me, and I made my way to the presentation area wearing a perfectly practiced look of disbelief. Danny gave me a huge smile when I got up there, not too revealing but so proud. Mr. Greene placed the crown over my head as I half real-cried, half faked a couple of tears. Cameras flashed and everyone applauded me and cheered my name over and over. What a moment: from supposed slut to shining superstar. I knew I had just become a part of SP history in the most magical way possible.

"And your King of Hearts . . . MR. CHAD BECK!"

This was fate's little way of trying to ruin the moment for me, but I wasn't going to let it happen. When Chad finally got up to the presentation area after like, five minutes of flexing his muscles and showboating, I pretended to be super-happy that I was about to slow dance with him in front of everyone. And really, despite Chad's presence, I was feeling fully fantastic right then. I had the perfect plan: just close my eyes and pretend like I was dancing with Danny.

"And now San Paulo, a very special surprise."

What?

"In the interest of promoting school-wide unity, your royal court

will lead you in not one, but two dances. Now, for the first time ever, seventh and eighth graders will dance together. So for this first dance, King, find your Princess. Queen, find your Prince."

Soooooo wait. What?! I was in total disbelief. So Danny and I had to dance with each other? In front of everybody? To promote school-wide unity?

As much of a curveball as this was, I wasn't about to let it get in the way of my amazing night. The music started playing, the crowd of people on the dance floor parted, and Danny took my hand. Together we walked into the center of the floor where Chad and Taylor already were. He put his hands around my waist, I put mine around his neck.

It was wonderful. We didn't get too close, for fear of looking like what we actually were, but he gave my hip a little extra squeeze, and I gently ran my hand over his spiky hair. It sounds so typical to say, but even though there were literally hundreds of people staring at us, I felt like it was just Danny and me. We were Tony and Maria. Just the two of us together, now and forever. I ached so badly to stand up on my tip-toes and give him a kiss. I almost did. I was feeling the moment that much. But I couldn't, not in front of everyone.

And then . . . well, then . . .

I don't want to talk about what happened next.

ay, chicle

¿ya luz?

that was the best thing to eva happen @ SP

wut abt the time gabi n hector got caught in the band room

o n wut about when guillermo tagged greene's car?

n we cant forget the lunch wen the east n westsiders fought over me

they were fighting over me!

¡no mames! theyd never fight over ur ugly face

wut abt ur big ass

better my ass then ur ass face

te amo

¡¡te amo!!

srsly that thing at the dance. that was the funniest thing.

wat a little coqueta

ya, hannah deserved that stuff

ya she's nice to us n stuff

but she cant get away wit that

ya we did wat we had 2 do

ya

te amo

te amo

22 • Jake Schwartz

Saturday, February 13

It's the rare person who can get his best friend and his sister to hate him forever in one night. I guess I'm just one of a kind.

Really, though, this all starts with Dorothy.

I thought she was going to show up at the dance. I did. That's the only reason I even went in the first place. She told me that her dad was pissed about her bad grade, yeah, but she also told me that she could get him to let her come, that she'd find a way to the dance no matter what. She even told me to wear gray and red. She said it'd go with what she was wearing.

So I decided to go. I was still nervous about the whole dancing part, and now I know I'll never go to another dance again, but tonight I figured that if I went with Dorothy, it'd be fun. She made studying for math fun.

As soon as all my sister's friends finished taking pictures on the back lawn and left the house, I went to my mom and asked her for a ride. She asked if I was sure I wanted to wear the bow tie. I said yes.

The immediate thing I noticed when I got to school was that everyone walking into the gym was paired off. You know how cartoon characters like Mickey and Donald always have a girlfriend who's basically just a girl version of them? That's what everyone looked like. The indie guys with straight black hair and eye makeup had indie dates with straight black hair and eye makeup. The tall, tan water-polo dudes had tall, tan water-polo dates. Only I, the loser in gray and red, had no fellow loser in gray and red to call my own.

I called Dorothy's house. No response. I tried her house again.

"Hello, friend, you have reached the Wu residence . . ."

After that, my communication options were limited, because believe it or not, D. Wu does not own a cell phone. Why? Who knows? Maybe because her dad won't let her have one. Maybe because she's secretly from the nineteenth century. But, hmm . . . then how would I explain her love of virtual pets? The girl's a mystery.

I waited outside for a long time. I don't know how long exactly. For sure over an hour. Long enough for me to develop some significant facial sweat from all my pacing back and forth, and I'm not usually a very sweaty guy. I thought Dorothy might be waiting for me in one of our usual spots. I checked the library, where we usually eat lunch. I checked behind this one portable classroom, where we sometimes eat lunch. Eventually I realized that, for whatever reason, she probably wasn't gonna show up. So then I thought, well, I might as well check out the dance.

As soon as I went inside, I regretted my decision. All the decorations were disgustingly cutesy and girly, like a Barbie Dream House covered in pink vomit. The music was just as bad, but in the complete opposite way. It was loud and angry and sexual. The dancing was even worse than the music. Jeez, from what I've learned this past week in health, I'd say some girls definitely got impregnated on the dance floor.

There was absolutely nobody around for me to dance with, not that I have groove anyway. I decided I'd do what all losers do at dances: get some punch and drink it while standing against the wall. As I was walking to the refreshments table, I saw Danny dancing up real close on a girl I didn't know. It was weird to see my lifelong best friend doing that, but at the same time it wasn't that weird because that's the kind of thing Danny does more and more of these days. Well, I thought, at least he's having fun. Get some, Danny.

Then I noticed something weird. Standing a few feet away from Danny was Hannah, and although I couldn't see very well with all the flashing lights, she was staring at Danny, and she had this look on her face. It's the same look she gives me when I call shotgun before her, only it was way more intense. Something was definitely up.

Then it dawned on me.

I realized that they must have gone to the dance together. After all, I hadn't seen who was in her group—I hid from them the whole time. It made sense for them to be dates, too. Danny and Hannah have become really good friends lately—I've seen her go to his room tons of times to hang out—and it's not like Hannah had a boyfriend to come with tonight. And it made sense that Danny wouldn't tell me, because mostly these days we just talk about basketball. So all the pieces fit together in my head. Danny and Hannah must have gone to the dance together, but then Hannah saw Danny freak dancing all nasty with some other girl. Of course she got really pissed about it, because hey, what kind of girl wants to see their date doing that, even if he is just a friend?

I saw Hannah turn and walk away, so I thought I'd find her and ask how her night's been so far, ask her about Danny. I had nothing better to do. Dorothy Wu wasn't walking through the door. I saw the table that Hannah was heading toward, and I actually ran there so I could get to it first. I wanted to make it so that she would have to talk to me.

This is when things got bizarre. I asked if I could speak with her real quick. She said no—understandable, since she is Hannah Schwartz and I am Jake and we were in public. I knew I'd only get time for one question, so I had to make it count. I asked if she and Danny were at the dance together.

Her eyes practically busted out of her sockets. I figured she must have misheard me. So I asked her again.

And then she said one of those things you never expect to hear, so you don't even believe it when you hear it. Something about her and Danny, and my room, and a bed.

So they were—no, it didn't seem possible—where did this come from?—did she just say that they were . . . boyfriend and girlfriend?

Before I could say anything else—before I could even react emotionally—Hannah basically pushed me away and ran off, and next thing I knew, everyone's attention was directed toward Mr. Greene at the front of the gym.

I didn't want to think about Danny and Hannah together,

so I didn't. This was all a huge misunderstanding, I told myself. This whole night was weird and confusing and not real. I blocked that image of them—on my bed—out of my mind. I kept completely focused on the royal court presentation.

Taylor Doran won Princess. Good for her I guess, but yeesh. She's no princess. She's in my social studies class, and we were in the same group for a project on Greek philosophers and she didn't do anything. I think that says a lot about you, how much effort you put in when you're part of a group project.

When Danny was named the Prince, I felt genuinely happy for him. Yeah, I'm probably the person who's suffered most by him becoming popular, but he deserves to be popular. He's such a great guy. I was just holding him back in elementary school.

Then, when Hannah got crowned Queen, I was even happier for her. I knew how much she had wanted to win, and now she had something to feel good about after all the bad stuff that's happened to her. At this point, I still refused to put Danny and Hannah together in my mind. I couldn't.

Then Hannah's ex-boyfriend won King, and then Mr. Greene said something weird about new traditions, and then Hannah and Danny started dancing together.

And then, for the first time, it really hit me.

I saw the way he looked at her, the way he rubbed his hand on her hips to the rhythm of the music. I saw the way she touched his hair all gently. As his lifelong best friend, and as her lifelong brother, I saw something that no one else could see: they were in love.

And wait—they hooked up?! On my bed?!?!

This was too much. How long had they been outright lying to me? How long had they been nice to my face while secretly talking bad about me behind my back? How long had they been sneaking into my room to do dirty things?

I had to do something. They couldn't just dance like this, in front of everyone, in front of me, and expect to get away with it. I had to tell someone the truth about the Queen and Prince of Hearts. I saw Hannah's friends standing in a clump, the gossipy ones, but I knew they wouldn't believe anything I told them. Plus, they all think she's hot for Chad.

Then I saw Danny's friends, Chicle and Luz. "Las Chismosas," he calls them. Danny once told me that those two could start a rumor at the beginning of passing period, and that by the bell for class, the office would already be calling someone's parents about it. They were just the girls for this job. I ran up to them and blurted it all at once:

"Hi-I'm-Jake-Hannah's-brother-Danny's-best-friend-maybe-ex-best-friend-I-don't-know-yet-LOOK-Danny-and-Hannah-are-together-I-mean-*together*-together-for-real-I-swear-it's-true-they-hooked-up-on-my-bed!"

I expected to have to repeat myself, but both of them just smiled at me. It was as if they'd known about Danny and Hannah all along, but they just needed a source to confirm it. Then Luz whispered something to Chicle and Chicle whispered something back to Luz, and they both giggled, and before I knew it they started to chant something, quietly at first, then louder.

"buchkwawa! buchkwawa! buchkwawa!"

Some other kids joined in. I couldn't tell what they were saying, but everyone who was chanting it was laughing and whispering and pointing at Danny and Hannah.

"BUMCHICKWAWA! BUMCHICKWAWA! BUM-CHICKWAWA!"

What were they saying? It was catching on like crazy, this phrase in an Eskimo language or whatever it was. I couldn't figure out how everyone knew to say this same thing. Before I knew it, what seemed like the entire gymnasium was chanting.

"BOM CHICKA WAH WAH! BOM CHICKA WAH WAH! BOM CHICKA WAH WAH!"

The chanting grew louder, much louder than the music. Hannah stopped swaying with Danny. She stepped away from him. Both of them looked at each other, then around the room. They didn't realize the chants were about them, not at first. They couldn't tell what was going on. I couldn't figure out what everyone was saying.

"BOM CHICKA WAH WAH! BOM CHICKA WAH WAH! BOM CHICKA WAH WAH!"

Then it hit me. *Bom chicka wah wah* . . . it's the sound that Hannah always makes when she talks about her friends Kristen and Alex, the ones who do intense boy-girl stuff. *Bom chicka wah wah* . . . the entire student body was making the sound of a guitar riff from a 1970s porn movie. Not that any of us have seen those movies, or, well, I guess *I* haven't seen those movies, but we all know what the sound means. . . .

Essentially, it means, you know, *"HANNAH SCHWARTZ IS A SLUT."*

And that's when it hit Hannah. It was a horrible, almost scary moment. In two seconds she turned redder than I've ever seen her before. Her forehead, her cheeks, her eyes. She put her hands to her head. She did a full 360-degree turn, looking around the entire room, everyone still screaming, the whole school mocking her in unison. Danny put a hand to her shoulder, but she slapped it away. Then she just took off.

I watched as Hannah raced out of the gym, trying her best not to cry, none of her friends running after her, no one going after her. I knew it was all my fault.

I ran outside as fast as I could, leaving the chanting behind me. I saw her crown on the ground near the exit door. I ran past it and out into the night. I saw Hannah sitting on the curb of the parking lot, already waiting for Mom, her head buried in her hands.

"Hannah!" I called as I ran madly up to her. "I'm sorry! I'm so sorry!"

She didn't respond. She was still looking down.

I made it to the curb. I just stood there above her. I was out of breath.

"I'm a jerk. I'm such a jerk, Hannah. I'm an asshole."

She didn't move for a few seconds. Then she rubbed her eyes with her hands. Then she nudged her head up to look at me. Her eyes met mine. They were wet and bloodshot and terrifying.

"I'm sorry! I'm an asshole. I didn't mean to. Well, I guess

I, what I did was, it was so stupid, I—"

She didn't say anything. She just stared at me. Her face was covered in blue and black makeup. Some of it dripped onto her dress. It's the kind of thing she normally would have cared about. But not now.

"It's just, you didn't tell me about you and Danny, so like, I don't know, I guess I felt like, I don't know . . ."

She didn't say anything to that either. She just sniffled. Then her eyes went sort of soft and dead. She wasn't looking at me anymore. She put her head in her hands again.

"I'm sorry, Hannah. That wasn't fair what happened. I didn't mean to—well, I mean, I did what I did for a reason maybe, but the whole thing was such an accident, you know? Hey, I can go back and get your crown if you want. You want me to do that? I can go do that. I'm sorry, okay?"

I'm not really good at knowing when to shut up.

Danny came out, but he didn't say anything to either of us. We didn't say anything to him. The three of us sat there in silence until my mom came to pick us up. In the car, we stayed silent.

Hannah will never talk to me again. Neither will Danny. And I still can't get through to Dorothy.

lilbeachbabe777: hey

lilbeachbabe777: i have to talk to you

getsome_danny24: ya ok

getsome_danny24: meet up at the spot in 5?

lilbeachbabe777: no i think we should talk here

lilbeachbabe777: online

getsome_danny24: o

getsome_danny24: ok

getsome_danny24: wats up

lilbeachbabe777: so . . . the dance

getsome_danny24: i kno

getsome_danny24: jakes fault

getsome_danny24: luz told me

getsome_danny24: im so pissed at him

getsome_danny24: cant even put it in words

lilbeachbabe777: yeah well

lilbeachbabe777: idk

lilbeachbabe777: i was thinkin about it

lilbeachbabe777: and like

lilbeachbabe777: idk maybe its better off this way

getsome_danny24: ?

getsome_danny24: wat do u mean

lilbeachbabe777: well this relationship

lilbeachbabe777: well

lilbeachbabe777: i dont think we can pull it off

lilbeachbabe777: what w/ our families

lilbeachbabe777: my friends

lilbeachbabe777: ur friends

lilbeachbabe777: jake

lilbeachbabe777: its better for both of us this way

getsome_danny24: u

getsome_danny24: ur breakin up wit me?

lilbeachbabe777: no

lilbeachbabe777: dont think of it like that

lilbeachbabe777: but i mean

lilbeachbabe777: yeah

getsome_danny24: ok so like

getsome-danny24: ya i guess people kno bout us now

getsome_danny24: why does that mean we have 2 break up?

lilbeachbabe777: well

lilbeachbabe777: if we break up now

lilbeachbabe777: i think we can pretend that there never was an us

getsome_danny24: wat?

lilbeachbabe777: we'll just pretend like the thing at the dance was a mean lie

lilbeachbabe777: pretend that luz was jealous i beat her for queen so she started the chant

lilbeachbabe777: the only one who knows the truth is jake

lilbeachbabe777: and if we end things now, he wont do anything

lilbeachbabe777: he feels so bad

lilbeachbabe777: we have to use that

lilbeachbabe777: its our only chance

getsome_danny24: but like

getsome_danny24: dont u like bein wit me?

lilbeachbabe777: of course i do

lilbeachbabe777: its not about that

lilbeachbabe777: its about how people see us

getsome_danny24: wat does that even mean?

lilbeachbabe777: you cant be the guy who hooked up with his best friends sister

lilbeachbabe777: and i cant be the slut

getsome_danny24: jakes not my best friend

lilbeachbabe777: trust me, danny

lilbeachbabe777: it hurts so much to do this

lilbeachbabe777: but i thought about it a lot

lilbeachbabe777: and its for the best

getsome_danny24: but hannah

getsome_danny24: i love you

getsome_danny24: <3

lilbeachbabe777 has signed off at 2:24 a.m.

getsome_danny24 has signed off at 2:38 a.m.

23 • Dorothy Wu

Thursday, February 18

I wake up far earlier than usual this morning, at 5:42 a.m. I ponder going back to sleep for a moment, but, bah, there is no point. I have not been able to sleep effectively for the last month or so. Methinks it is the growing pains.

One of the advantages of suddenly waking at random hours is that you can remember your dreams. In my dream this morning, I was Bruce Wayne, a.k.a. the Dark Knight. I snuck around the halls of San Paulo posting covert messages on the walls. The messages were secret logos, similar to hobo signs. I do not remember their significance. At the end of the dream, I was holding a secret meeting with other people from San Paulo who were also superheroes. Jake was Spider-Man. Coach Wade was the Incredible Hulk. Tyler Bell was Professor X. Mr. Morales was a made-up superhero who wears glasses, even though nerds are not generally heroic. I do not remember the subject of our meeting.

And, yes, I realize that my dream mixed Marvel and DC characters inappropriately. I have already given myself plenty of grief about it.

I spend the rest of my before-school morning watching assorted YouTube clips of *Rurouni Kenshin* and *Yu-Gi-Oh!* It is, as they say, "legit." However, in my enjoyment, I lose track of the time. My father walks into my room fourteen minutes before school to discover me still in pajamas, watching clips on my bed, giggling girlishly. He curses up a storm and threatens to take away my computer. It would not be surprising if he followed through on this threat. He has already taken away most of my civil liberties.

I arrive at math class seven minutes late. Luckily, however, Mr. Peterson does not assign me a detention. Ever since Mr. Peterson spoke to my father on the phone, I think he has realized that I already receive enough punishments at home. To assign me a detention as well would be unusual and cruel.

In health, we continue our unit on SEX. (Sometimes I like to say that word loudly to get people's attention. Hehe.) In today's class, we do an activity in which everyone walks around shaking each other's hands. When Jeremy Farnsworth shakes my hand, he gives my wrist a little scratch. After thirty seconds, Ms. Windler asks whoever got scratched by Jeremy to raise their hands. I do, along with five others. Then Ms. Windler asks anyone who shook the hand of anyone who got scratched by Jeremy to raise their hands. The entire class does. Ms. Windler says that if Jeremy had an STD, and if shaking hands was sex, and if we had not used protection, then right now we would all have STDs. Whoa.

English class is frustrating. We are reading *The Giver* by Lois Lowry, one of my all-time most-beloved books. Yet the lessons Mr. Morales assigns are so mundane! Today, all he tells us to do for the entire class period is to go through chapters 8–12, find twenty vocabulary words, and define them.

Shouldn't we be having fulfilling class discussions based on such prompts as "Imagine you live in Jonas's society. What would your role in the community be and why?" Or, "What is your opinion of the book's ambiguous ending? Use examples from the text to support your argument." But nay, Mr. Morales does not teach like I know he can. He is too focused on the basketball team, methinks. The man is in a funk. I wish he would get funky.

Spanish is also problematic, but this time it is all my fault. I absolutely cannot stand my Spanish class, so recently I checked the first-year Latin textbook out of the library and have been reading that during fourth period instead. Today's story in the Cambridge Latin Course is particularly exciting. Grumio the chef is carrying on a scandalous affair with the slave girl Melissa! However, just as I am nearing the tale's climax, Señor Cruz discovers that I am reading the wrong book, and he asks me what I am doing. I think about standing up to him. I think about saying right to his face that I would much rather study the nominative case than the preterite tense. I think about crying out to the world, "LATIN'S COOL! SPANISH DROOLS!" But instead I apologize quietly and put my book away. I wish I possessed *cajones*.

The last few lunches, Jake has been doing this annoying thing where instead of meeting me at one of our usual spots, he goes to some random, hard-to-find place without telling me, and so it takes me several minutes just to find him. I call it his "Waldo Phase." Yesterday I could not locate Jake at all. I wish he would just forgive my apology about the dance. My father caught me sneaking out. What was I supposed to do?

Today it takes me ten minutes to find Jake. After looking around the library, the portable buildings, and the Dumpsters, I discover him sitting outside the main office next to the tree that was dedicated to that boy who died. Jake does not want to talk much at lunch. The child has been so moody lately. Ah, perhaps he has finally started puberty?

Science is my third-least-favorite class behind math and P.E. I never pay attention unless we are talking about animals (preferably cats). Today we are not talking about animals. We are learning about plant reproduction, so I do not pay attention. Instead I think about my dream some more. I know I had that dream for a reason. Why?

In Social Studies we are continuing our unit on Asian history. This is good because Asia rules. It is bad because, as an Asian, I am expected to know everything about Asia. How can one know everything about Asia? Asia is bigger than everything.

In today's class we learn about a particularly rad concept: the samurai. We learn about how the samurai were a special class of Japanese military folk who had wicked swords and their own special code of ethics known as *Bushido*. They engaged in activities such as tea ceremonies, monochrome ink painting, and Zen rock-garden assembling. I, too, will master these three arts one day, mehopes. I wish I could be a samurai. I think everyone wishes that.

In P.E. it is that most dreaded of days: mile day. About halfway through my mile, I become very sleepy and almost collapse in the middle of the track. At first I fear that I am turning narcoleptic! Then I realize that I am tired because I have been sleeping so little lately. I determine that first thing after school, I must go home and rest.

Of course, I do not want to. I want to stay and hang out with Jake. But alas, he has hoops practice, and I doubt he wants to kick "it" with me anyway after the way I stood him up last Saturday night. Plus, bollocks, I'm still grounded for four more days. *No bueno.*

On my way home, I try to think of ways to get back in Jake's good graces. Also, I think that it would be nice to make Mr. Morales happy again. And it would be wonderful to have the writing club back, too.

Then—idea of all ideas!—I can combine those three things into one! Here is the plan: Together, Jake and I will secretly rebuild the writing club, better and stronger than before. We will generate anticipation by posting secret logos across the campus, just like in my dream. By doing this, we will recruit all kinds of cool new people. Then, when the club is popular enough, we kids will reveal ourselves to Mr. Morales, and together we can all bask in the kind of glow that only a creative community can provide.

What will we call ourselves? Hmm. Good question . . .

"Writing Club" is too boring. "Justice League" has already been taken. So has "The United Nations."

I know! I know! We shall be known as . . .

The Super Story Samurai.

cue epic music

Dorothy takes a bow
Jake kisses Dorothy on the lips
THE END.

I am sleepy.

24 • Danny Uribe

Friday, February 26

We'd been struggling all game. La Mesa's press was forcing Edgar into making a bunch of turnovers that he doesn't usually make. Guillermo was getting all kinds of fouls called on him and he even picked up a technical for arguing with the ref. Antonio turned an ankle early and couldn't play much after that. Jake airballed his one shot.

But still, we were in it. We had a chance to win at the end because, well, I was playing pretty good. And I wasn't just playing good because I knew Hannah was in the stands. I play good every game.

I looked up at the scoreboard. There was a minute left and we had the ball down three. Edgar passed me the ball at the top of the key. The guy on me was real slow, so I shook him easy with a crossover, drove hard to my left, went up like I was going for the shot, then threw a quick pass in to Rudy who laid it in. One-point game. The crowd went crazy. And okay, like, there weren't that many people there, but the ones who were there were mad into it. La Mesa's mostly Westsiders so everyone wanted us to dominate them.

Their point guard was nervous bringing the ball up. He kept looking over at their coach, trying to figure out what to do. I knew we could make him do something dumb. Edgar and I ran up and trapped him hard on the sideline. The scared fool picked up his dribble and looked up at the ref like he was begging for a foul. I slapped the ball away clean and took off with it, running hard with no one between me and the basket, no one between us and the win—

Then right before I was gonna score, stupid Mr. Morales had to go and call a time-out. I don't know why he's our coach. Dude needs to stick to writing or whatever he does.

In the huddle, Morales tried to draw up a play, but it didn't make any sense. The guys on the team were starting to argue about it with him, with each other—

"Give it to Guillermo, Coach. He's the biggest."

"No way, man. I got this!"

"Naw fool, you're worse than the Jew."

"Guys, if you could just be quiet for a second, I'm trying to focus."

"Why'd you call time-out, Coach?"

"Coach, this play sucks."

"You're gonna make us lose, Coach."

"What the hell, Coach?"

I couldn't take it anymore.

"*¡BASTA!*" I shouted at the guys. "*¡BASTA!*"

They looked at me. They shut up right away. I looked at Morales.

"Just give me the ball," I said. "I'll make it."

"Okay," Morales said. "Let's do that."

Javy inbounded the ball to me. There were fifteen seconds left, fourteen. . . . I was being guarded by the same guy I had just burned before. He looked like he was about to crap his pants. Ten seconds, nine . . . I took one hard dribble to my right like I was gonna drive in, and the guy went for it, but then I switched quick to my left between my legs, and when the fool tried to go after me, Guillermo clocked him hard with a screen. . . . Six seconds, five . . . I took one more dribble going to my left, picked the ball up, rose for the shot. . . . Three seconds, two . . . The ball had perfect rotation, I had perfect follow-through. . . . One second . . . no seconds . . .

Swish. Pirates win.

It was the coolest non-making-out moment of my life. I threw a big fist pump like Jordan and right away the whole team surrounded me, even Mr. Morales. They all hugged me and patted me on the back and jumped on me. When we went into the locker room, all the guys punched Jake on the arm. It's something everyone does before each of our games for luck and also after the game if we win. Sometimes if we lose, too. I'd never done it before since I don't really think Jake likes it that much, but after today's game I just had to. Went as hard as I could. Felt good.

Jake told me he was gonna shower at home, and he asked if I wanted to catch a ride back with him and Hannah and his mom. He's been trying to be all nice to me since the dance. I don't think he gets it. I told him I was gonna stay out and celebrate with the guys. He asked if I thought I was still gonna make it back in time for the screening of his dad's movie. I told him, "Easy man, it's only five thirty. Let me chill for a little, I'll be there." Not that it was him I wanted to see.

I watched the Schwartzes walk off and get into their Lexus. Hannah didn't turn around to look at me.

I was livin' large, though. "Señor Clutch," that's what everyone was calling me. After we showered and changed, Morales said he would take the team out for pizza. We all said we were busy, though, so he left. Then we went to Taco Bell.

At Taco Bell, it was really nice, everyone chipped in to pay for my Cheesy Gordita Crunch. And when Javy ordered it for me, he said to the guy, "And I want it with extra hot sauce because my man is *on fire!*" So tight.

The food was gross but in a tasty kind of way. After a tough win, there's really nothing better than some cheap, fake Mexican food. All of us were having the best time sitting around the table, remembering all the cool stuff we did during the game, making fun of those wack Westside guys from the other team, giving each other crazy nicknames.

After we'd been sitting around the table for a while, Guillermo, who we'd just given the name "Frida Kahlo," tapped me on the shoulder and he asked if the two of us could talk for a second. It made me feel kind of weird when he did that. I didn't know what to expect. At least I knew it couldn't be worse than the last time someone wanted to have "a talk" with me.

I followed Guillermo out to the alley behind the restaurant. I'm not gonna lie, when he first led me out there I actually got nervous for a second. Everyone knows the kinds of things that Guillermo's maybe done. But then he slapped hands and bumped fists with me and brought me in for a little hug, like a gangster kind of a hug.

"Danny," he said. "I wanna let you know something. I've noticed your leadership on this team. I respect the way you treat everyone right, even the white kid. Just wanted to let you know that if you ever wanna join the family, we'll make it good for you."

He gave me a nod. Then, just like that, he walked back into Taco Bell.

I'm still not really sure what to think. "The family . . ." Did Guillermo offer me to join the Raiders? And not just that, but like a legit position? Basically he said he would want me to be a leader, right? Like how I am on the team. The whole deal is crazy.

I went back inside, where we all hung out for a few more minutes. Then Javy and Carlos said everyone was invited to their house for a post-post-game celebration. There would be chips and girls and boxing on TV and maybe, if they could find them, some of their dad's Coronas. It sounded fun to me. I really wanted to go. But I'd already promised Jake that I'd be there for the movie at his house. Hannah would be at the movie, too. Not that she would talk to me or anything, but what if she did? I told the guys I had to peace. They said, "*Really*, Danielito?" I said really. They got on the bus headed for the Eastside and I got on the one to Seabrook.

When I walked into the Schwartz's TV room, the whole family was there, plus a couple of Hannah's friends. Also Dorothy from writing club. They were all already watching the movie. I looked at the screen. A T. rex was fighting a dragon. Keanu Reeves was riding the dragon. Mr. Schwartz was explaining how it took them like, five years to get the computer graphics on this scene just right. Jake turned back to me and said, in his most annoying voice possible, "You're thirty-five minutes late." Hannah didn't turn back at all.

I sat down to watch the movie. I guess it was pretty good, but after all that had happened to me today, it was hard to focus. It was a lot more fun to close my eyes and imagine that I was hitting the game-winning shot again. Or that I was making out with Hannah. Or that I was punching Jake in the arm.

25 • Hannah Schwartz

Tuesday, March 2

DiRTY LiTTLE SECRETS
San Paulo's Premier Gossip Blog
Always by Queen Hannah

Queen Hannah's How-to of the Day

How I Can Judge You Based Solely on Your Profile Picture

Who says I have to get to know you in order to know
everything about you? Using this handy guide, I can tell
exactly how awesome/lame/creepy you are within just one
second of looking at your FB profile pic. Remember, I don't
need a thousand words—just the picture.

Type of picture: You as an adorable baby/toddler.
What you're trying to say: "Look how cute I used to be!"
What you're really saying: "Not anymore!!"
Where you rank on the lameness scale: As lame as an after-
school playdate with one of those girls who your mom made
you be friends with because the girl had no other friends.

Type of picture: You among a large group of people.
What you're trying to say: "I have so many besties!"
What you're really saying: "I have no individual worth!"
Where you rank on the lameness scale: As lame as being the

400th girl to wear plaid to school. (Queen Hannah = cuh-learly the first.)

Type of picture: You with other members of your family.
What you're trying to say: "Family is the most important thing in my life!"
What you're really saying: "I'm homeschooled!"
Where you rank on the lameness scale: As lame as this sentence: "Teacher? I mean . . . Mom?"

Type of picture: You dropping a gangsta sign.
What you're trying to say: "Thug liiiiife!"
What you're really saying: "White girrrrl!"
Where you rank on the lameness scale: As lame as a homey from Seabrook.

Type of picture: You in nature.
What you're trying to say: "When I'm outside . . . yeah . . . that's when I feel the most free."
What you're really saying: "I like nature! I! Am! Inherently! Uninteresting!"
Where you rank on the lameness scale: As lame as a girl peeing outdoors.

Type of picture: Not a picture of you, but a picture of a well-known celebrity/cute animal.
What you're trying to say: "This isn't really me . . . but imagine if it were!"
What you're really saying: "This isn't really me . . . isn't it depressing that I wish I were Beyoncé . . . or a rabbit?"
Where you rank on the lameness scale: As lame as being insecure.

Rumor Mill

- An anonymous source confirms that Meghan Moore and Lauren Gardner-Smith made out at a sleepover last weekend. It remains unclear whether it was just late-night-let's-put-this-on-YouTube antics or a serious lesbian thing. My money's on the latter.

- Avery Sinclair was seen out shopping with his mom on Sunday afternoon. Allegedly he purchased new underwear . . . and bed-wetting pills.

- Nisha Patel was spotted walking into the principal's office this afternoon. In tears. Rumor has it that Little Ms. ASB President scored a little too well on her latest math test. *Stars! They Cheat Like Us!*

- Ashley Clarke was recently spotted at the movies canoodling with David Harmer, the youngest of the Harmer boys. That's all three of them now, isn't it, Ashley?

Queen Hannah's Words of Wisdom

Never start a legit relationship in middle school. We're ready for a little fun, but not the real thing. (Plus, you don't want to end up like Kristen and Alex. YECH.)
(P.S. No offense, Krist. Love you girl!)

HANNAH OUT.

So that is the fourth—and so far, juiciest—post of my all-new blog. It's only been up a few hours and already it's got 216 hits. Yeah, I know, basically I've reached phenomenon status.

Dirty Little Secrets is the biggest thing to hit San Paulo since Chicle Rodriguez's butt. Oooh, that's so harsh, I know. Once I get into gossip-blog mode, it's kinda hard for me to switch out.

I don't care, though. This thing has done wonders for my image. No one ever talks about my recent embarrassing moments anymore. And yeah, I guess maybe that's because the entire student body is too scared of me now to say anything. But hey, as Daddy says when he's negotiating with Hollywood people, It is better to be feared than loved.

I love my dad. For the whole week after the dance, I did not want to talk about what happened. Not with anyone. I couldn't talk to my mom because she can't know about Danny. I couldn't talk to my friends because *they* can't know about Danny. I couldn't talk to Jake because I refuse to ever speak to that little snitch again for as long as I live. And I couldn't talk to Danny. I just couldn't. I can't. He wouldn't understand.

And the other day, when Dad knocked on my door after a week of being down in L.A. doing Oscars press, I didn't really want to talk to him either.

"Please go away, Daddy," I told him.

"Heard you haven't been feeling so great," he said, through the door.

"Yeah," I said, "but I don't want to talk about it, okay?"

"You don't have to," he said. "But can I come in?"

"Maybe later," I said.

So of course he opened the door right then and came in

with the prettiest potted orchid wrapped in a big purple ribbon and my favorite skinny vanilla latte from Starbucks.

"What's going on?" he said, handing me the latte.

"Life sucks," I said.

So he said, "Well, why don't you do something about it?"

I said, "What do you mean, Dad?"

He said, "Get creative, Hannah."

So I did, and an Internet sensation was born.

Who knew I could be so powerful? I mean, DLS is literally me just typing down the things I used to say at lunch or in passing period. That's all it is. Only now, what I say matters so much more. Five minutes after I posted this latest entry, Jamie Mackintosh changed her profile pic from her as a baby to her in a bikini sitting on that Italian exchange student's lap. I can't wait to see what she'll do when I post tomorrow's entry: "Five ways your Facebook profile makes you look like a whore."

The other insane thing has been how little work I've had to put into this. I mean, obviously I write everything myself—who else is as sassily snarkified as me?—but I get all the rumors and stuff from outside sources. People will reveal the most scandalous secrets to me—in class, at club V-ball practice, by sending anonymous e-mails. It's like everyone was dying to spread this stuff all along. Now that they've got me, they have a way to make everyone's dirty laundry everyone's business.

Today Chad came up to me at lunch and said that my blog was the coolest thing to ever happen at San Paulo, even cooler than the time he went paintballing with his bros at midnight near a retirement community. Honestly, that's some pretty high praise. And I mean, obviously, yeah, Chad's opinion doesn't mean much to me, but it's still pretty awesome that he said that, you know?

Chad Beck is right. I'm back, slutbags, and better than ever. All that stuff that happened in the past is a distant memory. All anyone notices is what I'm doing now. I'm feared and I love it.

Jamie Boo,

Could there possibly be a more pointless class than journalism? I'm sitting here in seventh—twenty minutes till the bell—and I'm supposed to be writing this article about the wrestling team, but I know that no one will ever read it. No one cares about the newspaper at this school. After all, what's a newspaper when compared to a blog?

Hannah's post on DLS last night was brrrutal, wasn't it? She basically indirectly called you an ugly. And, well, no offense, but it's not like you were the cutest baby that ever lived. Redhead babies are weird. No offense. I mean, you're a total goddess now. It's good you changed your prof pic to that super-cute one of you on Marco's lap. There's nothing bad that Hannah can say about that, right?

BTW, how are you and Marco? Is he getting better at English or is he still all like, "Ciao, Bella! Pizza pizza, Mario Luigi!" LOL. But srsly, who cares how bad he is at our language? He's so hot it doesn't matter.

Ten mins till school gets out—which means only 24 hours and 10 mins till my mom takes us to get our mani-pedis! Ahhhh! BFF date! So excited. Can

we wear matching outfits to the spa and everythang?
I wanna do twin ponytails.

Soooooo bored right now in case you couldn't
tell. I have to write another article this week, and
there is srsly nothing newsworthy on this campus to
cover. Hannah already puts all the good juicy stuff
on her blog. I guess I could ask one of the Mexis in
our class what's going on w/ the gangsters. Those
guys r always up to something lol.

Actually maybe I could write something about all
those weird signs. You've seen them in the bathroom
stalls, right? The ones w/ the big picture of the sword
on them. They say "SSS" or something like that?
Creepy. I heard that the janitors keep taking them
down, but then the next day the signs keep popping
back up. No one knows how or why. I even heard
that the office is starting to get concerned. They
think it's like a cholo thing. Maybe Greene will take
a break from solving the seventh grade/eighth grade
crisis that's TEARING THIS SCHOOL APART
(eyeroll) long enough to check this sitch out.

Oh, there's the bell. Can't wait for our after
school adventure mañana! My fingernails and
toenails are so stoked.

All my love till the end of time,
Emily-Bear

Hannah,

I miss you. It's been a long time since we talked and I think we should get together sometime. It would be cool if we

Dear Hannah,

It's been more than a month since we talked. Don't you think that's a really long time? I don't understand

Hannah,

What happened at the dance sucked. Your brother ruined what we had. He ruined our lives. But really, don't you think we could

Dear Hannah,

We were a great couple. Even if people didn't know about us, I knew about us and that's why I'm so

Hannah,

I miss us. Don't you

Dear Hannah,

I don't know if you realize it, but I think you need me.

Hannah,
Remember Jake's room?

Dear Hannah,
I convinced Luz and Chicle that we weren't ever even a couple. Maybe if you want to

My Hannah,

Dear Hannah,
I know I'm never gonna find another girl like you again. It makes me

Hannah,

Hannah,

26 • Jake Schwartz

Wednesday, March 17

I forgot to wear green today. I woke up this morning, I saw that it was March 17th on my "This Day in History" calendar, and still I somehow failed to realize that it was St. Patrick's Day. I put on brown pants, my black New York Public Library T-shirt, and my gray hoodie, same as any normal day. No green. I would come to regret this decision.

On this day in history, 624 C.E., Muhammad and the Muslims of Medina defeated the Quraysh of Mecca in the Battle of Badr. It was a bad day for the Quraysh.

On this day in history, 1845 C.E., the rubber band was patented. It was a bad day for tree bark.

And on this day in history, today C.E., the absolute unluckiest day of my life, I was defeated by Guillermo Torres and the San Paulo Raiders in the Battle of Jake's Dignity. If only I'd worn green.

School wasn't so bad. Yeah, I had to deal with a few kids pinching me, and Brendan Wheeler kept bugging me during math by whispering things like, "Jews don't celebrate St. Patrick's Day! Unless you guys are the leprechauns! Beheheheh!" But honestly, it was fine. Whenever little things like that come up, I always remind myself: I have good friends, I have a good family, things could be a lot worse.

Then, after school happened. First Dorothy threw a huge hissy fit when I told her I had practice so I wouldn't be able to meet with her to plan the upcoming return of Writing Club. I explained that the team only has a few more practices before the big end-of-season county tournament, and that honestly, she and I probably aren't going to be able to successfully bring the club back anyway. But she wasn't having any of it.

"Jacob Schwartz!" she screamed in my face. "You, sir, are a cur!"

Cur. That's a new one.

Then, right before practice, I went up to Mr. Morales in the hall to ask him for some of his favorite creative-writing exercises. Dorothy made me do it on behalf of the SSS. Some of the guys overheard Mr. Morales and me as the two of us were talking about character sketches and simile circles.

"Nerd!" Rudy called me later as we were changing in the locker room.

"Dork!" shouted Javy.

"Pussy!" shouted Guillermo.

"Four-eyes!" shouted Antonio.

I tried to explain to Antonio that I can't be a four-eyes, seeing as I don't wear glasses. He responded by promptly walking over to me and thwomping my left arm with a hell of a hurtful punch, giving me a tender, grayish bruise. Two minutes later, I had seven tender, grayish bruises on my left arm. Everyone but Danny. Thanks, Danny.

Sometimes when my mom picks me up from practice, she notices I'm in an upset mood and she asks me, "Jake, why are you even doing this? Why is it so important for you to be on this team?" I tell her that I like Mr. Morales, I like hanging out with Danny, and I like the sport of basketball. Of course I like being on the team.

Well, I guess I'm not exactly the biggest fan of all the running we do. I don't really like the fact that I bring the team down by sucking so hard. I can't say I enjoy the name-calling. Or the pushing. Or the bruises.

All right, fine. I hate it. I mean, it's too late to quit now, and I'm not a quitter anyway. But yes, it's true, Mom, I hate being on the team.

And I especially hated today, March 17th.

Practice itself was the usual. Edgar didn't pass me the ball once during our scrimmage, and the one time Danny threw it to me, I got jumpy and shot the ball clear over the backboard. Guillermo basically body-slammed me when I was going for a loose ball, and when I hit the ground I heard a weird cracking noise that I don't wish to investigate. Antonio wouldn't stop calling me "Four-eyes." Then, when he got bored of that, it was *"Cuatros Ojos."* Finally, he started calling me "Little White Turd."

But really, I could deal with all that. It was after practice I couldn't deal with.

We were all heading to the locker room. Usually I prefer to get picked up straight after practice and shower at home, but my mom was going to be a few minutes late since she was at Hannah's club-volleyball game on the other side of town. Mr. Morales had to run into the main building and make some copies. That left me alone. With the guys.

Of course I was nervous about changing in front of everyone. But if only that had been all—I didn't even get to the locker room.

As we were walking off the courts, I saw Javy and Carlos whispering to each other and laughing. I figured it was about, I don't know, a girl or something. Then the two of them went up to Guillermo and whispered to him. Guillermo didn't laugh, but he kind of smirked and nodded.

I looked away from them and up at Danny. He was a few steps in front of me. I was going to ask him if maybe he wanted to—

And then, suddenly, I was being picked up. Carlos got my legs. Javy had my torso. Guillermo was holding my head and shoulders. Then the rest of the guys noticed and came over, and they all started carrying me too, above their heads like I was their sacrifice. Only Danny held back. He watched us.

Part of me wanted to try to fight them off, but the rest of me knew that resistance would be stupid. I had to hold back and let this run its course.

I had a random thought—maybe they were taking me somewhere fun. Maybe Danny had used his clout with them to organize some sort of special surprise for me, a big "I'm sorry" kind of thing. Maybe we could all emerge from this as amigos.

Nope.

We were never going to be friends. When did I come to this conclusion? Oh, I'd say it was when I felt my feet being lifted high above my head, then when I felt my body going upside-down vertical, then when I felt fourteen hands let go of me, then when I felt the stinging clang as my head crashed down hard against metal, and then when I smelled the rancid stench of half-eaten burrito mixed with days-old yogurt.

I had been dumped face-first into a trash can.

I'm not sure how long I was in there. Trash can time is sort of like dog years or time spent in deep space. It's all messed up. All I know is that it felt like forever and that I kept expecting Danny to yell, "Cut it out, guys!" or *"¡BASTA!"* But he never did.

I guess I could have tried to get out myself, but A) that would have been kind of difficult to pull off, actually, and B) I was afraid. Once I was in there, I couldn't hear the guys laughing or anything, but I could sense their presence—all of them standing around the trash can admiring what they'd done, this work of modern art they'd created, those short, skinny legs sticking out of the can, those blue gym shorts and size-too-big basketball shoes kicking and flailing pathetically. I bet it was kind of poetic in a life-ruining sort of way.

And I could sense Danny standing there, watching.

Finally, I heard a voice. It was Mr. Morales.

"Guys, what are you—what's going on? Is that *Jake?*"

He made them pull me out and he called all of us into the locker room, together. I imagine my hair still reeked of that disgusting, unidentifiable liquid that always seems to exist at the bottom of the trash.

Mr. Morales asked them to explain themselves. Guillermo

said that we had all been horsing around, me included. Mr. Morales told them that bullying is taken seriously at this school. If he found out that they were lying to him, he said, they could all get referrals. That's like a detention, plus they call your parents, plus it goes on your permanent record. For some of the guys who actually have permanent records, a referral is pretty bad news. For the ones who have been held back before, like Guillermo, a referral could mean yet another year at SP. Or maybe juvenile hall.

Mr. Morales asked me, smelly me, if what Guillermo had said was right. Had we all just been messing around?

"NO!" I wanted to scream out. "NO, YOU FREAKING IDIOT! NO!"

But I knew I couldn't be the one to tell the truth. Imagine what the guys would have done to me then. They're all Raiders, for crying out loud, except Danny.

Danny was my only hope. He had to be the one to tell Mr. Morales what really happened, what they had really done to me, or otherwise they were going to get away with this. I looked over at Danny. He wasn't looking back at me. He was staring off at the wall. He didn't say anything.

Thanks, Danny.

27 • Danny Uribe

Sunday, March 21

It happened last Saturday, but still I can't stop thinking about it.

I knew Hannah would be getting back from her movie around 11, so I snuck into her room at 10:30.

I know it sounds mad creepy, but I had a reason. I needed to talk to her. I couldn't get her to talk to me any other way. She never said nothing about all the cards and flowers I left in her room the few weeks before, and she's not gonna go talking to me at school where people would see us. Plus, I figured, you know, it all started in Jake's room. Maybe we could get it going again in Hannah's room. Then we'd see what happened in my room.

At first I thought I would just leave a letter in her room and that's it. But then I thought, You know what, I know she still wants me. If I talk to her one-on-one, she won't be able to deny the way she feels. If I can get her one-on-one, we'll for sure get back together.

Being in her room all alone made me feel like a stalker. I started to feel like maybe this wasn't such a good idea. But no. I wasn't there to take weird pictures of stuff or to steal her underwear. I was there to tell her how much I love her. I wasn't being creepy. I was being romantic. She'd see the difference.

The car came up the driveway. The front door of the house opened. Hannah said good night to her mom. Hannah's room door opened. Then Hannah saw me sitting on her bed, and that's when she screamed.

It was just one of those short screams, like seeing a spider. Not loud or long enough for anyone else to hear, which was good. But the way Hannah looked at me . . . it was worse than if she'd seen a spider.

She asked me what I was doing there. No. Wait. She asked me what the hell I was doing there.

I said, I have to talk to you. Why have you been pretending like you don't even know me, I asked, even here at your house? It's fake. It's BS. I know we want each other, that's what I said. What happened at the dance shouldn't change that.

Hannah said that the dance didn't change the way she felt about me, but that it changed the way she *thought* about things. That's how she put it. She said the dance made her realize that we couldn't be together. I asked her why.

She asked me if I had joined the Raiders. I said no. I mean, I said yeah, all my friends are doing it, so yeah, I've thought about it a little, but if that would keep us from getting together, then of course I would never join. She said, Well, that's the reason we can't be together, Danny. Think about what you just said.

But you still love me, I told her.

No, she said. The dance made her change the way she *thought* about me. And once she started thinking about me different, then that's when she started *feeling* different about me. That's what she told me. Then she said she never loved me. We're too young to love, she said. She used to like me a lot, Hannah said, and she still likes me, sure, but not in that way. Then she told me to leave her room.

One more kiss, I asked her. Please.

No, she said.

Don't do this, I said. Please don't do this.

Leave, she said.

So I left.

I hate Jake.

I hate his gay-ass voice. I hate how he thinks he's so much smarter than people. I hate what a freaking loser he is. I hate him and that's not going to change.

My mom made my family go to church for Easter. It's not like me to listen when I'm in church, or even to be awake, but when I was there this morning the priest was saying stuff that I really connected with. He was talking a lot about how Jesus got killed and then came back. I mostly care about the killing part.

Jesus died because he got betrayed by Judas, one of his closest homies. The reason Jesus got betrayed was real dumb, too. His friend basically called him out for being too popular. His friend was jealous.

At least Jesus knew what was coming. I never could have seen Jake becoming such a little bastard. I mean, we've been friends for life. We used to do everything together. And like yeah, it hasn't been the same this year, I guess. But there's a reason for that. I'm growing up and he's not.

I guess I always thought that after a while, Jake would just get over being a little kid. I thought that some time in seventh grade, Jake would have to start acting his age instead of the number of pit hairs that he has. I thought he would start being like everyone else at school. I always thought that when that happened, then we'd be tight again.

But then this year Jake started annoying the hell out of me any time I wanted to do something fun, complaining about how I always leave him behind. He started hanging out with Dorothy, and together they'd do nothing but watch cartoons like gay little babies. He started stealing my report cards from the mail and yelling at me about my grades, and like, no one gets to see my grades but me. I don't even show them to my parents. Plus, Jake still looks like he's eight. Sounds like he's eight. Plays ball like he's eight.

After he did what he did at the dance, it's obvious that he's still just a kid. Just a little retard who doesn't understand how his actions hurt the people around him. He'll never realize how he ruined my life, that's for sure. I hate him so much. I can never be friends with him again. So who cares how many trash cans he gets dumped in. That's the kind of thing a Judas deserves.

Instead of going home after church, I took my parents to Bella Vista. We went there with my cousins and aunt and uncle. Some of the Raiders and their families were chilling at the park. The little kids were looking for Easter eggs. All of the eggs were filled with confetti, and the kids were cracking them over their heads. It was just a Sunday afternoon BBQ. Everyone was clean, everyone was straight. Today my mom even said how nice all my friends were. She has no idea that all of them are gangsters. And I don't need to tell her, either.

When I got there, I saw all the guys from the basketball team and all the other fools that I know on the Raiders. It was cool to see them with their moms and nieces and stuff. They were mostly hanging on their own, though. I basically knew everyone there, which was tight. And they all seemed real happy to see me.

"Danielito!" shouted Chuy.

"Wassup, Señor Clutch?" said Edgar.

Guillermo looked at me and nodded.

Gordo, who I guess is out of juvie now, ran up to me smiling, and he gave me a big fat dude hug. He handed me a hot dog. He said he'd get me a beer when my mom wasn't looking.

"One thing, though," he said all smiling. "The Coronas are being saved for Raiders only."

Some of the guys around me made an "ooohhh" sound, like when a kid gets a slip to the principal's office.

"Well, what if I really want a cold one?" I said.

Gordo smiled. Everyone made another "ooohhh."

"You gonna be one of us now?" Javy asked me. "You gon be a Raider, cuz?"

I spoke before even thinking about it, really.

"Let me talk to Guillermo," I said.

It was like he'd been waiting for me. Guillermo got up from where he was sitting, on a park bench with a couple of high school *veteranos*, far away from the adults. He came up and met me. The two of us walked away from the group, over toward a swing set.

A couple of kids were making each other dizzy on the

swings, like me and Jake used to do when we were in second grade. I think one of the kids was Guillermo's nephew. When we got there, they ran off. It was just me and the shot-caller.

I stood up straighter than normal and I looked at him right in the eye. I'd never planned what I was about to say, but in a way I think I've had the words ready for a long time.

I didn't used to like who I was. I mean, I had a good life, I know that. But it wasn't really my life. I lived at Jake's house and I went to Jake's school. I did things with Jake's family and with Jake's money. I was Jake's friend. And I wasn't really anything else.

My friends get who I really am. They don't drag me along to their things. They let me do my own thing. They don't talk down to me. They look up to me. They don't have to try and understand me. They do understand me. They're just like me. They're a part of me. And I love them for that. And yeah, pretty much all of them are Raiders.

There were so many things keeping me from becoming a Raider. I didn't want to disappoint Jake. I didn't want to lose Hannah. And I didn't want to put myself in danger. I've seen what happens to the fools who first join the Raiders, the guys like Gordo who one day don't have records and then, just like that, end up in juvie. I'm not stupid. I'm not a follower. I don't want bad things happening to me for no reason.

But the more I think about it, the more I realize something. To really become a part of my friends, to really become a part of the Eastside, and to really show Javy and Carlos and Gordo and Edgar and Chuy and Guillermo and all those guys how much I love them, there's no choice for me but to become a Raider. And plus, since all the guys want me, and since I'm smart, and since I don't want to be disrespected like some random gang recruit, I realize something else. I can join on my terms.

"I'll be a Raider," I said to Guillermo when we were standing there at the swing set, "but not your pawn. I don't want to take the crap for stuff I don't do. I don't want to be Danielito. I want it to be like it is on the team. I want to be important. *¿Comprende?*"

Guillermo gave me a hard look. Then he stepped up close to me like we were about to make a drug deal handshake.

"Of course," he said, in a voice so low that I could barely hear. "You have my respect. You'll always have my respect. And you know what else? You can have my job."

Main recruiter. Guillermo had just made me the main recruiter. Only my first day and already I was a shot-caller.

Guillermo gave me another hard look. Then he grabbed my hand, shook it tight, and brought me in for a gangsta hug. He said one more thing.

"Welcome to the family."

Thirty Signs That You Suck

People constantly come up to me and ask, "Queen Hannah, how do I know if I'm cool?"

My answer is always the same: "Well, my humble subject, here's the thing: you're not cool. You suck."

"But I don't want to suck!" they tell me. "How can I avoid this terrible fate?"

"Well," I say, "the first step to not sucking is admitting that you suck."

"But how can I tell that I suck?" they ask me.

"Well," I say. "There are thirty signs. . . ."

You suck if . . .

1. You're named something boring like "Mark," "Paul," or "Rachel."

2. You named your dog something boring like "Shadow," "Midnight," or "Oreo."

3. You are described as "nice" when people have to sum you up in one word. "Nice" = not pretty nor funny nor cool = not interesting = you probably named your dog Oreo = you're boring.

4. You think the word "amazing" isn't used often enough. Uh-mayyyy-zeeng.

5. You read for fun. You can't wait to finish *Johnny Tremain* . . . so you can reread *Johnny Tremain!* Then you'll go online and hit up the *Johnny Tremain* message boards!

6. Your parents don't let you watch TV. Not even PBS.

7. You do nothing but watch TV. The couch cushion is conformed to your butt.

8. You have a passion for the outdoors. Your favorite hair accessory is a deer tick.

9. You and your best friend dress up as twins sometimes. You know, matching side ponytails and all that. To go with your matching lack of other friends.

10. You and your sibling(s) were forced to dress identically at some point in your lives. Just in case your parents were idiotic enough to maybe lose you at Disneyland.

11. You're a ginger.

12. You're a curly.

13. You spike your hair.

14. You bleach the tips.

15. You like to proudly display your thong and you plan on getting a lower back tattoo. A butterfly would be really cute and only historically slutty.

16. You walk around school wearing a basketball jersey with no shirt underneath.

17. You play basketball wearing a jersey *with* a shirt underneath.

18. You sometimes make your Facebook status a passage from the Bible. Just in case God's checking his News Feed.

19. You have, at some point in your life, uttered the sentence, "I live for the nights I'll never remember with the girls I'll never forget!" Or you plan to upon immediately joining the most mediocre sorority at your future college.

20. You say fake curse words like "fudge," "shoot," and "hecka."

21. You're a jelly bracelets kind of girl. (You know what they mean. . . .)

22. You write boring things in people's yearbooks, like "2 good + 2 be = 4gotten."

23. You ask your teachers to sign your yearbook.

24. Your only picture in the yearbook is your school picture.

25. You think it's funny to refer to someone named Hannah as "Hannah Banana." It never occurs to you that she's keeping a list of everyone who's ever done this, and that someday she will make them all pay. Perhaps on her popular and influential blog.

26. You're one of those people who smells weird for no reason.

27. You are cute-looking, but secretly an ass.

28. You look like an ass and are actually still an ass.

29. You think it's romantic to be creepy. You would hide in someone's room and wait for them to come in before you confessed your creepy love.

30. You think you know what love is.

Rumor Mill

- Math teachers Mr. Peterson and Ms. Montez just got engaged. Also, Ms. Montez has been looking kinda fat recently. Is 1+1 about to become 3? Or is Ms. Montez just fat?

- Brian Fenton (he of the hideous acne) just started dating this rando sevvy girl Chloe something. And now *she* has terrible acne. Or *is* it acne . . . ?

- Apparently, as a special birthday present, Jamie Mackintosh's parents are letting her have a small group of friends including Marco sleep over at her house. How do you say "gross" in Italian?

- Then again, it's not *so* gross given that Marco is totally 9,000 percent gay.

- And, in gangbanger news, word on "tha streets" is that Danny Uribe (a.k.a. Seabrook's Finest) recently became the hombre in charge of recruiting innocent babies to Los Raiders de San Paulo. Congratulations, Danny. Mama *y* Papa would be *muy* proud.

Queen Hannah's Words of Wisdom

When in doubt, no one cares about you.

HANNAH OUT.

Uribe Not Enough as Pirates Fall to La Mesa

By Emily Colman, *Pirate Press*

Friday, March 26th

Despite a truly heroic 33-point effort from team captain and super-sevvy Danny "Señor Clutch" Uribe, the San Paulo Pirates lost to the La Mesa Bulldogs 65–60 in the San Paulo County Middle School Boys' Basketball Championship game.

"I just thank my teammates for getting us this far," said Uribe after the game. "I'd be nothing without my brothers."

Early on, it appeared the Pirates would have no chance at victory. Near the end of the first half, San Paulo trailed La Mesa by 16 points after some unusual substitution patterns by Coach Ruben Morales.

With Uribe on their side, however, the Pirates never gave up. In the fourth quarter, the Prince of Hearts scored ten straight points to pull San Paulo to within two. While the Pirates ultimately lost, their spirits never flagged.

"These guys deserve to hold their heads high," said Coach Morales, a smile on his face. "What an outstanding group of leaders."

Guillermo Torres added 12 points and 10 rebounds for the 2nd place Pirates.

28 • Dorothy Wu

Tuesday, March 30

Starting a secret society is hard work! You have to make it popular enough so all the kids know about it, but secret enough so adults like the principal and your father do not find out about it. You have to recruit with all your energies. You have to locate a special meeting place. You have to create lesson plans that make people say "Aha!" and not "Ha-ha!"

It is very difficult to do all this when your cofounder has not been able to devote his full energies to the group because he has been too busy with his basketball team and with his preparations to become a Jewish adult. It is even harder to get anything done when he thinks that the endeavor is going to be a gigantic failure anyway. Ack.

And yet, despite all these tribulations, I have successfully done it. Thanks to my grueling efforts, the writing club once known as Write On! has been reborn as The Super Story Samurai. Like the phoenix from the ashes, or the Easter guy, the club has risen again.

Step one in becoming the hottest thing to hit the school since Hot Cheetos and cream cheese was generating "buzz." I posted secret signs advertising the club on the wall, like in my memorable dream. In doing this, I drew upon the stealth skills that I developed in the days when I used to leave locker gifts like Boo Radley.

It was a great thrill trying to post the signs so that no one would see me do it. Usually I would wait in the school's hallways, behind my favorite garbage can, until around five o'clock or so. I told my father that I had after-school tutoring until then. Then, when the time came, I would take action. The janitors would be left in the halls, but they would never take my signs down. Only our esteemed principal cares about doing that. I think he has made clubs illegal, but I am not sure. I hope he has. It makes this adventure all the more dangerous and, I must admit, sexy.

Of course, making this secret society happen took a lot more than signs that feature well-drawn pictures of swords. My future students had to know where and when to meet. So, in each of my classes, I passed around several notes that read:

Two days 'fore the day for the Norse god of war,
At exactly four hours before four,
At the place where there are gross smells galore,
There will be all kinds of writing in store!
SUPER STORY SAMURAI. HARD-CORE!

I also had Jake pass around the notes in his classes. I figured that the poem made it supremely obvious that our club would be meeting every Tuesday at lunch behind the Dumpsters (the one place I could think of where no administrator would ever look).

Yet, disappointingly, there were only three of us there at our first meeting: myself, Jake, and Tyler Bell. I was immensely discouraged, of course, but I tried my very acting best not to make it seem so. I led a lesson inspired by my failures at math-studying in which we took different letters of the alphabet and gave them different personalities. *B* is a kindly nurse or a female farmer, depending on who you ask. *G* is a wacky prankster who never manages to get the girl. (Actually, Jake said that *G* means something else in real life, but I told him we are making our own real life here.) *K* has a lot of money but does not want to spend it. *Z* is the fresh new guy in town with all the cool moves. *Q* and *U* are best girlfriends—*Q* is the leader and *U* is the second banana, only *U* is secretly much prettier and nicer than *Q*, but *Q* does not want anyone in Alphabet Town to know that.

It was wonderful. Both of the boys responded very well to my lesson. Laughs and good times were plentiful. I am a pretty boss teacher, if I do say so myself.

At our second Tuesday meeting, we had six writers there. Just like the old days! There was myself, Jake, Tyler, Whitney Dealy, Whitney's friend Leah, and Andrea Molina, a quiet girl with a well-defined jaw. Of course everyone there complained a great deal about the smelly smell, but once we started thinking and writing, no one seemed to care as much. Together, we wrote a "Choose Your Own Adventure" story that took place at an enchanted carnival. Here is a hint: When the carny offers you a choice between the sack of shiny gold and the old boot, take the boot! It will turn out much better for you that way.

At our third meeting, we had eleven (ELEVEN!) attendees. In addition to our previous members, we added Willy Kreutzkampf, Devon Adams, McKenzie Hall, Ross Hawkins, and Heather Kirby. Once again, everyone complained about the smell, but I turned those complaints into yet another kickin' writing exercise: Smelly Similes! Everyone had to write down ten things that the stench smelled like, and they were not allowed to say "trash." Jake suggested, "Krill that was recently regurgitated by a whale." Devon said, "Action figures marinated in garlic broth." I liked mine the best: "An overweight gypsy's scarf after a long trek through the desert."

Today was meeting number four. And *what* a meeting number four. A whoppin' *twenty-three* people came, including ASB President Nisha Patel and a few of Jake's sisters' friends—a.k.a. populars! The cool girls said they wanted to learn how to write so that they could start a revolutionary blog of their own. But here is the important part: they wanted to learn how to write from *me*. A lot people said that they had been missing Mr. Morales's cool lessons, but then they said they heard that my lessons were basically like the same thing. I think about what they said. I think about what they said a lot. For *me* to be compared with Ruben Apollo Morales . . . whoa.

(Note: I do not think his middle name is really Apollo. I do not actually know his middle name. But I like to pretend.)

Today's lesson was especially primo. I had everyone pair off. Each person had to share their most embarrassing story that has happened to them at San Paulo with their partner. Then, each person in the pair wrote down their partner's story in the partner's voice. At the end, a few people shared. We had some funny stories about pants-ripping, accidental gas-passings, and menstrual escapades. The only disappointing moment was when Jake refused to share his most embarrassing story with his partner. I do not understand why he was so sensitive. I mean, yes, the episode between Jake and myself in the hallway before winter break sure was humiliating. But you do not see me crying about it still.

That is the lovely thing about chillin' with the Super Story Samurai, though. Even when events do not go according to plan, we are able to adapt and have tons o' fun and learn, regardless. Everyone has such a sensational positive spirit.

I absolutely cannot wait to unveil our secret club to Mr. Morales. I love the Super Story Samurai. I love my friends.

Friday, April 2 at 3:50 p.m.

Rachel Sloan SPRING BREAK!!! omg yesss. if u need me im at the beach lol

about a minute ago · Comment · Like

Alex Masterson surf tennis golf sleep. surf tennis golf sleep.

3 minutes ago · Comment · Like

Ashley Clarke goin 2 cabo wit the fam 4 the week. wish i was legal :'(

4 minutes ago · Comment · Like

Tina Lin im looking for a quality beach read . . . can anyone recommend any good teen paranormal romances?

6 minutes ago · Comment · Like

Jake Schwartz why does my bar mitzvah need a theme? my personality doesn't have a theme.

9 minutes ago · Comment · Like

Jamie Mackintosh gelato w/ marco. mmmm . . .

12 minutes ago · Comment · Like

McKenzie Hall just finished writing the best story. thanks again D. Wu.

14 minutes ago · Comment · Like

Emily Colman the teen center sucks, meghan.

16 minutes ago · Comment · Like

Meghan Moore who wants to hang downtown? i hear the new teen center is kinda cool

16 minutes ago · Comment · Like

Chad Beck stoked for tomorrow. its not a date tho, i kno haha

18 minutes ago · Comment · Like

Corinne Allison music is so amazing

20 minutes ago · Comment · Like

David Harmer just became a yellow belt. what now.

21 minutes ago · Comment · Like

Nisha Patel ok i would never cheat on a test!! dont believe every lie you read

22 minutes ago · Comment · Like

Hannah Rose Schwartz its the 1-month anniversary of DLS! http://spdirtylittlesecrets.blogspot.com whose life will i ruin next? YOURS

23 minutes ago · Comment · Like

29 • Danny Uribe

Friday, April 2

The bell rang and it was time for spring break. But that's not what was important about today.

I got to the locker room. It's the first time I'd been back since we lost the county finals, but it's not like I give a crap about basketball now.

Pretty much the whole team was waiting for me. Guillermo, my cousins, Chuy, Edgar. Jake wasn't there, but we don't think of him as part of the team. There were the usual other guys too. Jaime, Junior, Gordo, all my other brothers. Everyone was wearing dark shirts, long shorts, high socks, baseball caps with the stickers still on. When we start school again next week, I'll be wearing that stuff, just like them. Underneath my hat, my head will be shaved too. Like Guillermo's.

I nodded at them. They nodded at me. We walked.

We walked past Truman Elementary. That's where I'll recruit after break. It's right in the middle of the city. The Destroyers think of it as their turf, but we know it's Eastside. I looked at the kids in front of the school, the kids waiting for their parents to come pick them up. They had their little backpacks with cartoons on them. They were playing little kid games. When we recruit, those aren't the ones we'll be going for.

We walked past the Teen Center. They built the Teen Center a few years ago, basically to stop gangsters from doing gangster stuff. I think it has bean bags and a big screen TV or something. Maybe an air hockey table. I didn't see anyone in there. Same as always.

We walked past Bella Vista. That's where we were going, but we had to make another stop first.

San Paulo High School. We walked through the parking lot. We walked past mad people making out in their cars. That's so sick that they do that in high school. We walked through the hallways, past the lockers, and over some lawns. We walked to the end of the basketball courts, to the edge of the campus, same place where the Mexicans hang out at the junior high.

There were five fools waiting for us. They were all big like Guillermo and they had mustaches, too. He went up and talked to them.

They were high school veteranos, Raiders since they were maybe ten years old. I don't know their names, but I will soon. They don't usually do stuff with us younger guys, but I guess Guillermo convinced them that it was going to be a good time. They came with us.

There were maybe fifteen of us by this point. When I thought about it like that, when I thought about what would happen with that many people, well, I didn't think about it. You can't wuss out at these times. You have to man up.

Normally when all these guys are together there's lots of talking and laughing and stuff. But today there was business to take care of.

We walked past a parked cop car on the way to Bella Vista. I thought maybe we were gonna change our direction or something, but the other guys kept walking. I followed them.

There was a little group of boys playing at the park when we got there. White kids. They were playing tag or some crap. Guillermo went up to them. He said something. They left.

We had the park to ourselves. I knew what was coming next. This was basically my last chance to get out if I wanted to. But I didn't want to. Everyone turned around and looked at me.

They made kind of a circle around me. I looked around at the different faces surrounding my body. Edgar was almost squinting. He was so serious. Gordo was the opposite. He had a little smile on his face. He kept shaking his head like he was remembering a funny story. Javy and Carlos looked at each other, then at me. I couldn't read anything into Guillermo's stare. The high school guys just looked huge.

All of them had one thing in common: they all seemed like they wanted to kick my ass. But I was ready for them. I was trying to be ready for them. At least I knew what was coming, and why.

Guillermo nodded at me. I nodded back. He nodded at the rest of them.

A punch to the back of my head was the first thing I felt and one of the last things I clearly remember. I think it was a couple hard shoves in the back that knocked me to my knees.

I remember I didn't want to fall completely to the ground. That shows weakness, and that's not what being a gangster's about. I stayed on my knees and I took every blow.

There was a kick to my chest. Two or three of them, maybe. Someone kneed me in the head. Someone else whacked the side of my face. Two punches hit both of my eyes at the same time. Then there was a punch to my balls. I bet it was Guillermo.

This was all before three seconds were through. The worst injuries I've ever had, and only three seconds in. But all I could do was count. They had told me not to try to defend myself. They told me just to count and not to fall to the ground.

I braced myself by putting a hand to the grass below me, but a stomp to my fingers made it so I wouldn't be going there again. Then there was a scratch all the way down my left arm. Another couple hard shoves. Then a kick. It was the kind of strike that would send in a goal from midfield. It hit me in the face.

I knew that my arm and my nose and my mouth were bleeding by this point. But I didn't care. All I cared about was seven more seconds.

Three or four punches to my gut. I wasn't breathing at this point. I was going in and out of feeling things. I knew they would leave me alive, but I didn't know how alive.

I was trying my hardest not to scream. I didn't scream. I was counting. Five more seconds, then a punch to my mouth, then four more seconds, then a whole body jumping with all of its weight onto my left leg, then three more seconds, and I felt fingers going into both of my eyeballs.

Two more seconds. There were punches all over my body.

Cheeks, chest, arm, stomach, balls again. One more second, and I felt like giving up completely even though there was just one more second. I honestly would have yelled stop if I'd thought about it. But I couldn't think. I just had to focus on counting, on staying up, on not crying. My whole body wanted to cry, but I didn't, and that's how I know I'm a man. I didn't scream. I didn't fall. I didn't cry. I didn't open my eyes.

Then time was up. Thirteen seconds were up. I was a Raider.

Then the guys all started beating me up again. That's what it felt like at first. My entire body was so bruised and bloody and sore and stupid from what they'd done that every touch felt like a knockout punch. But they weren't trying to hurt me anymore. They were slapping me on the back. They were giving me noogies. They were trying to give me fist pounds. I didn't mean to leave them hanging, but I couldn't lift my hand.

But the worst was over. They had jumped me in. They had made it count. Now I was one of them.

I couldn't move again without at least a little bit of me wanting to cry. Probably won't be able to do anything normal for weeks. But the rest of the day was so good. They gave me cold beers to ice my bruises with. They joked about all the sounds I made during the jump-in, even though they mostly seemed like they respected me. They showed me Raider stuff. The high school guys and Guillermo all showed me the same tattoo they have on their arm.

P/V. Stands for *por vida*. Eastside for life.

It was one of those afternoons that I'm always going to remember this year by. Not because of getting jumped in, either, but because of what it was like after. What I'll remember is what getting jumped in earned me. It earned me this day and it earned me these guys. We hung till way after dark, and we talked and drank, and the veteranos told us about high school, and we made plans to recruit and plans to chill.

At the end, as we were all leaving to go home, Guillermo asked me where I live. It was a weird moment for a second. Most of the guys know by now that my room is at the Schwartz house, but I've always tried to keep that stuff from Guillermo. I feel like he shouldn't know about that part of me.

So when Guillermo asked me where I live, I didn't say Seabrook. I told him something else. Something that feels way more true anyway. I told him Raider Territory.

30 • Hannah Schwartz

Thursday, April 8

It was really only a matter of time before they were going to shut me down. My dad always says that no one wants to hear the truth.

Well, in this case that's only partly true. Hundreds upon hundreds of people were checking my site every day to see who I would go after next, so obviously everyone who matters wanted to know *my* truth.

But I guess after a while, a few too many kids and their parents got a little too crybabyish about the whole thing, and so next thing I knew, Principal Greene was calling my house to set up a meeting with him and me and my parents.

The meeting happened last Friday, the last day before break, and it was hilarious. My dad's in between projects right now, so he was able to come, and that's what made it so awesome. Principal Slimeball began with this lame little speech about how school shouldn't be gossip and scandals but studying hard and following guidelines and the golden rule and all this BS, and then Daddy just straight-up interrupted him.

First my dad patted me on the shoulder, and he said that he was proud of the fact that I'd undertaken an outside project like my blog and that he loved seeing me be creative. He said one of the reasons he had been so happy with SP up until this point was that he felt like the teachers here allowed students to express themselves in unique ways. He talked about Jake's writing club and the teacher who started it and stuff. Then my dad said yes, maybe I had gone too far with the kinds of things I was saying online, but better too far than nothing at all.

This left Principal Nutless fully flabbergasted. He like, couldn't talk at first. He made a pathetic attempt to try and decide a proper punishment for me, but my dad interrupted him again and said that he and mom would set my sentence at home. "Hannah's punishment will fit the crime," Dad said, and then he winked at me. It was so obvious I had totally gotten away with everything. And then Principal Ferretface tried to get in one last thing, but my dad just said, "We're done here."

When Jeffrey Schwartz says it's done, it's done. Mom, Dad, and I walked out that door and I haven't heard anything from the office since.

My parents told me I had to take the blog down, but I said, "Mommy, Daddy, I like having my voice heard." My dad said he understood that. My mom said I could keep the site if I could figure out how to do it without hurting people's feelings.

It soon became clear what I had to do.

Every celebrity reaches a point where she doesn't want to be known anymore for the thing that made her famous. If she was an actress, she stops appearing in big blockbuster movies. If she was a supermodel, she stops photographing in lingerie. If she was a reality star, she stops pretending to date other reality stars. In all of these cases, no matter what their career was before, these stars go ahead and do the exact same thing: they make a difference. They spread awareness of a disease. They start a charity. They take pictures holding baby pandas.

I started Dirty Little Secrets because I wanted to hurt people. After the bad rumors about me at the beginning of the school year, and especially after the Sweethearts Dance, people acted like I was some kind of joke. Maybe they didn't learn what was actually going on with me and Danny, and maybe I ensured that they would never fully find out, but even still, that didn't stop every single person in the school from laughing at Hannah the slut on Saturday, February 13th. Worst moment of my life.

So I wanted to get back at every person who laughed at me that night. I wanted everyone at SP to know the shame that I felt, or to fear it. So yeah, I started my blog for less-than-noble reasons, and yeah, it worked to perfection. People totally respect me now. They tell me the most horrible things about their own best friends. They avoid eye contact in the halls, especially if they've just posted the status, "I love wearing Marco's shirts. Mmm . . ." I bet they stay awake at night, worrying about whose life I'll destroy next. I bet they even have nightmares about me. And you know what? Maybe I don't want to cause any more nightmares. I deserve respect, but maybe I'm tired of using cruelty to get it.

So this is what I have to do: I have to stop using my powers for evil. I have to get in touch with my soft side. DLS will be a gossip blog no more. I don't just want to be feared, I want to be loved. And to get that, I have to show the world that I can love too.

The more I think about it, the more I realize that I actually am a pretty loving person. Since I've decided to redo the blog, I've started thinking about my whole life in a different way. I've decided to make it up to all of the people that I've hurt the most.

Not Danny. I don't want to think about Danny. I don't want to think about him replacing his spiky hair with a vile skinhead look. I don't want to think about him coming to school with two black eyes and a bloody arm and a limp. Back when I used to be friends with Chicle and Luz, back before they betrayed me, back when I used to acknowledge their human existence, they told me what it means when a kid from the Eastside shows up looking like that—the shaved head, the cuts and bruises. I know about "jumping in." I know who Danny's "mobbing" with now. But I choose not to think about any of that stuff. I have no room in my brain to think about Danny.

No, instead I will prefer to think and talk and dream about a subject that, over the past few weeks, has strangely and shockingly become very near and dear to my heart:

Chad Beck.

Don't laugh at me. I mean, yeah, I would have laughed at myself a month ago, but don't laugh at me now. I swear he's changed. He's totally gotten better.

I just had him wrong the whole time. All those times I thought Chad was scarily stalking me, really he was just trying to apologize. Only I was too blind to see that because I was too obsessed with other stuff.

Chad wanted to say sorry. He just couldn't find the right opportunity. Every time he tried to talk to me in person, like at the Hanukkah party, I walked away from him. Every time he texted me, I ignored it. And I blocked him on AIM. And FB chat. And Gchat.

So then Chad got really into the idea of being King of Hearts at the dance, just like I wanted so bad to be Queen. He figured that if the two of us got to be alone in a slow dance together, in front of the whole school, then maybe some sparks would fly between us.

Obviously that didn't work out.

Chad didn't give up, though. He didn't give up because he really, truly, deeply cares for me. He started finding little times to come and talk to me in class. He made a new screen name and he used it to apologize to me and to praise my blog. We became friends again.

And then, one day, a few days before break started, it was after school and I was home by myself. Dad was in L.A. and Mom was watching Jake and Danny's team lose the big county tournament or whatever. I was just in my room, on the computer, when all of a sudden I started to hear some music coming from outside my bay window.

"Staring into the world inside your sapphire eyes, and running my hands through your beautiful brown, brown hair . . ."

"Song for Hannah." A new recording of it, acoustic-style. It sounded so incredible.

I looked outside my window where I could see iPod speakers resting on the ground. He had gone to the trouble of making an mp3 out of the song he wrote for me. Amazing. Then I looked at the checkered Vans standing next to those speakers. Then I looked up at the rest of the body. Faded jeans, a soft red plaid flannel, an adorable dimpled smile . . . and Chad was holding something, too. A big white sign:

I'M READY TO STOP THINKING
WITH MY DICK. I'M READY TO START
THINKING WITH MY HEART.

All right, a little vulgar perhaps, and it didn't quite make sense, but a very, very funny and cute gesture nonetheless. I appreciated it.

Then Chad flipped the sign over.

HANNAH SCHWARTZ—DATE ME
OR LOSE AT LIFE.

I put my hands to my mouth. I nodded really hard. I probably squealed. I ran out of my room and down the stairs and through the hallway and out the front door and down to the lawn, and this took quite a while actually, but Chad waited for me.

And then we kissed. And that's pretty much all we've done since then. Well, sometimes we hold hands. And sometimes we tickle each other. He knows all my best/worst spots. Sometimes we have long talks about nothing in particular.

It's been the best spring break. It's all been so absolutely beyond perfect. I may have lost my blog, but I got it back and it's going to be better than ever. And I gained a boy.

Dance. Love. Sing.
A Life Blog
By Hannah Schwartz

It's easy to ruin someone's reputation. It's easy to cheat on a test. It's easy to litter. But you know what's much cooler than taking the easy way out?

Doing what's right.

This blog is growing up. You can still expect the same Queen Hannah you always got, but now I'm actually living up to my lovely title—I'll be your Queen of Hearts for real.

I'm through with scaring you. I want to inspire you. So let's kick off the new and reformed DLS with . . .

Thirty Ways You Can Help This World

1. Make a photo collage of you and your best friends. Figure out who's not in the collage that should be. Give her a call.

2. Listen for people whistling. Sing along. Especially if you have a bad voice.

3. Eat the bottom of the muffin first. Give the top to a friend.

4. Talk to a homeless person. Treat him like a home person.

5. Plant a tree for each heart you've broken.

6. Ask a guy on a date. Hold the door open for him. Pay for the meal. Let him get dessert.

7. Give up Facebook for a month. If you really have to check it, then plant a tree afterward.

8. Find the kid at school with the driest lips. Give him ChapStick, and maybe a kiss.

9. Sneak into your parents' room. Leave their wedding photo on the bed.

10. Make yourself a friendship bracelet. Chevron pattern. (B/c your best friend is yourself.)

11. Go to school without makeup. On Picture Day.

12. Be silent for an entire lunch period. Learn to listen.

13. Watch a black-and-white movie with old people. Tolerate their nostalgia.

14. Play with fire. Get burned.

15. Have a bake sale for the poorest country you can think of.

16. Talk good about someone behind her back. Spread that she's the prettiest girl in school and not a slut at all.

17. Make signs. Read signs.

18. Find your boyfriend's most ticklish spot. Then tickle him in a surprise spot.

19. Don't buy exotic pets. Keep them in zoos.

20. If you see a lonely kid, let him share your iPod earbud.

21. Watch the news. Never forget.

22. Take something lame your brother says and make it the cool new slang.

23. Photoshop your head on to a fat body. Realize that it would be fine.

24. Find someone wearing cast with no signatures. Write a love letter on it.

25. Plant an imaginary garden.

26. Window-shop in a museum.

27. Stand on a street corner and ask people if they've forgotten something. They probably have.

28. Snore.

29. Sweat.

30. Experience.

31 • Dorothy Wu

The Club Chronicles
Part 41: The Legend of the League of Legends
By Dorothy Wu

Dorothy and Jacobim looked around helplessly. They had been ambushed in Secrets Canyon, and they were surrounded by every single baddie they had ever faced.

Dorothy looked up into the eyes of each villain. There was Moo-Dar, the pachydermic ogre alien. Then there was Poseidon, the spiteful Lord of the Sea. And of course there was Mibocaj, Prince Jacobim's evil twin, the one who had tricked Dorothy into entering the Maelstrom of Lost Souls.

All the other notable villains were there, too. Falcontooth, the dolphin-eating man-bird. Dr. Harmfellow, the cunning gnome professor. Not to mention Kragg, the sex dragon who breathed STDs.

Dorothy's forehead started to sweat copious amounts of worry-sweat, but it was too early to panic. She and Jacobim had been in jams like this before. She looked over at the Prince. He always came up with the most clever plans in these situations.

But then the unthinkable happened: Jacobim fainted!

"Zounds!" Dorothy muttered to herself. Now she was really doomed.

At the sight of the unconscious Jacobim, the villains all began to laugh.

"AAAALL BY YOOOURSELF NOOOW, EH, LITTLE GIRRRL?" Poseidon bellowed.

"At long last . . . I will be able to make you my slave!" Moo-Dar cackled.

"RAAAAAHHHHHH!" Kragg roared as he breathed a gigantic cloud of gonorrhea.

Dorothy deftly managed to roll out of the way of Kragg's contagious smoke puff, but still, she was helpless. Although she had escaped from impossible situations before, she had always had Jacobim beside her. Now that she was all alone, she wanted to cry. She thought about just giving up. She had no other choice.

But then—oh, but then!

Twenty streaks of white light shot through the sky, zoomed down into the canyon, and landed on the ground next to Dorothy. As soon as each light beam hit the ground, it reformed itself into a great hero.

Within nanomoments, Dorothy was surrounded by that most revered of fighting forces: the League of Legends. She looked at each famous face—Tylord Belltron, king of the droids. Whit-Neigh, tween centaur. Lady Heather, controller of weather. Madame McKenzie, the renowned seamstress/shapeshifter. Ross Hawkheart, the walking, talking Rubik's Cube. Tiny Tina, the four-inch girl. Neee-shaaa, president *of koalas . . . and oh, oh! so many more.*

They had all come to her aid when she most needed them. This supreme collection of her dearest friends was here to help Dorothy destroy evil once and for all.

Dorothy and the League joined hands in a circle.

"All right, comrades!" Dorothy shouted. "Let us do this . . . together!"

They all shouted that last word to the heavens: "TOGETHER!"

Normally I try not to base my stories too much on real life, but this time I must admit that I have found inspiration in the form of all my new friends. How could I not reimagine the Super Story Samurai as the League of Legends? They are all such wondrous people.

Friends . . . friends . . . friends . . . friends . . . Who ever would have guessed it? Of course I have always considered my fellow classmates and clubmates to be my chums, and Jake remains my true-blue buddy no matter how mopey he might get. But for me to have this many people who care about what I have to say and who laugh at my funnies and who hang out with me after school . . . all I can say is Holy Table.

Did I mention that my friends have started saying "Holy Table"? They have begun to say all of the things that I say. McKenzie even made a T-shirt that has a little stick figure (the stick figure is me) shouting all of my Dorothyisms, words like "Bah!" and "Zounds!" and "GROINS!" McKenzie gave me a copy of the T-shirt too. I must say, I did not ever think I would actually make it onto my own shirt, at least not at such a young age. Now I am like Big Dog, or the serious Latino man with the funny beret. That is one lifelong dream fulfilled, several to go!

(Next lifelong dream: Purchase my own forest and fill it with nothing but cats. Then observe as the cats form their own society. Then craft a best-selling work of nonfiction about my Jane Goodall–like experiences with forest cats. I will call it . . . *Tribal Purr: True Tales of Cat Murder.*)

I must admit, at first it worried me when I would make my friends laugh. I was concerned that they were laughing at me and not with me. But they all reassured me that they were laughing with.

"Yes, you are weird, D. Wu," they said, "but that is the reason we like you."

A big group of about fifteen of us from SSS had lots of swingin' hangouts over spring break. We went ice skating, bowling, movie-ing, ultimate Frisbee-ing—you name the activity! Jake could not attend most of the events because he got sick or something like that, so that was a bummer. But the great news is that my father does not even mind the group of us hanging out so much because so many of my new friends are geniuses. Ross, Tina, and Nisha are all Mathletes and Future Scientists and Engineers of America. I have been able to convince my father that by hanging out with them, I will develop better grades by hypnosis.

Osmosis. Ross keeps reminding me that the word is osmosis.

Today was the raddest—we all went to Laser Quest! There were seventeen of us and we got a bunch of parents to drive us there after school, and it was the funnest experience I have ever had in my life, methinks.

The first thing you do when you go to Laser Quest is you choose a code name. I made mine "Heather." It really confused the heck out of Heather! Everyone thought it was the zaniest thing. I am a trickster. That will be my code name next time: "Trixtor." See how I made it more future-y?

In our mission, I was on the green team. It was such a memorable experience. There was one moment when I cornered Devon and started firing my laser gun at him, but then McKenzie ambushed me—but then Leah ambushed McKenzie! Ambush sandwich! With McKenzie bread! Afterward, we all shared the heartiest laugh over it.

We played arcade games for like, two whole hours. I played Whac-A-Mole and Cruis'n Exotica and several games of Skee-Ball. On the whole I was quite unsuccessful. I only had enough prize tickets to buy two Ring Pops and a skeleton necklace. But on our way out, all the other guys and gals surprised me by giving me—oh, it was the coolest thing—I still cannot believe they did this—a magic set. And it cost, wait for it . . . 500 prize tickets! They had all combined their tickets to buy me something I would love. They said I deserved it for giving them the opportunity to write, for bringing us all together. I said, "Just wait until Mr. Morales gets his hands on us. I may have done a great job thus far, but I think we are finally ready to be his club again."

When I got home that evening, my mother said I had a message waiting for me on the machine. It was Jake. He said it is after school and he asked where I was and if we were going to hang out. Grr. What a dolt. I am fairly certain he knew about the plan to go to Laser Quest. It is just that he chooses not to get involved in these things, that is all.

CHAD2.0nicechad: hey

lilbeachbabe777: hey

CHAD2.0nicechad: sup

lilbeachbabe777: nm u?

CHAD2.0nicechad: nm

lilbeachbabe777: i had such a fun time tonight

CHAD2.0nicechad: yea

CHAD2.0nicechad: it was funny how alex and kristen were like

CHAD2.0nicechad: fighting

CHAD2.0nicechad: all the way thru dinner n the movie

CHAD2.0nicechad: n we were just like

CHAD2.0nicechad: chill

lilbeachbabe777: happy

lilbeachbabe777: yeah

lilbeachbabe777: krist and alex are like the couple from hell

CHAD2.0nicechad: yea

CHAD2.0nicechad: im so glad were not like them lol

lilbeachbabe777: yeah

lilbeachbabe777: i really like us

CHAD2.0nicechad: yea

lilbeachbabe777: about us, actually

CHAD2.0nicechad: ?

CHAD2.0nicechad: somethin wrong?

lilbeachbabe777: well

lilbeachbabe777: i think we should become official

CHAD2.0nicechad: were not official?

lilbeachbabe777: well

lilbeachbabe777: i think we should go public

CHAD2.0nicechad: were not public?

lilbeachbabe777: chad

lilbeachbabe777: i want my parents to know about us

CHAD2.0nicechad: o

CHAD2.0nicechad: o

CHAD2.0nicechad: thats awesome

lilbeachbabe777: yeah

lilbeachbabe777: well i think youre pretty awesome

CHAD2.0nicechad: thanks babe

lilbeachbabe777: lol dont call me babe tho

CHAD2.0nicechad: ok

CHAD2.0nicechad: hannah then

lilbeachbabe777: :)

lilbeachbabe777: i have to go to bed

lilbeachbabe777: i wonder who im gonna think about

lilbeachbabe777: while im dreaming

lilbeachbabe777: ;)

CHAD2.0nicechad: me probly lol

lilbeachbabe777: yes chad

lilbeachbabe777: you

lilbeachbabe777: good night

lilbeachbabe777: <3

CHAD2.0nicechad: night

lilbeachbabe777 has signed off at 11:39 p.m.

CHAD2.0nicechad has signed off at 11:43 p.m.

Miss Emily-Bear,

Sitting here in science and every five seconds I almost fall asleep, and the only thing keeping me awake is looking at Marco across the room . . . omg . . . his skin is so olive-colored and perfect . . . the two of us would have the tannest babies . . .

Be honest with me: I don't think about Marco too much, do I?

Oh—I can't believe I forgot to mention this at nutrition break—HAVE YOU SEEN THE NEW DLS??? <u>What</u> is going on inside Hannah's mind?! So one second she's calling me "Ginger Spawn of Satan" in her blog, and now she's all, "Help the world. Save the trees. Make signs. Read signs." I mean, what is up with that? Who does she think she is, Oprah? Wtf is happening?

Do u believe that Hannah's really changed? I don't. Not for, like, a second.

First off, she's back with Chad. That says a lot. The other day, Marco called Chad a "deek" (LMAO) and he was totes right. Chad Beck is a complete dick, and truly nice girls do not date dicks. It's like how in Grease, Sandy was only allowed to hook up with Danny Zuko once she got that slutty leather jacket and that whorish perm. Because Danny Zuko was a dick.

(Almost as much of a dick as Danny Uribe. Bom chicka wah wah . . . hahahahahahah . . . I don't know why, but that's still hilarious. . . .)

And, I mean, Hannah just doesn't seem like she's changed. Like, I still see the way she looks at me during lunch, with those

255

judgy eyes of hers. I still see how she whispers stuff to Chad and then the two of them laugh. This one time, I swear they were making fun of Marco. Eff them. Eff them and eff her so hard.

I srsly doubt that Hannah has become a new person. A catty tiger can't change its nasty stripes. U can write something online, yeah, whatever, but u have to back it up in real life.

Wowww, I did not think this would turn into such a Hannah rant! Lo siento, girl! Next note I write, I owe u like a 5,000 word ode about how bangin' your butt looks in your new jeans! Even Marco texted me to say u look hot. (See? He's NOT. GAY.)

I will always love u,
Jamie Boo

32 • Jake Schwartz

Tuesday, April 27

Hannah had her bat mitzvah two years ago. The theme of it was basically THE WORLD REVOLVES AROUND HANNAH SCHWARTZ. It was so big and expensive and out of control. MTV had a film crew there. My dad had a Ferris wheel and a go-kart racetrack installed in our backyard. Snoop Dogg serenaded Hannah, and Maya Angelou wrote her a special poem about womanhood. Dad commissioned this Lego artist to make a gigantic Lego sculpture of Hannah in her party dress, and when Hannah said it was ugly and that she hated the way her skin looked all yellow, we didn't even display the sculpture at the party.

Lego Hannah aside, my sister loved that night. She was as happy as I've ever seen anyone ever. She smiled and giggled and hugged people constantly, she rapped along with Snoop and cried at Maya's poem, she had like, twenty girls following her around at all times, and even if her skin wasn't Lego yellow, it sure was glowing.

I've been thinking about Hannah's bat mitzvah more and more as my big day approaches. Somehow, a little over a month from now, according to Jewish tradition, in order for me to become a man, a giant party just like Hannah's must be thrown in my honor.

But I don't want what Hannah got. I don't want my dad to invite any of the pro athletes or Victoria's Secret models he keeps on suggesting. I don't want him bringing his hundreds of large-headed and shiny-faced Hollywood friends who will undoubtedly have to come purely as favors to him. I don't want anyone. I don't even really want any kids my age to be there. They'll just party in spite of me, not because of me. They'll make fun of whatever I say in my "Today I am a man" speech. And when I chant Torah at the ceremony, they'll make fun of my high voice. They'll call it gay.

Obviously Hannah will have to be there, and I guess she can bring Chad, but I feel kind of strange about other kids who might maybe come. I definitely feel that way about Danny. Man, I even feel that way about Dorothy.

I wish I could just fast-forward to the day after June 5th. Or maybe, when the big day comes, I could just stay inside in my room, under the covers, where my stuffed animals can protect me. Or maybe I could go up to my parents and the rabbi right now and say, "You know what, guys? Thanks, but no thanks, I'm fine with never being a man."

I don't want to do this. I'm not ready. I don't want to be celebrated. I guess I'd like a Lego version of me, but that's it.

I've been thinking about all this a lot because of what happened today. The thing that really got me thinking about Hannah's bat mitzvah was watching the way she interacted with her friends at lunch.

Wait. That sounds weird. Let me explain.

I didn't want to go to Super Story Samurai. I just didn't

feel like it. In third period this morning, Dorothy told me about this hot new lesson plan she'd just designed—*Write a story about yourself in which you are a mythical beast of the opposite sex*—and I guess it sounded neat and everything, but after fourth, I decided not to meet her and the others at the Dumpsters.

I'm happy for Dorothy. I really am. She has what she always wanted: people who like her. I don't think she ever even had a friend before me, and now she's got a whole crew of cool, interesting, nice people. I'm proud of her.

I do think it's curious that I wasn't invited to laser tag with everyone else. I don't think they excluded me or anything, it wasn't like that. But they didn't remember me, either.

It's just funny. Super Story Samurai was supposed to be mine and Dorothy's. We designed the lesson plans together and everything, and I was there for her at the beginning, when it was just a tiny club with only three people, and I stuck by her, because that's what a good friend does. And then it got popular, which, yeah, is cool, and then all of a sudden it became the D. Wu Show, and again, that's fine. I just think it's interesting. I was the first one to really notice D. Wu—I was the guy who saw how kooky and entertaining she is, and what a great friend she can be, all that stuff—and now I'm the only one out of the entire club who wasn't invited to laser tag. It's just funny.

But seriously, I'm proud of Dorothy. For me, it's the same situation as when Danny got cool friends. I didn't stand in his way or demand he stay true to me or whatever. I just let him be cool. It's the least I can do.

So, no, I didn't go to Super Story Samurai at lunch today, but it wasn't a big deal.

I don't know why I did what I did instead, but I did it. I ate lunch on the blacktop.

I just sort of wandered there. I left fourth period without any sort of plan—except for making sure that Dorothy didn't see me—and I walked around the campus for a while. Before long, I ended up on the blacktop. I've never spent much time there before. A different kind of crowd tends to congregate on the blacktop. A cool and attractive crowd. A Facebook-obsessed, water polo–playing, Leadership sweatshirt–wearing, and sometimes, I think, alcohol-drinking crowd. My sister's crowd. Not exactly my kind of people. I guess I was curious to see what they were like.

My sister truly is the queen of her friends. It was fascinating, watching her. Watching everybody else watch her. None of her friends laughed at a joke until she laughed first, and if she rolled her eyes at a joke, then the laughter stopped immediately. All kinds of girls lined up before her, waiting to be complimented, or at least spoken to.

I know the feeling, girls. Hannah hasn't talked to me in over two months.

She looked so happy. That's what reminded me of her bat mitzvah day, just seeing that expression of sheer joy on her face as she made a sassy remark to put down one of her friends, or as she got a cheek kiss from Chad, or, better yet, a jealous look from another girl. She seemed totally in her element. I know Hannah's been making a big thing lately of being all kind and empathetic, what with her new humanitarian blog and stuff, but part of me thinks she'll always love being the queen most of all.

It's insane to me that the two of us are related, that we share the same genetic makeup. Watching her on the blacktop today, watching her be the absolute center of the coolest possible attention, I didn't exactly see myself.

She wasn't the only person I watched, either.

Sitting up against the fence, where Hannah's friends couldn't quite see me, I also had a view of the basketball courts. This gave me a view of a different crowd.

I didn't enjoy this other view.

Whoever that was, hanging out with the Raiders, wearing a humongous black T-shirt and with those horrible cuts still all over his face, it did not look like Danny to me. Danny wouldn't stand the way that guy was standing. His hand gestures are different from that guy's. And Danny wouldn't shave his head. Danny has hair. Danny has cool hair that he likes to gel and spike. Danny loves his cool hair. That wasn't Danny out there on the courts, and whoever it was, I wasn't going to watch him thugging out with his criminal friends.

I just have to bring myself to not care about Danny. I mean, he doesn't care about me. So yeah, I got curious, and yeah, I looked across the fence, but I didn't look at Danny and those guys for more than two seconds. Why the hell would I?

By this point, I didn't much feel like watching Hannah and her friends anymore, either. And I definitely didn't want to think about my bar mitzvah. And I definitely definitely didn't want to think about what the Super Story Samurai were up to. So I just focused on my food.

My mom made me a really awesome PB & J today, and she packed my favorite flavor of Capri Sun—Surfer Cooler—to go along with it. Not to mention, a surprise bag of Peach Rings. And a note.

To Jake,
As long as I'm living, my baby you'll be.
XOXO
Mom
P.S. Share the candy with your friends!

I'm glad no one was with me to see the note. That would have been embarrassing.

The PB&J had the crusts cut off. Classic. The Capri Sun really hit the spot, too. And the Peach Rings tasted delicious. I haven't gotten to enjoy a full bag in a while.

It was a good lunch.

33 • Dorothy Wu

Monday, May 3

I have the most frabjous news. It is not to be believed.

I have finally—*finally*—FINALLY convinced Ruben Apollo Morales to assume the position that is rightfully his: Supreme Overlord of the Super Story Samurai!

He is going to be our writing teacher again! WA-WA-WA-WAAAAAHOOOOOOOOOO!!!!!!!!!!

Each day he found a new way of saying nay. At first he said he was too busy. Then he started saying that the club's time has passed, and that it is getting to be the end of the year anyway, so we should move on to other things. Then he went back to too busy. Then he said that he wanted to come back, but that he was worried about what that scoundrel Greene might do to him. (He did not say scoundrel, I said scoundrel. But he meant scoundrel.)

But then today at nutrition break—wonder of wonders, miracle of miracles—Mr. Morales agreed to return! He said he had thought much of the matter over the weekend, and then he thanked me and he said that I was right. He said he should do what he wants to do. He said that starting tomorrow, we can have the club in his room at lunch every single day for the rest of the year. And he said that he has learned much from me, Dorothy Wu. Heart flutter!

When I reported the news to the gang today at the

Dumpsters, they were all much excited. I spent most of lunchtime's forty-five minutes regaling them with stories of Morales's greatest moments.

Right in the middle of one of our biggest group laughs of the whole lunch period, I noticed that Jake was not there. Jake's absence has actually been a usual occurrence over the last many lunches, but I decided that he needed to know the news about Morales right now, and so I left the group early. I ran off without saying anything. "Oh well," I bet they all said. "That is just D. Wu being D. Wu."

Jake proved exceedingly difficult to locate. He is most definitely back in his Waldo phase. At first I thought he might be somewhere where he could be lonely and feel bad about himself, like the library. So I checked there as well as the portable buildings and Angel's Tree. But, alas, he was nowhere to be found.

On my walk back to the Dumpsters, a scant five minutes before the bell rang, I suddenly spotted Jake in the most unlikely of places: on the blacktop, where the populars eat. And I do not mean populars as in people who have a higher-than-average amount of friends like me. I mean popular like so popular that the whole entire school knows who you are. Popular like King Chad Beck. Popular like Queen Hannah Schwartz. Popular like the mascot.

Jake was not sitting amongst a group of the social elite. He does not even like those people. He was sitting up against a fence, by himself, just sort of watching them all. I actually thought he looked quite weird, almost disturbing. This is coming from someone who loves watching people!

It was the look on his face. He looked so downtrodden, as if he would never be happy again, like a cat who has just been bathed. In human terms, I would say he was "brooding," like the male protagonist in a Jane Austen novel. Or Eeyore.

Only I, the ever-loveable D. Wu, could cheer him up! I ran up to the fence, plopped down on the ground next to him, and started making a series of strange and cute sounds.

"Ehh ehh! Ehh ehh oh ehh ehh! Ehh ahh ehh ehh ehh!"

"Dorothy, what are you doing?" he said.

I held up my palms in a playful manner and I shouted, "I am communicating with you via echolocation!" I thought that by invoking the memory of the dolphins, which is quite possibly mine and Jake's happiest memory together, that I could make him feel better.

"Why are you doing that? What are you saying?"

"It is a really great message!" I told him. "But you have to translate it!"

He looked at me like, "Are you for serious?"

"Ehh ehh ehh! Oh oh ehh ehh ehh!" I cried.

This is probably when some people started to look over at us. I do not know. I was very focused on Jake.

"Just tell me."

"Ehh ehh ehh! Oh ehh ehh oh ehh!"

"Dorothy, you look retarded."

I wanted to scold him for using such a word, but I knew that the best way to get him to stop being cross with me was to just tell him.

"Ohhh, all right, Doctor Cornelius Moodypants! Fine, fine. Here is the news. Ready for it? Ready? Drumroll . . . drumroll . . . Mr. Morales . . . is . . . coming back to teach us!"

"Cool," Jake said.

"Aaaaaaand . . . ?" I replied.

"I don't know," he said. "Good for you."

"Aaaaaaand . . . ?" I replied.

"Well, I'm not gonna thank you," he said. He half rolled his eyes as he said it.

All right, that made me a little mad. If I were the Hulk, this is where my toes would have started turning green.

"You know, Jake, it is not all about you all of the time."

"I could say the same for you."

Now my whole lower body was the shade of limeade.

"You could at least *try* acting like a friend sometimes."

"You've got friends to spare."

Now my whole torso was green with green rage. This is also, if I were the Hulk, when my rippling muscles would have started to emerge, when my shirt would have ripped.

"Jacobim," I said. I did not mean to say it.

"Who's Jacobim?" he interrupted. "What does that even mean?"

"Nothing. Jacobim means nothing."

"Is that supposed to be me?"

"No, it is—"

"Is that like, from one of your stupid stories?"

No, he did not say, he did not just say, I could not believe he said—

I had to unleash the beast.

I grabbed his shoulders and I clenched them hard and I brought my face his into his personal space. But I was not going in for an aggressive kiss, as it may have appeared. I was going in for the kill.

"JACOB EMANUEL SCHWARTZ!" I screamed so loud that the ladies in the office could hear me, even without their hearing aids. "YOU ARE PATHETIC AND EVERYONE IN THIS ENTIRE SCHOOL KNOWS IT. YOU ARE A LOSER, YOU ARE NOT CUTE, AND IN MY OPINION—YOU ARE A LITTLE GIRL! I HATE YOU!"

I screamed with so much fury that I think some saliva flew out of my mouth and hit him in the face. But I did not stop to check. I stood up, I turned around, and, with everyone still watching me, I took myself to fifth period.

adm u heard right?
lil bit. heard the worst stuff
well like it couldve maybe been worse
did n e of ours get caught?
no but one of theirs
ADM wut if G ever got caught?
that cant happen
none of ours got hurt or nothing, ya? danny n gordo n all them?
theyre fine i think
wut abt los bebes
theyre not THAT little
theyre SO little! they become bangers b4 theyre like 10
well theyre all fine too i think
k
ya
thats good
ya
¿ay luz?
¿ya chicle?
te amo
te amo también

34 • Danny Uribe

Friday, May 7

Six months ago it was my birthday. I can still remember Jake waking me up all early and me wanting to punch him in the face. I remember going to the set, seeing what it's like to make a movie. That's also like, the day I got real close to Hannah. Man, feels like so long ago. I've changed so much since then.

It's funny how I can remember all kinds of stuff from months ago, even though I'm so different now compared to how I was. But, like, I can't remember any of the stuff I was supposed to learn at school today. They don't teach the Mexicans nothing.

I do remember what happened after school today, though. Can't forget something like your first brawl.

Me and Guillermo and the other guys had been planning it for a while, ever since spring break. It was meant to mostly be a recruiting trip, but we were doing it at Truman Elementary, right near where the Destroyers hang out. So we knew it was gonna turn into something else.

We all left right when school got out. It was a serious crew. We ran like, twelve deep. The walk over to Truman was badass. I imagined we were all walking in slow-mo and like some dope heavy metal or sick rap was playing. It was

269

so tight, all of us walking in a group, knowing what we were about to do. Everyone who saw us walking knew who we were.

We got to the fence in the back of the school. We saw the kids we were there to see. I was surprised by how little they looked. I don't believe I looked like them a year ago. There was like ten or eleven of them and also this random other girl. As soon as we got there, she ran off. Guillermo said that would happen.

We took a few steps up to the fence.

"Guillermo," one of the little kids said. He was wearing a big silver cross that looked pretty thug, but his hair was all gelled like his mom did it. He pointed at me. "Who's this fool?"

"This is the *cholo* I was telling you about," Guillermo said. "The one who owns everybody at ball."

"Señor Clutch?" another one said, looking at me. He was real short, like four feet tall, and kinda chubby. Fat baby cheeks. "Is it true you dropped forty points on Viejo?"

I didn't know what to say. I didn't want to brag about myself to these kids. They're so little, I thought, they'd believe anything I said.

"Damn right it's true," Guillermo said. "And he was MVP of the city play-offs. If the refs hadn't been so messed up, and if our coach wasn't such a dumbass, we would've been champs."

The kids all looked impressed. I have to say it made me feel pretty tight.

"And now," Guillermo added. "Now he's one of us. He's part of the family. So if you all wanna roll over to our hood sometime, maybe he could teach you some moves. You know what? Matter of fact, we just headin' there right now."

I felt a little weird during all this. Yeah, it was cool that Guillermo had already told them all about me, but wasn't it maybe kinda messed up for him to use my rep to try and get them to join with the Raiders? These were little kids, right? Babies, right?

But then I had to remind myself: I didn't feel like a baby when I was their age. And I looked at them again. They were all standing there, heads up, eyes narrow. They were all listening, but none of them was smiling. They had the look.

"We know you haven't decided if you're gonna be Raiders or Destroyers," Guillermo said. "And that's fine. Y'all are free agents. But we just want to help you make up your minds. Once you see what we can do, you'll see why you got to be one of us."

He reached his hand into his pocket. I thought he was gonna pull something out, but he just left his hand in there.

Then I noticed something in the distance. It was the random little girl who had just run away, and she was coming back. She was walking toward us, and behind her there was a crew of maybe like, fifteen *cholos* in blue and white. They were walking with the same swag as us. Guillermo told the sixth graders to get behind the fence. He said watch what we're about to do.

All part of his plan.

The Destroyers came up to like, ten feet away from us.

Then one walked in closer. Guillermo went up to him.

"Thought we told you *putas* to stay away from here," the guy said. He had a super fresh Dodgers cap and messed-up teeth. Guillermo's told me about this *cholo*. His name is Arturo. The two of them went to kindergarten together. I guess Arturo's teeth are so janked because Guillermo punched him hard in the mouth when they were little. I don't know if I believe that, though. There are a lot of stories about Guillermo. They can't all be true. I don't think they can all be true. I mean, some of them are real bad.

"This is our turf," Guillermo said all up in Arturo's face. He wasn't playing games. "You leave, or we stomp your asses."

"Naw. You can't just come up in here, man."

"Why not? These kids want to join up with us."

"They're Destroyers by blood."

"Why don't you ask them what they are?"

"Ask me."

Guillermo smiled. He took his hand out of his pocket. "You sure you want this?"

"Whatever, man, yeah. Do what you do. We'll take you."

Then, without giving any warning, Guillermo went. He threw his fist mad hard into Arturo's stomach with one hand and slapped hard across Arturo's face with the other. Then the Destroyers were running right at us, and then we were running right at them.

We all split up into smaller matchups. The first guy I ran up to was probably high school age. He was tall and he had a full mustache. But he also looked like a puss. I knew I could take him. I dove at him hard and tackled him to the ground, where I pinned him down and gave him two hard punches right in the cheek. Then another one in his eye. That's how the Raiders do it.

I jumped up and I saw that Chuy was having some trouble with Juan Salcido. Juan's in a couple classes with me and I actually know him better than Chuy, but Chuy's my brother and I had to defend my brother. I ran up behind Juan when he wasn't looking, and then when Chuy charged at him, Juan turned around to run away—only he ran right into me. I grabbed on to his shirt with my hands and flung him down to the ground, where Chuy took over. Two quick kicks to the chest and Juan wasn't gonna get up.

I'm not gonna lie. During all this, I felt good. I was just going up to fools, whaling on them, then going for the next target. It's the same feeling I get when I'm in the middle of a basketball game and I can't miss.

The rest of our guys weren't doing quite as good as me, but we were hanging tough. It was an even fight. I got a surprise when right after I knocked the fattest Destroyer to the ground, I felt a punch on my back. Not a hard one, it didn't hurt. It was kind of low on my back, too. I turned around and I saw one of the sixth graders. It was one of the kids we were trying to recruit. Then I looked around the whole scene. All the little kids were fighting. Half of them for us, half of them for the Destroyers. They were doing their thing. They were in the zone too.

It was like that for a few more minutes. Crazy. Just going after anyone wearing blue, or anyone who was going after any of us. Even the little kids. I sort of forgot what even started the fight in the first place, but you can't stop when you're in the middle of a fight, you know?

Then, right away, everyone did just stop. At first I thought, Oh no. The cops.

But I didn't hear sirens or see no one running away. Everyone was looking a little ways away from us, over near the trash cans at the end of the fence. What were they looking at?

Guillermo. He had his arms wrapped tight around the sixth grader with the silver cross. The little kid was squirming. Then Guillermo pulled something brown from his pocket. I couldn't tell what it was. I had an idea, though. Real quick he pressed a button on the thing and there was a flash of silver and he brought it up damn close to the little kid's throat, an inch away. And all of a sudden it got real, real quiet.

"All right, come on Guillermo, don't mess around!" Arturo shouted.

"There's little kids here!" shouted another Destroyer. "No weapons!"

Guillermo stared them down. No talking, just staring. He looked down the line at what seemed like every one of the Destroyers. Then he waited some more. He smiled again.

Then out of nowhere, he slapped the silver cross kid mad hard against the face with his hand that wasn't holding the knife. The kid started to sniffle. Mad tears started to go down his face, like tears that he couldn't control. Then, finally, Guillermo talked.

"Give them to us, Arturo," he said. He said it real smooth, like he had it practiced. "Surrender this turf, and leave these kids to us. They're ours, all right? They're ours. And don't try to play games with us. Don't make one of them a spy or something like that."

Guillermo gave a hard look to all the other Destroyers. Then turned back to Arturo. Then he said his next thing.

"You know what happened last time you sent us a snitch."

Arturo's eyes got big.

"You remember what we did when we found out he was ratting on us, ratting on his homies."

I thought there was no way Guillermo was gonna say what he said next. He's my friend. You don't expect your friends to say certain stuff, because they're your friends. Even when you've heard bad rumors. But I guess I don't know Guillermo as well as I thought. Not based on what he said to Arturo.

"You remember Angel."

Angel. Angel Calderon, the kid who was found stabbed to death on the Westside last year. My cousins knew him pretty good. He would've been in eighth grade this year.

I didn't want to think about what Guillermo just said, what he meant by it. There wasn't time to think anyway. I had to be ready. Couldn't let a thing like Angel happen again.

Guillermo and Arturo kept staring at each other. Guillermo inched the knife closer to the little kid's neck. Now it was pressing up against him, pressing hard, starting to make a little cut. There was some blood, like the kid's face was leaking red. No one else moved. No one else made a sound. My heart was the one thing I could hear. It was pounding. It hurt.

After all of us stood there for I don't know how long, I suddenly saw that same little girl from before running toward us all crazy. She was screaming.

"THE COPS ARE COMING! THE COPS ARE COMING! TURO, I CALLED THE COPS! THEY'RE COMING!"

Five seconds later, the area was empty. We all cleared completely, before the police had time to show up. I don't know, maybe one person got caught. One of the Destroyers. Serves that fool right, whoever he is.

Some of the little kids ran with us, some with the Destroyers. About half and half. Maybe that's the way it should have been the whole time.

That night me and the guys hung out at at Javy and Carlos's. We welcomed the new recruits to the family. We gave the sixth graders their first sips of beer, and we all had a good time, laughing and telling them crazy stories. Those kids are so scared about getting jumped-in. We went on for a long time about how hard we're gonna whup them. So funny.

It was as tight as a night can get. Remembering things about the fight, bragging about our best-ever hookups, giving all the new recruits wack nicknames. Like this one new kid's pants fell down in the fight so we called him "Buttcrack." Stuff like that. We had the best night. All those guys, it's not fair to just call them gangsters and leave it at that. They're my best friends. They're the reason I'm a Raider for life. They're my *hermanos*.

Plus, there's this. When I got home late tonight, I got one more reason that reminded me why I'm a Raider. As I was sneaking into my room close to midnight, I heard some high-pitched noises coming from the Schwartz's pool. I walked over to see what the sound was.

It was Hannah. I guess she heated the pool up or something, like we used to back in the day. It was all steaming, like a giant Jacuzzi. She was laughing real hard in there, so hard it sounded kinda like snorts. She was in her red string bikini. She was laughing, splashing around with that guy Chad who won King at the dance. The same fool who broke her heart by saying such mean stuff about her at the beginning of the year.

I watched them swim. I watched her float over to him and whisper something in his ear. Then I watched them make out.

Girls are whores. They will drive you crazy, lie to you, leave you just like that. But you've always got your boys.

I lost a friend this year.

He didn't move. He didn't go to a new school. He didn't die.

He joined a gang.

I understand why someone would want to join a gang. I do. Gangs give you friends. They give you power. I want those things too. We all do. Wanting those things doesn't make you a bad person.

I even get why gangs make bad stuff seem okay. When you're with your friends, and when you're having fun, you feel like you can get away with anything. Doing drugs doesn't feel as bad. Selling them doesn't feel as bad. Saying mean things about people seems fine. Even hurting people. It all feels more okay. You're with your friends.

That's the thing, though. You're not with your real friends. Those are the people you left behind when you got jumped-in.

Your real friends are the people who really have your back. They're the ones telling you that you can't go on living like this. You could get caught. You could go to juvie, maybe someday jail. You could do something truly wrong. You could really hurt someone. You could get really hurt.

But you don't care. You've got your *familia* now, and you don't care about anyone else. You can be as selfish and as hurtful and as evil as you want, and the rest of us just have to take it.

But not me.

I lost a friend, yeah, but I'm not losing this war. Those of us who have been hurt by the existence of gangs, we can't just accept it. We have to stand together. Comment to this post. Write about your experiences of friends and family members that you've lost. Share your stories. Send this post to all the gangsters you know. Help them see the light.

We can do it. We can fight the power of gangs.

HANNAH OUT.

---

alexsgurlie805
posted May 13 at 8:22 p.m.

like x 1000000. u said it hannah. gangs r the WORST!!!!!
the only way we can stop them is thru people like you. your making such a difference! you inspire me.

Reply

QueenHannahDLS
posted May 13 at 8:26 p.m.

Thanks, Krist. Just trying to do my part.

Reply

MargotMackintosh
posted May 13 at 8:45 p.m.

Hi Hannah,

This is Margot Mackintosh—Jamie's mom. Based on some of the things my daughter has said, I was expecting something different from your blog. Yet what you've written here is thoughtful and moving. I plan on taking your message to this month's PTA meeting.

You should be very proud of yourself.
—Margot M. (Jamie's mom)

Reply

QueenHannahDLS
posted May 13 at 8:49 p.m.

Thank you so much, Mrs. Mackintosh. I'm going to keep writing and fighting.

Reply

---

iluvLUZi
posted May 13 at 9:01 p.m.

we kno gangs do bad things. we dont need u to save the world for us.

Reply

QueenHannahDLS
posted May 13 at 9:08 p.m.

Thank you for your comment, Luz.
You say: "we dont need u to save the world for us."
I say: why can't we try?

Reply

---

lilbeachbabe777: hey honey

CHAD2.0nicechad: honey bunch

CHAD2.0nicechad: honey bunches of oats

CHAD2.0nicechad: lol

lilbeachbabe777: lol yeah

lilbeachbabe777: whats ^?

CHAD2.0nicechad: nm

CHAD2.0nicechad: well idk

CHAD2.0nicechad: im kinda pissed

lilbeachbabe777: why?

CHAD2.0nicechad: ok like

CHAD2.0nicechad: me al and avery had this plan 4 after school

CHAD2.0nicechad: we were gon walk to BV and chill there

CHAD2.0nicechad: maybe toss the disc around

CHAD2.0nicechad: whatever

CHAD2.0nicechad: but when we got there

CHAD2.0nicechad: like there were all these mexicans

lilbeachbabe777: the raiders?

CHAD2.0nicechad: ya

CHAD2.0nicechad: n that one dude danny

CHAD2.0nicechad: u no the dude that lives at ur house?

lilbeachbabe777: yes chad, i know danny

CHAD2.0nicechad: he just gets up in our face and hes like get off our turf

CHAD2.0nicechad: n i kinda wanted to kick his ass for like

CHAD2.0nicechad: bein disrespectful

CHAD2.0nicechad: but we bounced

CHAD2.0nicechad: cuz i was all like

CHAD2.0nicechad: i dont wanna go messin around with those dudes

CHAD2.0nicechad: not with a bunch of wetbacks

lilbeachbabe777: chad

lilbeachbabe777: dont use that word

CHAD2.0nicechad: wetback?

CHAD2.0nicechad: why

CHAD2.0nicechad: wetback

CHAD2.0nicechad: theyre just a bunch of bangers

CHAD2.0nicechad: they were messed up to us

CHAD2.0nicechad: theyre like that to everyone

lilbeachbabe777: yeah but still

lilbeachbabe777: just cause you dont like them doesnt mean you call them that

CHAD2.0nicechad: but thats what they are

CHAD2.0nicechad: u dont like them either

CHAD2.0nicechad: i saw ur little blog thing

CHAD2.0nicechad: u no wat wetback means right?

lilbeachbabe777: chad

lilbeachbabe777: just plz stop

CHAD2.0nicechad: why

CHAD2.0nicechad: why babe?

CHAD2.0nicechad: wetback

lilbeachbabe777: good night chad

lilbeachbabe777 has signed off at 7:21 p.m.

CHAD2.0nicechad has signed off at 7:39 p.m.

35 • Jake Schwartz

Sunday, May 23

Putting together your own bar mitzvah slide show is a pretty strange process. I'm not sure whether I recommend it.

I'm an idiot, first of all. My parents told me that they would go ahead and hire someone to make a great video for me. My dad was all, "Should I give Robert a ring? You know, Robert . . . *Zemeckis?*" But I insisted—no, I *demanded* to make the thing myself. I thought that by putting together my own slide show, that I could, I don't know, it just felt like something I should do. I thought that maybe I'd get . . . something out of it?

All I've learned is what a loser I am.

Danny's in like, every picture. Every single freaking one. Well, not the photos that have been taken this year, obviously, but there haven't been very many taken this year. Who wants awkward pictures of themselves in seventh grade? Even if the photos don't look all that different from pics of me in fourth grade.

It's going to be so brutal, having to sit there while everyone watches this entire thing, all fourteen minutes and twenty-two seconds of it. Fourteen minutes and twenty-two seconds of CELEBRATING JAKE SCHWARTZ'S MANHOOD. They'll probably all hate my song choices, too.

"Elton John? What are you, gay?"

"Beatles? What are you, a walking cliché?"

"'Memory' from *Cats*? What are you, a walking gay cliché?"

(Hmm. Maybe my imaginary bullies make a good point with that last one.)

It's going to be so embarrassing seeing all the pictures one after another. Only my mom will enjoy it, and that's because she took most of the shots, and because her favorite pastime is kvelling at stuff that pains me. And . . . well, okay, it's not like I hate the memories themselves. I do actually like a bunch of the photos when they're on their own. I like them a lot. I mean, I did pick them out.

The first picture in the slide show is probably my favorite picture of me ever. It's from when I was seven, which is the year I met Danny, and it's this picture of us at our second-grade Thanksgiving celebration. He's wearing like a little construction paper Pilgrim hat and I've got this pretend head-dress thing on. We're shaking hands just like they teach you the Pilgrims and Indians did. Oh, and both of our faces are absolutely covered in gravy. Hilarious.

Then, right when the song switches from "Forever Young" to "I Want to Break Free," there's another really really awesome pic. It's from Splash Mountain at Disneyland. It's one of those pictures they take of you right at the end, just as you're dropping down the waterfall. I remember I was eight and I was too chicken to go on the ride at first, and I got so scared and embarrassed that I started crying, but then Danny went on and he loved it so much that he made me go on it with him right after, and the man operating the ride had seen me crying before so he let us go straight to the front of the line, no questions asked.

In the picture, I have both of my hands clutching my hair so hard because obviously I was freaked out of my mind, you know? But I've got this look of pure exhilaration on my face because I was so happy that I had been brave enough to go on the ride. And Danny just looks totally cool—he's wearing sunglasses and one of those little Goofy hats that they sell, the ones with the ears. Hannah's not in the picture since she was on the teacups with my mom.

Oh, dude, and I couldn't forget to include the picture of us on the fifth-grade class trip to D.C. It's the craziest. It's the two of us wading through the freaking Reflecting Pool, for crying out loud. I think that's like a federal offense, but both of us jumped in anyway, just long enough for the picture, and it was worth it because it's such a sweet shot. Danny's splashing water on me and I have this look on my face like I'm about to tackle him into the pool. Of course I didn't do that because I didn't want to like, make Zombie Martin Luther King, Jr. mad or something, but man. What a day.

Oh, and I think I forgot what my actual favorite picture is. It's from Halloween three years ago, when me and Danny dressed up as each other. He's wearing my standard gray hoodie and a ridiculous afro wig, and I'm wearing one of those little white polos that Danny's mom used to always make him wear in elementary school, back before he started wearing silver and black 24/7. My hair is all slicked down in the picture too, because Danny used to have hair.

So all the way up through this past summer, yeah, there's just classic photo after classic photo. Crap—I almost forgot to mention the shot of us from the Europe trip where we're pretending to hold up the Leaning Tower of Pisa with our butts! And then there's us holding up the Eiffel Tower with our butts, and Tower of London butts, and even Stonehenge butts. There were going to be so many other butts photos too. We had all these ideas.

And then seventh grade happened.

I guess this whole past year, I've done a pretty good job of blocking out all the good times. I've basically made myself believe that I've always been a loser, that being a loner is just like normal for me. It can be easier to think that way. For sure. When a friend leaves me, I can just try and pretend like they didn't mean that much to me. It helps numb the pain.

But it's fake. I can't pretend like Disneyland and the Reflecting Pool and the Butt Towers and all that stuff never happened. And Danny shouldn't be able to, either. Just because he hasn't spoken to me since St. Patrick's Day, the day all of his friends made me eat garbage, doesn't mean that our connection should be broken forever. Just because he wants to hang out with his gangbanging crew more than me doesn't mean that he should be able to betray his roots. It's not right. I'm his family.

I don't know. I guess right now I'm just hoping that at the end of my bar mitzvah, when I have to give my speech, that

Danny will listen. I don't know when else he's going to hear me talk. He needs to hear what I have to say.

I don't think I'm a very superstitious person, but I haven't been able to stop myself from wishing on stuff lately. I've been blowing eyelashes and dandelion spores. I've been holding my breath in tunnels and at 11:11. I've been throwing pennies in fountains and salt over my shoulder. And I've got birthday candles coming up, so that's a big one.

I know that what I'm birthday-wishing for is obvious, but I can't say it, because I need for it to come true. I'm willing to forgive everything that's happened. I just want my wish.

And I know saying that makes me sound like a lame little kid, and I don't care, because that's what I am. I need this wish.

36 • Hannah Schwartz

Thursday, May 27

It was last Saturday night. We walked all the way to the edge of the pier. The movie had been pretty funny, and definitely very romantic. It was starting to get dark. I gazed up at the sky. I could see Venus and the North Star and a few others that my brother can name. It was chilly so Chad gave me his jacket. So comfy.

I held both of Chad's hands in mine. I looked up into his green-blue eyes. I knew that this was the right moment.

I took a deep breath. I exhaled.

"We have to end this."

He definitely did not believe me at first. "Don't eff with me," he said, only he didn't say "eff."

I said, "Chad, I'm not the kind of person who effs with people," and I did in fact say "eff." I asked him if he wanted the full explanation. He said yeah.

So I told Chad straight up that, yeah, it's over. And it's all his fault. Somehow I was too dumb to see it before, but I realized it in the last few days: he sucks. I'm so over his constant need for "guy time." I've had enough of having to be the one who calls, of having to organize every hang-out, of having to ensure that not every hang-out is a hookup. Most of all, I cannot stand his stupidly simpleminded view of looking at the world. Not everyone's a fag. Not everyone's a wetback. Not everyone's a slut. And like, even if he thinks that someone is one of those things, who cares? Those labels are cruel and they aren't important. Sort of like my now-ex-boyfriend.

Chad tried to fight it for a few minutes, but he didn't last long. He knows he's a horrible companion. He knows he's got miles to go before I can think of him as being anywhere close to an okay person. He may be good at the big gestures, and, fine, I guess his eyes and his butt aren't too shabby. But still. There's more to life than eyes and butt.

So I dumped the chump. I busted his heart and hopefully his balls, and now I'm just not going to worry about boys for a very long time.

Number two on my list of things to do: complete.

I already got number one checked off when I made that latest DLS post. It was something that had been in my heart for a long time. Now the world knows how I feel about gangs. I think the world agrees, too. Eighty-four commenters can't be wrong.

Today, it was time for the third and most important thing that I had to do: the apology.

No, I didn't apologize to Danny. He's doing just fine, thank you. He's rolling with his homies and he's happy being a delinquent, and even if I did say sorry to him, he wouldn't listen to me, so there's no point.

Not Danny. I had to apologize to someone who actually deserves it. Someone I've genuinely hurt.

I had to apologize to my brother.

I know it's taken me beyond forever to even realize that this was something I had to do, but it is. And it was so hard to get up the courage to walk into his room and admit that I was wrong—because, come on, I'm rarely wrong. But I had to.

Jake was practicing his Torah portion when I walked up to his door. I didn't want to disturb him, so I stood outside for a few minutes and waited for him to finish.

He actually sounded really good. Some of the notes he was reaching . . . there's no way that I went that high at my bat mitzvah, and I'm a girl. His vocal range is just . . . like, he could totally be a little choirboy or a member of the Jackson 5 if he wanted to. Not that anyone wants to be either of those things, but whatever. That still qualifies as a compliment, right?

Jake's been working so, so hard on all his bar mitzvah stuff. I kind of want to tell him that it's not that big a deal. I mean, you get the money no matter how good you are. But I shouldn't get in his way. If working this hard makes him happy, then he should stay in his room and work on stuff by himself all the time.

When he finished with his chanting, I knocked softly on the door.

"Not now, Mom!" he shouted.

"It's Hannah."

He didn't say anything to that, so I walked in.

I didn't realize it until I entered, but it was the first time I'd been back in Jake's room since that one night. Everything was exactly the same. Jake's room hasn't changed in like, six years. There are still hundreds of bobblehead dolls all awkwardly staring at you from his desk. There's still the Nerf basketball hoop that him and Danny used to play on for like entire summers. There's still the gigantic world map with thumbtacks in all the places he wants to visit. (Iceland? Sri Lanka? Easter Island? Honestly, who is my brother?)

I kept looking around his room for a little while. I mean, once I walked in, I realized that I had no idea how to say what I wanted to say. When it's been so long since you've had a real conversation with your little brother, you kind of forget how to speak his language.

Luckily, he spoke first.

"I'm sorry," he said.

No!

"No!" I told him. "*I'm* sorry!"

He insisted that he was more sorry, for everything—for the Sweethearts Dance and the whole thing with Danny and for being so lame. I told him that's ridiculous—*I'm* more sorry for blaming stuff on him that's all my fault, for stealing his best friend, for treating him like a nobody even though he's my brother, for God's sake.

I knew we'd find a way to turn a heartfelt talk into a stupid siblings argument.

But it was a really good talk. Once we decided that we were both equally victims and victimizers, we moved on to other subjects. School and teachers and friends and family . . . and I know it sounds super-generic, but, I mean, we did talk about all that stuff. It's not as if we'd ever covered those topics before. Jake and I really do have those things in common. I never realized it before this, but like, maybe my little brother and I are friends?

Okay, that's going too far. But what I'm trying to say is that some day in the future, I could maybe possibly sort of accept Jake's Facebook friend request.

He gave me a sneak peak at the bar mitzvah slide show he's making, which was unexpectedly the best. I had to help him de-lame the music choices, obviously, but there's a ton of the cutest pictures. Like this one of me, Jake, and Danny at the premiere of one of Dad's movies when we're all really young. The two of them are wearing little tuxes, and I've got this shiny silver dress on that makes me look like a disco ball. It's so funny. It's awesome.

I'd left my phone in my room, so I'm not sure how long I hung out in Jake's. But it was light when I went in there and dark when I left, and I actually think that's pretty cool, that I was in there for that long. I mean, it's horribly lame, yeah, but underneath all that embarrassingness there's like, a milligram of secret cool.

The only other thing to report is something weird I found on my phone when I did get back to my room. It was a text. I didn't recognize the number.

ur gon 2 regret wat u did.

Okay, that's pathetic even for Chad. Does he seriously think that he still matters to me? Like, at all? Honestly, wtf.

Wednesday, June 2 at 7:12 p.m.

Kristen Duffy nvm, only 8.5 days left . . . last days a min. day
2 minutes ago · Comment · Like

Kristen Duffy 9 days left of middle school . . .
3 minutes ago · Comment · Like

Jamie Mackintosh cant believe marco's goin back 2 italy :'(i will never love again
3 minutes ago · Comment · Like

Chad Beck if im already tan then does that mean this summer my skins gonna turn mexican? lol
5 minutes ago · Comment · Like

Brian Fenton ANYONE ELSE DOING KAYAK CAMP?
6 minutes ago · Comment · Like

Nisha Patel needs to write the best grad speech ever . . . help me d. wu
7 minutes ago · Comment · Like

Lauren Gardner-Smith omg meghan u need to reserve me like 4 pgs in ur yearbook bffs
9 minutes ago · Comment · Like

Meghan Moore omg lauren u need to reserve me like 4 pgs in ur yearbook bffs
9 minutes ago · Comment · Like

Avery Sinclair lakers suck lakers r gay

12 minutes ago · Comment · Like

Ashley Clarke the rumors are NOT true . . . well some of them might be ;)

13 minutes ago · Comment · Like

Tyler Bell goin to the beach. hit me up ladies xoxo

15 minutes ago · Comment · Like

Hannah Schwartz thinks some people should just be real for once.

15 minutes ago · Comment · Like

Bryce Sherman LETS GO LAKE SHOW! game 2 tonight MAKE IT TIGHT!

17 minutes ago · Comment · Like

37 • Dorothy Wu

Saturday, June 5

In my next incarnation, I am most definitely coming back as a Jew! Bar mitzvahs, bar mitzvahs . . . who knew?!

I had a very bad feeling about today. Jake did not return either of my good-luck (or, as they say, "Matzoh Tov!") phone calls. In fact, he has not returned any of my calls since I spat in his face. Because of our friend feud, I thought he might be flustered when he looked out and saw me in the audience today. Because he would be flustered, I thought that he would potentially start sobbing. But Jake did not cry one solitary tear. Nay. Rather, he did something that none of us expected.

I arrived at the service early in order to see the sights. The whole event was held in the massive backyard of the Schwartz house, which was decorated to perfection. The chairs were white, the little circular hats that all the men and some of the women wore were light blue, and I was dressed in pretty, pretty pink. It was a flower design that I purchased months ago, as soon as I received the invitation for this occasion. I also bought a small trinket to wear on this day. It is a silver necklace with a small dolphin charm that I purchased from renowned jewelry boutique Claire's. I figured that when Jake saw me, it would remind him of our happier times. For real this time.

When it came time for everyone to take their seats,

I looked up at Jake sitting stoically on the stage. I became quite intimidated. He looked very serious and focused, like Abraham Lincoln or that stern Indian that Pocahontas was supposed to marry. Perhaps that makes sense. After all, the theme of his party was "This Day in History."

Luckily, I did not stay intimidated by Jake for long. For you see, I noticed the most adorable thing. Lining the whole front of the stage were dozens and dozens of pairs of shoes, going from little baby tennis shoes on the left all the way up to the ginormous basketball shoes that are much too big for Jake's feet on the right. I overheard two ladies behind me talking about them. Apparently, Jake's mother has kept every single pair of shoes he has ever worn since he was born. This reminded me that Jake is still a little boy, and thinking about that makes me smile.

And then the service began. And Jake stood up, and Jake wrapped a white-and-blue shawl around his shoulders, and Jake started to chant things in Hebrew, and this was the point at which I realized something that I never thought I would realize: Could it be that my little boy is now something of a man?!

Holy Table! His voice . . . it was so low! Not low in an ugly way either, like a troll or Muzzy, but low like a smooth, cool man. Low like how milk chocolate would talk if milk chocolate had a voice.

And it was not just his voice. For the first time in the history of man, Jake Schwartz stood up straight. He is taller than one realizes. Not as tall as Danny, but tall like his father. Certainly taller-seeming than Tom Cruise, who was sitting in front of me. Mr. Cruise's surprising lack of height was all that the ladies behind me could talk about.

Jake's hair-poof was gone, also. He has opted for a much shorter, sleeker look that causes him to resemble a Roman centurion. I like it. I love Jake's "fro" more than anything, yes it is true, but this new cut makes him look much older, and also I am sure that it was much easier for him to keep his little hat on his head with the shortened hair.

And it was the way Jake walked. There is a part in the service in which the bar mitzvah boy-man takes hold of the "Torah" (the giant scroll that he reads his story from, for all you ignorami), and he has to walk with it all the way through the audience while people touch their Hebrew books to the Torah and then kiss their books.

I would have been so, SO, so, SO nervous if I had to carry that thing. Back when Jake and I used to converse on a regular basis, back during the golden era of our friendship, he told me that if you drop the Torah, you are not allowed to eat during daylight for forty days! And I think he was telling the truth when he told me that, unlike the time he told me that the hamburgers from the school cafeteria are actually made of whale.

What I am trying to say is that Jake held on to that Torah strong, and he walked hard. He did not drop it and he made us all very proud.

Then Jake chanted from the Torah, and he was perfect. His voice deftly mixed the inspiring confidence of Nelson Mandela with the melodious range of Jigglypuff. I do not think he made any mistakes, and even if he did err, then he covered his boo-boos flawlessly, which is perhaps even more impressive I think. The only problem was that I could not understand any of the Hebrew things that he was chanting. But then he gave a speech in my native tongue of English and . . . whoa. No one who was there for his speech will ever forget it. It was heartwarming and haunting.

Shortly after the speech, there was a delightful moment when everyone in the audience was given wrapped candies, and we got to throw them at Jake. One of the candies, which I think was thrown by one of Madonna's children, hit Jake squarely in the eye—*yowch*. But Jake did not cry.

After the service ended, everyone went up to the bar mitzvah boy-man to congratulate him. Everyone except me. Too many butterflies. I had the following thought process: I know that eventually I will have my opportunity to tell Jake how wondrous he was and how wondrous he is. However, I feel like he still thinks of me as a poor friend. I just need to find the right moment.

I went home and played Final Fantasy VII for four hours. I tried to avoid thinking about Jake during this time. I tried to keep my focus on Sephiroth.

In the evening, I returned to the Schwartz home for the grand party. Again, the decorations were awe-inspiring. There were two Statue of Liberty statues at the end of the driveway. There was a large cardboard cutout of Mount Rushmore with a hole where Theodore Roosevelt's face should be where you could have your picture taken. And all of the waiters were dressed as Revolutionary War people, with the tricornered hats and the drums and the fifes and everything.

I came dressed as Charlie Chaplin. I was under the impression that since the party was history-themed, that everyone would be dressed as something fun from the past. But the people there were only wearing modern-style shirts and ties and dresses. One of Hannah's friends came up to me and asked me why I had a Hitler mustache. Erggh. That vexed me to peeve proportions. I did not want others to say such things to me, so I washed my mustache off with swimming pool water and I hid my bowler behind a tree. For the remainder of the evening, I was just a girl wearing all black. Just like every other day.

Primarily I watched others enjoy themselves. Why? I just was not in a groovin' mood, that is all. You can refuse to dance and this does not make you a loser.

Jake did an excellent job of not being a loser. He was front and center for every single group dance—"YMCA," "Macarena," "Have a Nagila"—everything. I especially enjoyed watching him get lifted up on a chair by adults. What an enjoyable culture.

There was one moment when I wanted to approach Jake especially much. The DJ announced that we were going to play a game called Pepsi 7-Up. In this game, everyone splits up into teams of one boy and one girl, and then the teams have to do ridiculous shenanigans on the dance floor. Jake and I would have been the ideal tandem for this game since ridiculous shenanigans are probably our number-one pastime. In addition, Jake did not even have very many friends of his own at the party—I do not think he truly considers my Super Story Samurai pals to be his friends as well, so most every kid in attendance was a Hannah bud, almost as if he had turned over the guest invitation duties to her completely.

I was titillated, therefore, as Jake's only true-blue play-fellow in attendance, to play Pepsi 7-Up with him. However, before I could walk even two steps toward my former prince, Hannah had already claimed him as her partner. Perhaps that makes sense since they are family. But they are not even friends. Harrumph.

For the briefest of moments I thought I could make Jake envious by partnering with his former best amigo, Danny Uribe, but while I had observed Danny sitting in the back row with his family during the ceremony and speech (mostly texting—ruuuude!), I did not catch a sight-whiff of him at the nighttime party. He was probably with his family.

I did finally speak to Jake before my father picked me up. I walked up to him on the floor in the middle of "Billie Jean," and I did not look him in the eyes, and I told him, "Thank you for inviting me, I was very proud of you, you are very special, you are not a little girl, I am sorry."

I then turned around very quickly and walked away very quickly. Jake did not chase after me, so I do not know where that leaves us.

I am fine. If I cannot be Jake's best friend, or at least his good friend, or at least his friend, then I am content to be an admirer from afar.

June 5th

My Speech

Shabbat Shalom to family and friends. Thank you everyone for coming.

It is the duty of every bar mitzvah boy, on his big day, to read a story in Hebrew from the Torah, otherwise known as the Old Testament. That is what I just did. We must then give a speech in which we compare the story to our own lives, no matter how far-fetched the comparison between Biblical and modern times might seem. That is what I'm doing right now. It's all part of having a bar mitzvah, all part of becoming a man.

We do not get to choose the story. It is chosen for us according to our date of birth. The portion of the Torah that I just read to you is called Parashat Sh'ach. It is a story from the book of Numbers. The Book of Numbers is, no offense Moses, known for being a pretty boring book. Basically, all that happens in the stories is that people get counted, categorized, ranked, and made to do random things.

This is exactly what happens in my story. Moses and the Jews are wandering through the desert when God tells Moses to send one man from each of the twelve tribes to go observe the land of Canaan. The men do just this, they spy on Canaan, and when they come back, two of the men really like what they've seen. Joshua and Caleb. These guys call Canaan the "land of milk and honey," and they want Moses and all of the Jews to go there as soon as possible. They want to fight the men who live there for the right to live there. This is what God wants too.

But the other spies aren't so sure. They witnessed some seriously strong and scary people in Canaan, and they argue that the Jews would maybe be better off just going back to Egypt.

God responds by killing all of the spies except for Joshua and Caleb, and what's more, he threatens to kill every single one of the Jews wandering in the desert. Moses convinces God not to do this. So God says, "Fine, Moses, I won't kill your people, and yes, I will guide them into the land of milk and honey, but there is a catch— you'll never get to go there yourself."

The end. That's the end of my Torah portion.

So . . . what could any of that possibly have to do with me?

Actually, I think, a whole lot. Let's recap.

For starters, the Book of Numbers basically involves a bunch of categorizing, ranking, and people being made to do random things. I see no difference between that and junior high.

And in my story, different "tribes" of people are encouraged to fight over the same piece of land: the land of milk and honey. Well, I don't think there's much milk and honey in San Paulo, and we don't exactly call these kinds of groups "tribes" anymore—we have a different name for them: gangs. So, as we can see, there's a connection there too.

So what about the meaning of the story itself? What is it and what could it possibly have to do with today?

Well, I think it's a story about not fighting. I know that that sort of contradicts what Old Testament God said and did, and I know it doesn't seem very bar mitzvah-ish for me to say that God was wrong. So I'm sorry in advance, God, and if I get smote then I'll know why.

But let's look at the facts as they stand today. In our modern world, the land of Canaan still exists. It's called Israel, and there are Jews there, and there are lots of other people there, and there's still a lot of fighting there, and it sort of seems like it's going to be that way forever. Everyone wants some of that milk and honey.

I think that there are Canaans, there are Israels all over the world, even today. Places that lots of people want for various reasons, and so these people go to great lengths to try and get those places. Lots of times there's fighting, lots of times there's death. In San Paulo, we see this. We see our local "tribes," we see violence, and yes, we see death.

Yet I think everyone's got the whole thing wrong. Moses, Joshua, Caleb, everyone today . . . they're all after the wrong thing. Yes, I do believe that the land of milk and honey exists like God says it does in the book of Numbers.

But what makes us so sure that it's an actual physical land?

I've learned a lot about metaphors this year at school—shout-out to Mr. Morales, who's here in the audience—and I think the Bible's filled with them. And so I ask this: what if the land of milk and honey is a metaphor?

What if all the fighting—from whatever year Numbers is supposed to have happened all the way up until today—what if it's really supposed to teach us not to fight?

That's what I think. The promised land isn't a game of Risk or Settlers of Catan. It isn't just some territory you can claim all for yourself and hold on to for as long as possible. In fact, it can't be reached by force at all.

The promised land is a place we can only get to if we collectively decide that fighting—for any reason—is stupid. It's a place we can only get to if we decide that spending all of our time categorizing and ranking people is stupid.

And maybe, like Moses, we'll never reach the supposed land of milk and honey. Maybe us even thinking that we can get there one day is just stupid.

But we have to keep trying. That's what I've learned.

Today I am a man.

Thank you.

SAN PAULO JUNIOR HIGH SCHOOL
MORNING ANNOUNCEMENTS—THURSDAY, JUNE 10

Congratulations on finishing your finals, San Paulo! Only one more day until summer vacation!

Tomorrow is a MINIMUM DAY. All seventh grade students will be dismissed from classes at 12:30 p.m. Those who wish to be released at 11 in order to attend the graduation ceremony may ask their teachers if they can do so.

Eighth grade students, tomorrow, **June 11**, is your graduation day! Remember to wear nice clothes to school and to bring your smile.

Graduation Calendar of Events for Eighth Grade Students:
8:00–8:30 a.m.: Meet in 1st period classrooms.
8:30–9:30 a.m.: Graduation practice on the main field.
9:30–10:45 a.m.: 8th grade activities and yearbook signing.
11 a.m.–12:30 p.m.: Graduation ceremony. Please tell your family and friends to arrive early for good seats!
12:30 p.m.–???: CELEBRATE!

PLEASE turn in all *overdue library books*! If you are in eighth grade and you still have books checked out, you will not be allowed to walk at the graduation ceremony.

Summer school begins Monday, June 21. Get excited for summer learning!

And, for the FINAL TIME, San Paulo is a no gum, no iPods, no cell phones, no skateboards, no video games, no laser pointers, no pocket knives, no jelly bracelets school! Those found with any of the aforementioned items will be given a detention. **No exceptions.**

38 • Hannah Schwartz

Friday, June 11

I hate how graduation speeches are always like, "Who are we going to be twenty years from now? How will we change the world?" Honestly, the kids who graduated today didn't even know what they were going to do this afternoon. If I've learned anything in junior high, I've learned that. And I didn't learn it till today.

Graduation was, like everything else at this stupid school, typical. The marching band sucked hard. So many parents brought all these balloons and leis and homemade signs and foghorns, and they all just seemed a little too proud of their kids for graduating freaking middle school. Greene gave a way-too-intense speech, where he was like, "It's not a matter of *if* you will make a difference—it's *when!*" Obviously, all of my friends cried their eyes out, because they seem to be forgetting that we'll be going to school together next year and seeing each other at the beach all summer long in the meantime.

I guess I just hate how fake graduation is. Like, there's no real reason why on the last day of eighth grade we should have to wear ugly square hats with dowdy tassels and pretend like we're moving on to the next chapter of our lives. But we do. And some people love getting really into that, but I know that nothing matters until at least high school anyway.

Of course the King of the Fakes was having the best day of his life. Chad did the following Shameful Heinous Idiot Things:

S.H.I.T. #1. When he got his diploma, he jumped up in the air and screamed, "PIRATES FOR LIFE! YAAAHHH!"

S.H.I.T. #2. He snuck two flattened beach balls into the ceremony, blew them up, and threw each of them into the air, distracting everyone. One of them while I was getting my diploma.

S.H.I.T. #3. During the pre-graduation yearbook-signing period, I saw Chad kiss two different girls. Although I have to admit, kissing Corinne Allison and Ashley Clarke is really like kissing thirty guys. Hehe.

I think it's fair to say I'm over him, yeah? Finally, right? Finally I can stop being such a stupid. Finally I can stop falling for the wrong boys. Boys who don't communicate at all except through vicious bathroom lies and jerky jerkface texts.

That was the thing that really sealed it for me and Chad— that weird text I got from him. Even if, as it turns out, the text wasn't from him.

I met up with my family after the ceremony. Actually my dad couldn't be there because he had some major meetings with top agents this morning, but his plan was to make it back for a big dinner tonight.

Mom and Jake were so super-nice. I mean, they didn't make the hugest deal out of me graduating eighth grade because it's not like I'm one of those dropout kind of kids and this is the highest level of education I'll ever reach. But still, they made me feel special. Jake Photoshopped me a cute card with some of the choicest pictures from his slide show. It was more than a little awesome.

That said, I didn't feel too special for too long. Mom had to leave right away to meet with a "celebrity client," and Jake also had to go. I actually asked him if he wanted to hang out. Pathetic, I know, but I can't help it if I'm a nice person. But Jake said he couldn't, that he had been owing his friend Dorothy a proper minimum day for a long time now, whatever that meant.

I guess I could have gone to the pool party at Kristen's. But I didn't feel like hours of yearbook signing and gossip and games of Truth or Dare where the girls only pick truth and the guys only pick dare. I wanted something real.

That's when Danny walked over to me. He came the split second after Mom and Jake left, like he had been watching them and waiting for them to leave. He was wearing his nice black button-up from the Hanukkah party. And I didn't realize it until he showed up, because it's honestly been so long since I've really thought about him, but right at that moment Danny was really the person I wanted to be real with.

Okay. I didn't want him like that. God no. I'm so past that, isn't it obvious? I just wanted to talk to him. As friends. It was time.

He suggested we go on a walk. I said where. He said Bella Vista. I said beautiful sight.

Obviously it was über-awkward at first. Danny talked

about how nice and sunny it was, and how it was "tight" that the weather could be so nice on my graduation day. Only his voice cracked when he said "graduation day." I laughed and I said that reminds me of the time in Jake's room.

I know I made it more uncomfortable. But still. I'm allowed to make people uncomfortable on my day, especially when it's funny.

Danny asked me how come I broke it off. I told him the truth, which is that there were just too many differences between us. And obviously, I reminded him, that's become more true since he became a full-on, black-eyed, drug-running gangbanger. I asked Danny if he listened to Jake's bar mitzvah speech. I asked him if he read my blog entry. Those were for you, you know, I said.

The whole time I talked, Danny kept his eyes on me. This is new for him. I've never seen him hold eye contact with someone for more than like, five seconds. I don't know, maybe it was a tactic they taught him at gangster initiation. Whatever. It wasn't working on me.

Danny asked me why I got back together with Chad.

I said, "How did you know about me and Chad?"

He said, "Doesn't matter."

I said I honestly couldn't give him a good answer, beyond just that I'm an idiot. "But hey," I said, "at least I dumped the bastard."

Danny seemed surprised by that news. We kept walking.

I asked him if he'd really meant it when he said he loved me. I probably shouldn't have, but it fit with the conversation we were having and I wanted to know.

Danny said yes, he was in love. "That was the whole problem," he said. He really was in love.

I said, "Okay, you're in seventh grade. You don't know what love is."

He said eighth grade. He's in eighth grade. We kept walking.

A couple blocks away from the park, Danny asked me if I felt bad for the way I had treated him. I said I felt bad that he took it the way he did. He asked me again. Did I feel bad for the way I treated him? I said, "I wouldn't change anything, if that's what you mean." He said okay. We kept walking.

As we got close to Bella Vista, I could see that there were already people there. A bunch of Danny's gang friends. Some of them were wearing their finest graduation clothes. Some of them were wearing baller hats and those stupid Scotsmen socks.

"Um, Danny," I said. "It looks like the park's taken. We should go."

"No," he said. "We need to talk to you. Give us one minute."

"This isn't a good idea—"

"It's important."

"I definitely shouldn't—"

"It'll be fine," he said. "Hannah, trust me. I promise nothing will happen to you." Then he looked at me with that same constant look he had given me before. "You owe me."

That was a debatable point, and this was clearly a stupid

situation to get involved in, but I trusted Danny. If he said nothing was going to happen to me, then nothing would.

Plus, by that point I didn't much like my chances of getting away, anyhow.

We walked slowly up to the group. One of them stepped forward and nodded at Danny. He was the tallest one. He hadn't even had the decency to dress up for his graduation. He had two thick lines of black hair on his face, one above his eyes and one above his upper lip. I recognized him as Guillermo Torres. Back when Luz and Chicle were gossip associates of mine, they used to talk about him all the time. The rumors they spread about him . . . well, they can't be true. He'd be in jail right now. Not even juvie. *Jail.*

Guillermo looked down at me, his hands in his pants pockets.

"Why'd you write that thing on the Internet?"

I'd been expecting something like this sooner or later. I was thinking maybe something in e-mail form and not like, right after graduation. Totally awful thing of Danny to do, by the way, basically luring me here to talk about it. But honestly, it wasn't like I hadn't been expecting this shoe to drop eventually. It was fine. I'd deal with it, I'd own up to my words, and then Danny and I could go home.

"You guys know what you are," I said. "What did I write that wasn't true?"

"You shouldn't be talking about stuff you don't know nothing about," Guillermo said. Some of the others nodded and murmured in agreement, the way suck-ups do.

"I'm sorry," I said. "I'll take the piece down. It won't happen again."

"Yeah," Guillermo said, almost in a whisper but loud enough. "But how do we make sure?"

Guillermo looked straight at me, unblinking, and he reached his hand into his pocket.

Danny jumped forward faster than I could think.

"¡BASTA!" he shouted. The hand stopped.

Guillermo looked at me. Then, just as quickly, he wasn't looking at me anymore. He was looking off into the distance, past me.

I turned around to see what he saw.

Jake.

39 • Danny Uribe

Friday, June 11

It started with the thing she wrote online. None of the Raiders read her Web site or anything. We've got other stuff to do. But I remember Luz showed Carlos what Hannah wrote on that blog, and Carlos showed me, and I showed Guillermo and we were like, we have to do something.

It wasn't meant to be anything, though. Just a scare. Just like, back off, you know? It wasn't meant to be what it turned out to be.

It was her own fault. First the kind of stuff she was saying, then the way she ran around with that Chad fool. That was a dumb-slut thing to do.

So I said okay to Guillermo's plan. He promised me we weren't gonna hurt her. We were just gonna make her think we might.

I sat through Hannah's whole graduation. What a joke. There were a bunch of Mexicans in it who hadn't passed enough classes to graduate yet. The office is making them do summer school to graduate for real. SP just wants to get rid of them, make us the high school's problem.

At first I thought the Hannah plan wouldn't work. I thought she wouldn't want to hang with me. She's chilled with like every other person besides me these last few months, even her brother, who she's never even liked. But this after-noon when I went up to her after her family left, she was like, yeah, you're the exact person I want to be with right now. Kinda made me feel weird.

Kind of made me feel like, oh, I shouldn't be doing this. But I couldn't let her hotness distract me. She had to see that the fool things she does can get her in trouble. Words matter.

Our walk was our first time being together in a long time. She made it weird real quick by bringing up the old days.

I kept it cool. I didn't get all emotional or nothing. I was just like, okay, I'm gonna ask her these questions, and if she gives me the right answers then maybe she won't even have to deal with Guillermo. For real, I would have stopped us before we got to BV. I would have taken her home.

But she didn't give the right answers. She talked like some-one who hadn't learned a single damn thing this whole damn year. So the Raiders had to teach her a lesson.

She's smart and stuff, so she knew something was up right away. But she trusted me. I think she was smart to trust me too. I wasn't gonna let nothing bad happen to her.

So we got to BV. It was okay at first. Guillermo did the thing where he reaches into his pocket, but he does that with everyone. You have to really piss him off to see what's in there. Hannah was being a good girl, so when Guillermo did the reaching thing I told him to stop right away. He did. He respects me.

And then—

What the hell was Jake doing there? He knows better than

to come up to me and my scene. I've been telling him to stay away all year.

Guillermo smiled big when he saw Jake. Like, too big.

"Trash Boy!" he said. "Forgot your name. Forgot your face too. Just remember those little shoes. I missed you, Trash Boy. What are you doing here? Basketball season is over."

I gave Jake a look like, "Get out of here, man." I didn't want to say anything.

Jake didn't do what was best for him, though. He didn't peace. He walked down the sidewalk, onto the grass, and halfway across the field to where we were.

"Leave her alone." The way he said it, I don't know. Didn't seem like Jake.

Maybe the reason it didn't seem like him is because it was stupid.

"Get out of here, Jake," Hannah said.

"Oooooh—what is this?" Guillermo jumped in. "You two like boyfriend-girlfriend?"

"We're siblings," Jake said. And then—and I do not know what made him do this, he added, "Asshole."

I got that feeling when your blood gets cold in just your arms and your face. I couldn't see the other guys because I was standing in front of them. But I know the rest of them got that blood rush too. We were all going back in our minds to the last time some kid made this mistake.

"Yeah, Guillermo, you're an asshole." Jake stepped forward. "And maybe they're all too afraid to say it, but Hannah said it online. I'll say it now."

Guillermo smiled again. He smiled big. The corners of his mouth stretched out to the ends of his face, farther than his eyebrow goes.

"Tell me how I'm an asshole," he said.

Jake didn't say anything to that. Maybe he realized what he had gotten himself into.

"Come on, Trash Boy. You're smart, right? You must have all kinds of reasons."

Jake looked down at the ground, then up at the sky. He looked at Hannah. He didn't look at me.

"You're gonna tell me why I'm an asshole." Guillermo moved his hand near his pocket a little. "You're gonna do it."

Jake looked at Hannah again. She wanted him to shut up. But I could see that this mattered to Jake, and when something matters to him, he doesn't shut up about it.

So he decided to tell Guillermo. I remember every word.

"All right," he said. "All right. Listen, guys. So . . . I don't think any of you are bad people." He still wasn't looking at me.

"You're cool. The Raiders are cool. Kids look up to you. They want to be like you. And like, even though I could never be like you—because I belong in the trash, after all—"

A few guys laughed behind me.

"Even though I could never be like you, I remember thinking during basketball how much I wanted to be one of you. Hanging out after practice, going out to eat as one big group, punching little wimps in the arm . . . yeah. Yeah, that all seems like fun stuff to do.

"But I'm not one of you. I could never be. And that allows

me to see something very important, and that's this: you guys are too cool.

"You're so cool that it makes you think you can get away with anything, and I guess maybe you can, but that doesn't mean you should.

"Yeah, you guys are Raiders. But you're also Pirates. Well, I guess a raider can be a type of pirate, but you know what I mean. You guys aren't just disrespected gangsters. You're students and friends and boyfriends and sons and brothers. You all have plenty of people who love you outside the gang. And when we see you getting together with only each other, when we see you cutting class and giving up on school and selling stuff and, well, you know, all the other stuff you do . . . all the, you know, really hurtful stuff, and for no reason . . . well . . . that's what makes us think that yes, you are assholes."

I looked over at Hannah and she was smiling her real smile that she hardly ever shows. She couldn't hide it. I wasn't smiling. I couldn't. But some of the hairs on my arm did start standing on their own. It was the same feeling I got during Jake's speech last weekend, even though I didn't like that speech.

The other guys too, I knew they were getting that feeling. I could tell. They had listened to Jake's words and found something true in them.

Even Guillermo looked different.

"So . . . all the times we think we're being family," Guillermo said, all slow, "really, what we're doing . . . is we're hurting all our other friends . . . and letting down our real families."

Jake nodded.

"And . . . that's what makes us assholes."

Jake nodded again.

Guillermo stood there still and quiet. He was looking at Jake. He opened his mouth and then closed it. He blinked his eyes hard. Then he blinked his eyes hard again.

"I'm sorry about Angel," he said. "I think about him every day. It was a mistake, you know? I never meant for him to get hurt bad."

"You were just trying to scare him," Jake said.

"Yeah," Guillermo said. "Yeah."

"But you were a Raider, and he was a Destroyer," Jake said.

Guillermo started off slow. It seemed like it was hard for him to think of the words he wanted to say. "He was a Destroyer, yeah. But he was my boy, you know?"

His voice went up a little as he said it. It was all shaky and stuff. It wasn't like it cracked or anything, but more like he was choking back tears or something. Didn't sound like Guillermo Torres. Then he said something else, faster this time. It was like he'd wanted to say it for a while.

"I loved Angel. I love all you guys."

He stopped for a while again. He looked at Jake. His look had respect in it. It was the way he looks at me. He blinked and he shook his head and he lifted his shoulders and he sighed.

"But, Jake," Guillermo said.

"Yeah?"

"We're assholes, right?"

"You don't have to be," Jake said.

"But we are. And me most of all, right? I've been like, such a bad person this whole time."

"You don't have to be."

Guillermo slumped his shoulders and closed his eyes.

Jake looked over at me for the first time all day. All month, I guess. Maybe for the first time since I joined the Raiders. He nodded at me. It was a quick thing, but I forgot how good that felt. How good it felt for Jake to look over at me.

Then I heard Guillermo sigh again. He reached into his pocket. He pulled out something dark. He turned around, holding it in his hand. He looked straight at Hannah.

No.

I was not going to let that happen to her. I promised. I jumped in front of her, right between the two of them. I shot Guillermo a look. I didn't have a weapon, but I was going to defend her with everything I had.

Guillermo pressed the button on his handle. The blade flew into place. He raised the knife up in the air, holding it out in front of his chest, the blade pointed at me. He wasn't more than five feet away. I could hear fast breathing coming from behind me.

He looked at me. He narrowed his eyes, just like he must have done before he got Angel. I shook my head no. He kept looking at me. I shook my head no again. And again.

"*Basta,*" I said, in a low, quiet voice. Then I shook my head one more time.

Finally Guillermo widened his eyes. He didn't widen them fast like he was about to strike, but he did it slow like he was giving up. He blinked a couple times too, like he was waking up from a dream or a nightmare. Like he had to put one last scare in Hannah, just to prove he was boss. Just to prove that the Raiders still had some cred. But now he was done. He took his time bringing the knife down.

I squeezed Hannah's hand.

Then Guillermo spun around, ran two steps back, grabbed Jake's shoulder with his left hand, swung his right hand back, and plunged the knife deep into Jake's stomach. Jake's eyes rolled to the back of his head right away as he fell to the ground.

Everything went cold so fast. I don't remember anything I felt after that happened, just everything I did.

I threw myself at Guillermo, all my weight. Knocked him to the ground like a linebacker. His head hit real hard but I didn't give a damn about him. I pinned him to the grass, my knees pressing against his chest. He looked up at me like wtf.

I punched him in the face with my right. Then with my left. Then with my right. Then I punched him in the stomach. Then I kneed him down low. Then I punched him in the face again. I punched him till he looked different. I punched him till he didn't wake up.

I crawled over to Jake, lying on the ground a few feet away. He was in even worse shape than Guillermo. I couldn't tell what was going on. Hannah was screaming behind me. The guys just stood there, watching in shock. I tried to feel Jake for breathing or a heartbeat. There was so much blood all over his polo shirt.

I picked Jake up. I held my brother in my arms.

Hey McKenzie,
I didn't get to know you that well this year, but it was cool having math and Spanish with you. You are really smart. HAGS and see you in high school.
-David

Bryce—
2 good + 2 be = 4gotten
xoxo Avery P.

EMILY'S PAGE! NO ONE ELSE WRITE N E THING HERE!
Jamie Boo,
OMG what a cray-cray yr. First the Marco drama, then the Hannah drama, then a lil more Marco drama. SO DRAMATIC LOL. But u were my girl thru n thru n I luv u 4eva. I kno this isnt good-bye cause I'll be seeing u so much this summa. LULAS.
Always n 4eva,
Emily-Bear
P.S. who's that hottie on pg. 74? :p

Tina,
It was a real pleasure having you in English and then writing club in May and June. You are a phenomenal student and a very talented writer. I especially loved the two-voice poem you and Dorothy wrote about fathers and daughters. I feel very lucky to have been your teacher.
Ruben Morales

Alex—
It has truly been an amazing yr 4 me w/ u. There is
probly no one else who I will <u>ever</u> love again like you.
That's what makes this so hard, but I am using this
space to say that it's finally over between us. 4 the
last time. We just aren't ready, we're not—I'm sorry
this is too hard to finish
Kristen

Whitney,
Good times this yr! From rockin out in writing
club to that time we talked on the bus, I feel
like we were always up to something! You are
a really awesome girl and a very talented writer.
I'd love to get together to read each other's
stuff sometime. Call/text me.
—Tyler

Rachel Sloan,
I'm looking at you right now. Weeeeeird. Never trust an
angry cactus, that's what I say!
Sincerely, Brian Fenton

¡AMIGAS POR VIDA!
Besos, Luz

HEATHER,
BEST YEAR EVER? NO DOUBT.
<3 NISHA

Jake,

I don't know if you'll ever get this, but

Jake,

I hope you're okay. The doctors haven't told us anything. I pray that you're okay, man. I want

Jake,

I can't explain everything from this year. I don't know how. But I want you to understand

Jake,

I'm a Raider. But I can still be your friend

Jake,

Don't let this be the last thing I ever say to you. Don't

Jake,

You will always be important to me.

Jake,

I know you think I turned my back on you. It's not like that

Jake,
When I held you in my arms, that was

Jake,
I'm sorry.

Jake,
I feel bad. I feel so bad. But I can't be sorry, because

Jake,

40 • Jake Schwartz

Saturday, June 12

The first thing was I had to figure out whether I was alive or not. When you're barely a hundred pounds and you lose over two pints of blood, it can really go either way.

The hospital doctors told me I was alive when I asked. I didn't feel alive, but I tried to trust them since they're doctors. They told me it's a miracle that I'm alive, that if the knife had even so much as grazed any of my major organs, that I'd be dead right now. I told them I am dead right now. They said no you're not. They said just relax. I'm not very good at relaxing, though, so I lay there in my bed and thought. I thought about how I got here.

Well, I suppose it all started when my mom met my dad. They met at a party in college and hit it off, and dated, and got married, and if what we learned in health is true at all, before long, millions of his sperm were making their way into her uterine wall and—

Jeez. What kinds of drugs do they have me on?

Okay, I can remember Hannah's graduation. Dad couldn't come. The ceremony was boring except for a couple of beach balls. Hannah wanted to hang out with me after, but I'd already promised Dorothy.

D. Wu and I had a plan to finish up that minimum day we

never really got to have way back when. The day after my bar mitzvah, she called me up with the idea and it sounded fun to me. I was ready to spend time with her again. I missed her. So, today, we brought all the same foods with us as last time, and we were going to have just the most classic Jake-Dorothy picnic at BV.

But when we got there, we saw Hannah. She was with all the guys from basketball. It didn't look right to me.

I said, "Dorothy, we should tell the office about this." She said good idea and started running back to school as fast as she could. I wanted to call after her and say wait don't go yet, but I didn't want to be so loud as to blow my cover. And I couldn't run after her because I didn't want to leave Hannah. And I couldn't call Dorothy's cell phone because such a thing does not exist.

So there I was, by myself, watching my sister standing amid a group of gangsters for some reason, trying to make sure nothing went wrong.

And then I saw Guillermo reach inside his jacket. I jumped out instinctively and Guillermo spotted me. A little shrimp standing hundreds of feet away. He smiled when he saw me. I remember he had that same smile on St. Patrick's Day. I had no choice but to walk up to him.

Guillermo started asking me a bunch of questions, and I started talking—telling the truth no less—which was most likely stupid. But I was thinking that maybe in this situation, stupid was the smart way to go.

See, when I was on the team, the reason none of those

guys respected me is because I never did anything to earn their respect. The only ones they looked up to were guys like Guillermo and Danny, dudes who acted mean and tough. The Raiders had to see someone step up and be confident without being an ass about it. And Danny had to see me step up, period.

So I figured I'd fight a verbal fight. Best-case scenario would be if I radically shifted the perspectives of everyone in the gang, causing them to see for the first time that they have severely misinterpreted what the concept of brotherhood means. I thought that the worst-case scenario would be, I don't know, a few bruises on my arm, or another trip to the trash can. Somehow, I couldn't foresee what was, looking back, a much more realistic worst-case scenario.

I know they listened to me. I know they did. Even Guillermo, I know he heard what I said. Even though he stabbed me. He only did that because he felt like he had to.

Did it hurt? That's what everyone's been asking me. What a question. Yes, it hurt.

Guillermo treated my stomach like a steak. He ripped a hole in me. Flesh is not supposed to slice like that. Blood is not supposed to empty from my body like that. I don't know if I cried or screamed or what. Whatever I did, I wasn't supposed to do it.

I can't believe I used to wish that I could feel what it would be like to get kicked in the balls. After getting carved down to my guts, I never want to feel more than a paper cut ever again.

Luckily, I did only feel this pain for a few seconds. I passed out from shock almost right away, and it's pretty difficult to remember much of anything after that.

I guess Danny stepped up and defended me. Only about nine months too late. Then apparently Dorothy came back to the scene after not too long, and with her she had school officials and cops and EMTs and all kinds of people. She saved me too.

I was doing okay there in the ambulance until I looked down and noticed that the knife was still sticking out of me. Then I saw that about half of my body was completely drenched in red. I fainted again.

I had one of those long, long completely dreamless sleeps, like when it's the first night back in your bed after a month of camp. For all I know, I really was dead during this period. For all I know, I hung out in the afterlife for a while and kicked it with God, and he told me, "Good bar mitzvah speech, man, but go easy on me next time." Then maybe I chilled with some saints, or whatever it is that Jews have instead. Hilarious old rabbi ghosts? And then maybe I spent time in a train station with Dumbledore and a slimy Voldemort fetus? This all happened when I was dead.

But then I guess my body decided to live. Maybe it wanted to grow some peach fuzz before it died.

When I woke up in the hospital bed, the first thing I saw was, well, my dad's strong chin. There are more pleasant sights. But the look on my dad's face when he saw that I was apparently not dead . . . it's a look I don't think he puts on display in Hollywood too often. Maybe on Oscar night.

My mom freaked out. I'm not sure what there was more of, my blood or her tears. She told me over and over again how proud of me she is, how much she loves me, how smart I am, how funny I am, how handsome I am, how brave I am, how she wasn't ready to let me go. She's not gonna let me go, I know that much. She's a Jewish mother. After this, I may never be allowed outside again. At least not without a helmet.

It was just funny to me, seeing everyone like this. Funny in one of those ways where you've got a dumb smile on your face the whole time because everything feels so good, because you've gotten about as close as you can get to losing everything forever. That sounds cliché, but hey, I just got stabbed.

Hannah could barely talk when she came up to me. Her eyes were dripping wet and puffed up like the éclairs the caterers serve at Dad's parties. She's never looked worse, but in a way, I thought she looked even better than she did at graduation. She just stood there looking down at me, just looking, then she came in for a big hug and she rested her head against my chest. Didn't say a word.

"What is this," I said, "the silent treatment again? Haven't we been down this road before?"

She laughed at that, but with her right on top of me, her laughter made my stomach wound hurt, so I had to tell her to stop. She told me to stop being such a little wiener.

I love my sister.

I had to spend the night in the hospital, obviously, but it wasn't so bad. I got a bunch of ice cream, and the nurses said they liked my hair, and a couple of dad's movies were on TNT. I watched *Class Dismissed*, the one about a famous rapper who has to teach in an inner-city high school as part of his community service. It's based on a true story. Oh man. I hope my dad doesn't make my story into a movie. He totally would. Reminder to self: that can't happen.

This morning was the best. Dorothy came to visit. She had a dress on for some reason, and her hair was all smooth and sheen-y, as if she had actually showered and straightened it and everything. Impressive.

She gave me a stack of like, a thousand papers. She told me that there was once a time when me reading these papers was her worst, deepest fear, but that now I needed to see them.

I asked her what *The Club Chronicles: A Saga in 57 Phantasmagoric Parts* was all about. She said, "Do you really want to know?" I said sure. "Really, do you want to know?" she asked. Yes, I said. Really? Yes. Really? Yes. REEEEEEALLY? YESSSSSS.

Then she threw her arms wide open, shouted, "Whatever you say!" and came in for a gigantic hug.

Only it wasn't a hug. It was a kiss. And I was not ready for it.

I drooled, like, all over myself. Copious amounts of drool. An ocean of drool. I had no control over it. So embarrassing.

Dorothy started laughing. "First tears, then blood, now drool. Jacob Schwartz, what is it with you and your bodily fluids?"

I stopped to consider that statement, but one nanosecond into my thought process, there she was kissing me again.

And I didn't drool this time. I kissed back. And now I know what it feels like.

It feels great! It feels just like the guys in my cabin at camp described it. Warm and slimy, but good slimy, like candy that has flavored goo inside. But it was like interactive candy—candy that tastes you while you taste it. It was the best candy in the world. It was candy that I will most definitely be trying again.

Normally when D. Wu and I hang out, we're just talking and laughing the whole time. This was, um, well, a different experience. But in my opinion, it was equally frabjous.

She had to leave before lunch because she only got a B-plus on her math final, so her dad's only letting her out of the house for three hours a day for the first month of summer. But it's going to be a pretty nice three hours each day.

I couldn't stop thinking about Dorothy after she left. Her shimmery black hair, her witch's cackle of a laugh, her totally loony facial expressions when she thinks no one's watching. . . . I guess I'm just glad to have such a fun and unique person for a friend. No, scratch that—best friend. Or, well, I guess—girlfriend.

All through lunch and the afternoon, I thought about Dorothy. I fell asleep thinking about all the cool places I'm gonna show her this summer, all the adventures we're gonna go on.

Then I woke up from my nap, and there was Danny.

Danny was there to tell me some stuff. He told me that Guillermo's going to juvie and then maybe prison, and that by the time he gets out, I'll probably be in college, if not older. So that's good. Then Danny said that he might actually have to end up going to juvie for some Raider stuff, but probably not for very long. That's good too.

But Danny wasn't saying this stuff like it was good news. He was all quiet, all sad, like he was delivering some eulogy. I asked him, "Come on man, what's up?"

Danny said that honestly, he felt weird for ratting Guillermo out. He said he told the cops everything he knew about Angel Calderon's death, and that he knew it was the right thing to do, but at the same time he didn't know, you know?

I said I didn't know.

There was a pretty long pause, him just standing there, me just lying there. It was one of those awkward silences that can only happen between two people who know each other really well.

And it was on Danny to break the silence. I mean, come on, I was in a hospital bed. And he could have done something to prevent that, but he didn't.

There were a couple times where it looked like he wanted to say something to me. He didn't have to say much. All I really wanted was something along the lines of sorry. I miss you, maybe. But I didn't need some grand gesture or speech or whatever. I didn't need some big sign of best friendship. Just something. Maybe he could've asked to see my scar. I could've shown him that. It's cool-looking. Maybe he'd want to talk about my bar mitzvah speech, or the slide show. Maybe we could just catch up. Talk about basketball, video games, elementary school. I don't know.

Danny leaned over a little, and I thought it was going to be for a hug. He's not a big hugger or anything, but in the past he's done it sometimes. He's done it when he felt good. When we felt good together.

But he just held his fist out. He wasn't holding anything in it. It was just his fist.

I bumped it with my fist and he walked out the door.

I guess he's back at the house right now. I have no idea what he's up to. I'm not sure I care.

Local Gangs Come Together for Day of Peace

By Aaron Marcuse, *San Paulo Spectator*

Tuesday, January 15th

On Monday, several members of local youth gangs put their "beefs" on hold and chose instead to grill beef in a community-wide BBQ for Peace. The event, which was held at Bella Vista Park, saw over two hundred people attend.

Gang representatives say that while the event was organized in the wake of last Friday's stabbing, such an event has been a long time coming.

"This is something we should have done after Angel," said Arturo Fausto, a member of the Westside Destroyers, in reference to last year's gang-related murder of 13-year-old Angel Calderon.

Although members of gangs such as the Destroyers and the Raiders did not go so far as to declare a permanent truce, several gang representatives and community members stated that in light of recent events, a break from violence is necessary.

"I don't think there should be fighting for a while, maybe ever. It doesn't seem like there's a reason for it," said Martín "Gordo" Padilla, a member of the Eastside Raiders.

Still, despite this outpouring of good will, not all in attendance at the barbecue were completely sold on the reality of permanent peace between the gangs.

"I'll believe it when I see it," said Lt. Craig Shaw, one of several San Paulo police officers who were on hand to prevent any violence from breaking out.

Added Shaw, "I've been to a few of these things before."

getsome_danny24: hey

lilbeachbabe777: hi danny

getsome_danny24: sup?

lilbeachbabe777: wait

lilbeachbabe777: are u srsly asking me whats up?

getsome_danny24: o well like

getsome_danny24: i dont have to if u dont want

getsome_danny24: like i can just sign off

lilbeachbabe777: no dont do that

lilbeachbabe777: u dont have to do that

lilbeachbabe777: its just u dont have to start the convo w/ "sup"

lilbeachbabe777: we kno each other way too well

lilbeachbabe777: we have way too many things to say

getsome_danny24: o

getsome_danny24: ya

getsome_danny24: um . . . soooo

getsome_danny24: sup?

lilbeachbabe777: lol

lilbeachbabe777: nm u?

getsome_danny24: nm

getsome_danny24: well like

getsome_danny24: i guess

getsome_danny24: ok like

getsome_danny24: i want to say sorry

getsome_danny24: for how ive been

getsome_danny24: all the raider stuff

getsome_danny24: and like what happened to jake

lilbeachbabe777: oh danny

lilbeachbabe777: i accept your apology

lilbeachbabe777: yes. you made mistakes.

lilbeachbabe777: big mistakes

lilbeachbabe777: but we all did

lilbeachbabe777: and i can tell that you feel bad

getsome_danny24: i deserve to feel bad

getsome_danny24: i messed everythin up

lilbeachbabe777: look

lilbeachbabe777: jakes okay

lilbeachbabe777: and the reason he's ok is b/c u saved him

lilbeachbabe777: and dont forget u stepped in front of me too

getsome_danny24: no i kno

getsome_danny24: but like i feel bad

lilbeachbabe777: danny

lilbeachbabe777: i forgive u

getsome_danny24: ok

getsome_danny24: so

lilbeachbabe777: so

getsome_danny24: soooo

getsome_danny24: u want to maybe hang out sometime?

lilbeachbabe777: oh

lilbeachbabe777: danny

lilbeachbabe777: like what do u mean by hang out

getsome_danny24: idk

getsome_danny24: like old times

lilbeachbabe777: like which old times?

getsome_danny24: idk

getsome_danny24: i guess like umm

getsome_danny24: idk

lilbeachbabe777: like jakes room?

getsome_danny24: umm

getsome_danny24: ya

lilbeachbabe777: so ur asking

lilbeachbabe777: do i want to make out with u on jakes bed?

lilbeachbabe777: no, danny

lilbeachbabe777: i do not

getsome_danny24: no thats not how i meant it

lilbeachbabe777: really?

getsome_danny24: ya

lilbeachbabe777: so u have no interest in dating me?

getsome_danny24: no

lilbeachbabe777: not even a little?

getsome_danny24: well like

lilbeachbabe777: ?

getsome_danny24: i guess maybe like a little

getsome_danny24: yeah

lilbeachbabe777: ohhhhhhh boys

lilbeachbabe777: boys, boys, boys

getsome_danny24: wat?

getsome_danny24: wat does that mean?

lilbeachbabe777: it means

lilbeachbabe777: sorry danny

lilbeachbabe777: i dont want a bf until at least 10th grade

getsome_danny24: o

getsome_danny24: no no thats cool

getsome_danny24: like i want to be friends

getsome_danny24: i want to chill and talk and stuff

lilbeachbabe777: awesome

lilbeachbabe777: thats exactly what i want

lilbeachbabe777: and danny?

getsome_danny24: ya

lilbeachbabe777: good night

lilbeachbabe777 has signed off at 11:08 p.m.

getsome_danny24 has signed off at 11:42 p.m.

The Club Chronicles
THE FINAL EPILOGUE: Serendipity's Spit
By Dorothy Wu

He lay crumpled in a heap, the katana *protruding from his chest. His former friend had figuratively backstabbed him, his archenemy had literally chest-stabbed him, and then the two of them had run off with their cruel crew, the Pillagers, leaving Prince Jacobim all by himself in a puddle of blood-red blood. Though just a young man, he had been left on Death's doorstep.*

And Death had just been ding-dong ditched.

Princess Dorothy feared she was too late. She ran desperately to the top of the hill where Jacobim's body lay. She held the sword wound antidote in her hand, but she knew that the bottle of silver fluid would be of no use if Jacobim was already dead.

And he was already dead. She could see it before she even crouched down next to him. The brightness was gone from his maple eyes, the spring was gone from his curls. Her life mate, her lover, her kindred soul had already breathed his final breath, and she had not been there to feel its warm waft against her face.

She threw herself onto his body and began to sob such sobs. It was a violent kind of crying. Each tear subtracted large amounts of energy points from her overall total.

Dorothy cried and cried for minutes and hours and through the night and into the next morning. During the early part of this crying marathon, she maintained the naive hope that perhaps her tears could somehow bring Jacobim back to life, like in a children's movie. Yet all her crying did was make his face wet. His beautiful face.

She looked down at the face, and though it was now the face of a carcass, she longed to kiss it once more.

And then—an idea! A kiss! A kiss could rejuvenate him! After all, kisses from princes saved the lives of Snow White and Sleeping Beauty and that frog girl. Surely a smooch from a princess could rescue Jacobim.

Dorothy grabbed his face with eager hands. She closed her eyes, she took in the deepest of breaths, and she plunged her head downward. Her lips met his.

And nothing happened.

Dorothy sat back up. She did not cry. Rather, she sat in shocked silence. Her mouth hung open like a dumbfounded cow's.

So Jake was really gone. After all this, dead. She tried to contemplate her future without him. She could not. She had always imagined herself with him, ever since the day of the dolphins, and even through the dark times. Even when he did not love her, and even when she became distracted by lesser things, she still knew that their destiny was each other. And now that dream was never to be.

She was not sad like before, just stupefied. She was so stunned that she did not even notice when an excess amount of saliva built up in her hanging-open mouth. She did not feel the spit slide off her tongue and she did not see as it fell through the air and splashed against Jake's dead face.

And she had no way of knowing that spit of all things was the thing to bring him back to life.

Jake blinked his eyes open. They were very tired, but not too tired to smile. Dorothy gasped and smiled back and cried again. She leaned over and pressed her body tightly against his. Their chests were one. What a glorious feeling it was for Dorothy to embrace her beloved once more. What a miracle of a gift of a wish of a dream to have Jake back in her life. What a beautiful moment.

They made out furiously.

September 1st

Dear Jake,

Hi, it's Jake. You're writing this letter to yourself on the first day of seventh grade and you're not going to read it for a whole year. Here goes.

Here are some facts about yourself in case you forget: you're twelve years old. You're five feet if you say you are. You weigh a hundred and ten pounds.

All right, fine. You weigh ninety-eight pounds. But you do weigh a hundred and ten pounds on Neptune, which is your favorite planet. Hmm, Neptune sounds pretty good right about now. They don't have seventh grade on Neptune, do they?

You have two parents, an older sister, and no pets besides koi fish. Your parents are allergic to real pets. You have a normal group of friends including a best friend.

You have brown curly hair that people are obsessed with. You guess they're obsessed with it in a good way, but it's not that fun when people see you in the hallways and go, "Ch-ch-ch-ch-Chia!" Well, at least that's better than when they call you "Pube Head," which did happen one time.

It's probably worth mentioning that that one time was like, two hours ago, right after your first class of seventh grade.

Okay, you're not going to let that one experience ruin your day or your year or anything. It was just one of Hannah's stupid friends, and those guys are all overgrown four-year-olds.

Mr. Morales said that this writing exercise is all about seeing how much you can and will change in a year. But honestly, it's everyone else who's been changing. Not you. Stuff just seems different now. The guys came to school this year with baggier pants, and the girls have tighter tops, and Danny looks like someone stretched him out with a medieval torture device.

But you've got to remember that those changes are just physical. People can't change who they really are just because they want to. That's like the whole reason everyone hates junior high—because people know exactly who you are right away, and they don't let you change it, and they never let you forget it.

Like me. I'm not cool. It's common knowledge that Hannah has a dorky little brother who embarrasses her and tries too hard in his classes. I'm fine with that. If that's where I am a year from now, that's good.

I hope it's a good year. Danny and I were talking last night about what kinds of things we want this year. I said the usual stuff: good grades, good memories (with funny photos that go along with those memories), and for my bar mitzvah to go off without my voice cracking. Danny said that what he wanted—besides a bunch of girls, haha—was to figure out what makes him happy and go for it. I like that. I guess that means that Danny's going to be eating a bunch of pizza this year.

I wonder what it's going to be like reading this a year from now. I'll probably laugh a lot, like at the part where I wrote "Pube." That was pretty funny.

I just hope I don't cry. I do that too much. It's embarrassing for everyone. Danny says that when I cry it makes me seem like a little boy who's freaking out because his friends have all already learned how to ride bicycles, but he's still stuck riding a trike. I didn't point out to Danny that I was that little boy, only I didn't care about being on a trike because trikes are cool. And I wasn't ready for a bike yet. And really, trikes are cool! Still, I guess it's not a very seventh-grade attitude to have.

Seventh grade. Wow. Seventh grade . . . then

346

eighth grade. Then high school. Then college. Then whatever it is you do right after college. Then marriage, I guess. Then career and family. Then midlife crisis. Then the senior discount at the movie theater. Then grandkids. Then me and Danny getting so old that we get to play bingo and shuffleboard in the same retirement home every day. That'll be fun. But I've got to make sure I enjoy every minute up until then.

Okay, I can stop crying now. It's time for fourth period.

Here's to a good year.

Sincerely,
Jake

ACKNOWLEDGMENTS

I am preposterously grateful to the following people:

Christian Trimmer, my editor at Disney-Hyperion, for changing my life with one phone call and for being so insightful and hilarious on every other call. • Alex Glass, my agent at Trident Media Group, for offering to fly to L.A. just to meet me and for always going to the moon and back for me. Also to Michael Ferrante at Trident. • The dream team at Hyperion: Suzanne Murphy, Stephanie Lurie, Marci Senders, Ricardo Mejias, and the fantastic copyediting, production, and marketing folks. • My early readers: Sophie Carter-Kahn, Lindsey Toiaivao, Zoë Georgakis, and Andrew "Andrea" Molina. • My Stanford mentors: Dan Klein, Wendy Goldberg, and especially John L'Heureux, who paid this book its highest-ever compliment when he called it "publishable." • All of my phenomenal teachers in Santa Barbara, and in particular Mrs. Chancer, Mrs. Bachman, Mr. Battle, Ms. Carey, Ms. West, and Ms. Mason. • Tim Federle, for taking this earthbound manuscript and helping it become a winged bear of a novel. • Michael Weldon for the cover art, Ray Liu for the photos, Diogenes Brito for the Web site, Amber Sweeney for the designs, Jason Richman for the showbiz secrets, and to Fallon Leung for being Fallon. • Chiba, Delmy, Lupe, and Eva, for being such big parts of my family over the years. • Courtney, for being my three-hours-each-day back when I was first working on this book, and for being my twenty-four-hours-each-day now. • Kit, for showing me how to be a real writer. • Brian, for marrying Kit. • Emma, for coming up with most of the best jokes in this book. • Dad, for driving me to school every day of seventh grade and for always letting me win at one-on-one. • And, finally, Mom, for all of the hours she spent brainstorming with me, for all of the times she woke up at four a.m. to re-read this book for no reason, and for all of her millions of ideas—especially the ones I said were stupid. • They really weren't, Mom. I promise.

Okay, fine. Some of them were.